IS SHE LYING?

FRANCES LUCAS

Other Bella Books by Frances Lucas

Can I Trust Her?

About the Author

Frances Lucas discovered her passion for young adult novels through her students, establishing an after-school book club and free little library in her classroom. She taught animation, technology, and filmmaking in Anchorage, Alaska for many years and cofounded the Black Bear Film Festival for middle and high school students in 2012. She now lives in Southern Colorado with her wife and dogs and spends her days writing, reading, and exploring Colorado's many small mountain towns.

IS SHE LYING?

FRANCES LUCAS

2023

CHAPTER ONE

Katie

Nothing is the same and it's all Jason's fault. Matty, who's usually easygoing, is sniping at my girlfriend, Virginia. His boyfriend, Tom, is directing an ugly scowl across the school cafeteria at Jason who, with his fists on his hips, seems to be arguing with the guy who wipes down the tables. And Tally is staring at her phone. *Who the hell is E.D.? A new girlfriend she hasn't bothered mentioning to the rest of us?* I take a peek at her text string, but I'm unable to make anything of it.

Only Yoon-hi, the only straight one in our group, is making any effort at a regular conversation, saying something about a math student she's going to tutor after school. Me? I've given up. I'm not listening to anyone anymore. Just let the bell ring and put us all out of our misery. Because in ninety seconds, maybe less, Jason Gonzalez is going to head this way and make things worse.

"Virginia. I told you. Tom's father is disabled." Former drag queen Matty slaps the table hard enough to shake loose a fake red nail and jar me from my thoughts.

A blush rises from her collar. "I thought I'd heard—"

"It's okay," Tom intervenes. "My dad was diagnosed with MS a couple of years ago. He hated giving up his pilot's license, but he's head groundskeeper at McKinley now."

"The golf course?" I pat Virginia's knee under the table sympathetically.

"That's right."

Matty takes a beat, then offers a small, conciliatory shrug. He should. Virginia has been his best friend since they were freshmen. We could make this better by sitting at another table or eating in the library, but I'm not in charge. Virginia's the boss at this table, and I don't mind that a bit. When my family moved away from Anchorage my eighth-grade year, I felt lost without her. Last year we solved a murder and reconnected. Now anything that keeps me in her orbit is worth putting up with.

I don't feel the same about Matty, though. *Dude, come on. Tom or Jason, make a choice.* The problem started three weeks ago when Jason, Matty's former boyfriend, reenrolled at North. That very afternoon at lunch, he swished up to our table as if time had stood still in his yearlong absence. "Hello, people. Anybody miss me? Silly me. Of course you did. Matty, love, introduce me to your friends."

Matty's drag career became collateral damage due to last year's murder, but he still maintains a popular clothing review blog called Matty's Fishy Fashion Fixes. He's usually self-confident, but he can't handle confrontation—unless he starts it. Shifting subtly away from his current boyfriend, Tom, he mumbled, "Um, well, you know Virginia, right? This is Katie, Tally, Yoon-hi, and um, Tom."

"How's it going, guys?" Jason gave us each a semifriendly smile. "Tom, scoot over. Let me sit next to my boyfriend."

"You mean *my* boyfriend?" Tom wouldn't budge.

It went downhill from there and ended in a brawl last week when the woman who serves hoagies in the à la carte line asked him to pick up tray of sandwich buns he'd dropped. Jason pretended not to hear her.

"Bro, the lady's talking to you," Tom offered unhelpfully.

"Go to hell, *bruh*," Jason shot back, adding snarkily to her, "Christ, lady. Go away. Can't you see I'm eating lunch?"

"But the buns…" Her heavy jowls trembled like she was about to cry. I feel sorry for her. She's too old to have to work alongside an ill-mannered high school student.

Jason didn't see it that way. He flicked his fingers at her dismissively, saying, "They're your job. You work here, remember? Go on now. Scurry on back into the kitchen and stop embarrassing yourself."

The thing is, they're his job too, and he's the one who ought to be embarrassed. Jason used to help out in his father's tour boat business in Talkeetna. When the company went bankrupt, his unemployed father couldn't afford to pay his lunch tab and Jason had to work off his debt by cleaning up in the kitchen. I've no doubt it's demeaning for him, but it's no excuse for being rude.

I wasn't the only one disgusted. Matty grew a pair for once and told him to stop. Virginia asked if his parents never taught him the meaning of respect.

Tom, though, was the most outspoken. "Once a deadbeat, always an ass," he announced loud enough for everyone to hear. He was clearly goading Jason, and it worked.

Jason flew across the table at him. They punched and slapped each other and rolled across the floor. Kids from other tables egged them on until our three hundred fifty-pound security guard yanked them to their feet and dragged them to the principal's office.

No surprise, they were both suspended five days for fighting.

Today is their first day back and part of me hopes Jason will do the smart thing and find another group to hang with. No such luck. Ninety seconds later and right on cue, he rips off his hairnet, marches over and plops down on a stool.

"Well, haven't I had just the week. You too, Tom?"

Tom gazes at the table, pink spots blooming on his cheeks. "You could say that."

"Believe I did. Didn't you hear me?" The meanness in Jason's eyes softens into something else. "I think what you really mean is all's fair in love and war, right? No hard feelings?"

Tom has little choice but to shake the hand extended across the table. "Listen, man. About the other day—"

"When you stuck your nose in my business?" The softness, I see now, is a smirk.

"No. I mean, I just wanted to say I'm sorry for my part. And you know, hopefully we can move past it." Tom's Adam's apple bobs up and down his throat.

Dumbass Matty claps his hands in delight. "I think that's an excellent idea. So now that we're all friends again, I need opinions about my outfit. Blue or yellow?" I don't get what he means until he flips his collar and I note the inside of his tailored blouse with frills down the front is daisy yellow.

"Reversible?" Tally tucks her phone into a pocket and runs her fingers down a sleeve.

"Yup. I'll wash it tonight and see if it comes out wrinkly. For now, it gets a four-star rating."

"Only four?" Yoon-hi inspects it, too.

"Good design, but bulky. Thoughts?"

"I think it's really neat." Virginia winks at me. It's an inside joke between us. My beautiful girlfriend knows I love her occasional nerdiness.

Matty puckers his lips and takes a couple of selfies. When Tom nods as if he agrees with Virginia, I start to hope we can make it through lunch without another disaster. Jason, though, has other ideas. He snaps open his ridiculous *My Little Pony* metal lunchbox and sets a paper plate of homemade Lunchables on the table. "By the way, guys. Thanks for not waiting for me as usual. So nice to know my friends love me."

I let loose a quiet breath because I don't love him. I don't even consider him a friend. But Matty says, "Jas, honey. Don't be like that. You know we get here before you. I'll wait for you tomorrow, if you'd like."

We all go still. Will this set him off? But all he says is, "Don't bother."

He pops open a can of Diet Coke and stuffs a tiny sandwich of meat and cheese in his mouth, making mewing sounds in the back of his throat. "Mm. Delicious. Anyone want one?"

"No thanks." Several of us shake our heads.

"Oh, come on. How about you, Tom? You don't mind taking stuff that belongs to someone else."

And there it is, that moment of silence that follows a social blunder, which in this case is a challenge to Tom for "stealing" Matty from him. Tom wisely keeps his mouth shut. Matty's blue eyes turn to slits, but he stays quiet, too.

Virginia, the extrovert who's always trying to keep the peace at our table, starts to say something, but I bump her leg with my knee to stop her. A *don't engage* strategy I learned from dealing with my criminal father. Talking things out doesn't always make a situation better. I learned that the hard way.

Jason finishes off his lunch with the smirk still plastered on his face, and mercifully the bell rings. He rises and abruptly drops back to the stool. Blood trickles out of his left nostril. A few drops, then a stream. He wipes a knuckle across his upper lip and gazes at his hand with a *what the hell?* expression.

"Tissue?" Yoon-hi grabs one from her messenger bag and holds it out.

His eyes go round and shiny and his fingers snake forward for the tissue. Then all at once he falls backward off the stool and his whole body convulses.

CHAPTER TWO

Virginia

I've never seen anything like it and for a moment I'm frozen to my spot. Tally and Yoon-hi run for help. Kids from other tables scramble out of their chairs. Some offer advice. Others simply stand there, taking in the ghoulish scene. I finally unfreeze enough to grab the tissue Yoon-hi dropped, press it to Jason's nose, and roll him on his side so he won't bite his tongue or aspirate on his foamy vomit. Dad insisted I take CPR when I joined the ski team freshman year. The thing is, Jason is still breathing so I don't know what to do. I look to Katie for advice, but she stares back as clueless as I am.

"Is he sick? Does he take any sort of medication?" I yell at Matty who fans his chin with his fingers and screams, "His heart!"

Meaning he's having a heart attack? That can't be right. I've seen TV actors simulate heart attacks. They usually rub their chests and stammer about chest pains before crumpling on the floor. Jason's body jerks explosively.

"I'll check his backpack." Katie dumps the contents, scattering books and pens and loose-leaf notebook paper. "There's nothing here!"

"Jason." I lower my voice to a level I hope sounds soothing. "Tell me what I can do to help."

The spasms seem to lessen. "…sit up…"

I don't know if that's a good idea. His face is turning yellow. Before I can decide, Yoon-hi comes running back with our principal, Mrs. Foster, and the school security guard. "Tally went to get the nurse," she tells us. "An ambulance is on the way."

Mrs. Foster lowers herself to the floor, tucking her polyester floral skirt around her knees. "Please, everyone. We don't need an audience. Go to class." A few students leave but most stay put. They don't want to miss the show.

She rubs Jason's back in small, circular motions. "Jason, sweetheart. Your father is on his way. In the meantime, can you speak? Do you have any allergies? Or are you taking any medication? Any drugs we ought to know about?"

I'm guessing she means the illegal kind but is too polite to come right out and say it. He shakes his head and mumbles, "Can I have a drink of water?"

Katie hands me a bottle of water. I unscrew the cap and hold it to his lips. It dribbles down his chin as he starts seizing again.

"Jas, hold on." Matty rocks back and forth on three-inch patent leather heels above him. His tears send mascara running down his cheeks.

"You're gonna be okay," Tom murmurs a bit half-heartedly in my opinion. He stands several feet back with the cafeteria employees who came out when the commotion started. The cafeteria supervisor, Miss Jamie, looks distraught. Mrs. Lorner, the lady from the hoagie line, rubs her hands together like she's kneading bread dough. Lindley, the guy Jason was fussing with earlier, pulls out a stool and manspreads, his dark face blank.

When the EMTs arrive, Mrs. Foster steps aside. "Fetu, will you please gather Jason's things and take them to the security office?" The guard does as he's directed, picking up Jason's backpack, lunchbox, and empty plate.

"You," she goes on to the rest of us. "All of you who were sitting at the table, please come to my office with me. Everyone else, go to class. Now," she adds more forcefully when no one moves. "I'll make an announcement shortly to excuse your tardies."

Slowly everyone shuffles out. I look back in time to see two medics load Jason onto a stretcher. Most of his face is obscured by an oxygen mask. His yellow skin looks ghostly gray now, and his body is no longer shaking.

"Do you think he's going to be okay?" Katie whispers.

I curl my fingers around hers. I have no idea, but if I were to be honest, I think probably not. "Let's hope so," I reply.

The next several minutes feel eerily similar to last week when Tom and Jason had their fight and we were called into Mrs. Foster's office. Each of us was asked to give an account, including the hoagie lady, Mrs. Lorner, who kept shoving her thick, smudged glasses up the bridge of her nose and saying stuff like, "Oh, dear. I'm afraid I didn't see much of anything." And then, "I haven't worked here very long, but I will say it's normally a pleasant environment. When my dear husband was alive, he used to say that you see a man's true colors when he's under duress. Not that children have the same sensibilities, but they learn, and that's what important, don't you think?" Obviously useless. Mrs. Foster sent her on her way.

Katie and I did our best not to take sides. Yoon-hi and Tally, who had gone for help, were immediately dismissed. Tom and Jason stared sullenly at one another, each claiming the other one had started it, while my best friend, Matty, kept jumping in to defend whoever was talking. I love the guy, but he isn't great in a crisis.

This time, Tom decides to preempt all questions by saying loudly, "I didn't touch him."

Mrs. Foster pats her desk. "Nobody is accusing you of anything, young man. But I think it might be a good idea for you to call your folks. Here, use my phone."

She pushes the clunky desk phone toward him, making it clear he needs to do it now. She has Jason's medical chart in front of her. Our school nurse hovers behind her while the security guard blocks the door, in the event one of us tries to make a break for it, I guess.

"Let me see. No reported allergies. No previous epilepsy episodes. You say he had a heart condition?" Foster's question is directed at Matty.

"When he was a baby." He squeezes out more tears, which she ignores, directing her attention to Jason's chart.

"And more recently?"

"Nothing that I know of."

"Okay, then. Did he choke? Or perhaps eat something out of the ordinary?"

"He definitely didn't choke because he was already done eating," says Yoon-hi. She's probably the most observant one of our group. She and I started a tutoring service back in July at our NHS sponsor's suggestion.

"And just his usual," Katie adds. "Some sort of deli meat between two slices of cheese."

"Turkey or chicken, and always cheddar cheese. Four little sandwiches," says Matty, holding his thumb and forefinger a couple of inches apart to demonstrate the size. "Also, a Diet Coke."

"But no applesauce," says Tally. Then, "What?" when we all turn and stare at her. "He usually has applesauce." She's right, but I'm not sure it's important. Tally and I dated at the beginning of junior year before Katie returned to Alaska.

Mrs. Foster doesn't seem to think it's relevant either and moves on. "How soon after he finished eating did the seizures start?"

I look at Katie, and we both shrug. "Ten minutes?" she ventures.

"But the nosebleed started first," I say, glancing at the bloody tissue still twisted in my fingers. "Oh!" I drop it like it's a wasp about to sting me, suddenly recalling a video we watched in freshman health about bloodborne pathogens. Matty bends over as if to pick the crumpled tissue up.

"Don't!" The nurse starts forward. "Don't anyone touch it. Virginia, go wash your hands." She looks to Mrs. Foster as if to ask if it's okay to give me directions.

Mrs. Foster nods. "That's an excellent idea. In fact, all of you, go wash your hands. And then…" Her pause makes me wonder if she's going to make us talk about the fight last week again, but all she says is, "Then head on back to class."

CHAPTER THREE

Katie

Five minutes later, Tally is done washing her hands. We all are, except for Virginia who scrubs each finger up and down and front and back, over and over, like a doctor preparing for surgery.

"It's gotta be Ebola. Or that monkey virus, what's it called?" says Tally.

"Covid?" Yoon-hi tosses a paper towel into the trash can.

"I don't think so." Tally cocks her head as if she thinks Yoon-hi is serious. Sometimes I wonder how she gets out of bed on her own each morning. She's such a ditz.

She makes my case for me when she says, "Oh, my god, do you think the rest of us could be infected?" Grabbing her phone from her pocket, she unlocks it, makes a quick search, then reads aloud from the screen. "'Ebola is spread by animal bites or insect stings. By touching a contaminated surface, or by saliva. Like sharing drinks or kissing.' Well, I know I didn't kiss him. Gross! 'Symptoms include fever, headaches, vomiting, and coughing blood.' Huh. Jason did have quite a nose—"

"Tally, stop," Yoon-hi orders with a quick glance at Virginia. "Jason doesn't have Ebola."

"So, what then? It sure didn't look like a heart attack. You think he was poisoned?"

Yoon-hi steals another sideways peek at Virginia who finally dries her hands. Her fingers look like raw ground beef. "I don't know. I guess food poisoning is a possibility. I heard a couple of other kids have gotten sick at lunch."

"Yeah, but not like that." Tally blinks. I want to stuff a paper towel in her mouth. *Let it go.* Can't she see one of us is slightly panicked?

I wrap an arm around Virginia's waist. "Let me see." She splays her fingers in my direction. "No visible cuts or wounds," I say, after a close examination. "How do you feel?"

"Okay, I guess." Virginia is supremely self-confident, one of the many things I love about her, so it's unnerving to see her looking worried.

I tickle the tip of her nose with a finger. "No stomachaches or nosebleeds?"

She giggles. "I haven't had a bloody nose since second grade."

"Good. Then don't start now. I pronounce you well and healed, a perfect specimen." I kiss her fingers one by one. She gives me a heavy-lidded smile, the kind that sends my heart racing, and moves in close enough our breasts touch.

"Oh, for godsakes, get a room," Tally grumbles.

I bite my lip to keep from saying something back. I don't believe she still has feelings for my girlfriend, but seeing us together may make her wish she had someone to kiss her fingers. I think back to the texts on her phone.

Will you come see me at Caseo's?

If I can. –E.D.

E.D. Why do those initials seem familiar? Is there a new girl in her life?

Tally likes to sing at Caseo's, our favorite coffeehouse, on open mike nights. She'd planned to perform last Wednesday. When most of us couldn't go, she ended up canceling.

Yoon-hi glances at the time on her phone. "Speaking of rooms, Virginia. I'm supposed to meet Shanice Kennedy in the Little Bear conference room after school for pre-calc tutoring, but I just missed my physics quiz. Can you take her so I can make it up?"

"Sure. No problem."

Her thumbs tap across her phone. "Thanks. I'm letting her know."

The bell rings, and the four of us file out of the restroom into the hall. "See you later," Virginia calls to Yoon-hi and Tally as they head off to their lockers. Then she pulls me aside for a kiss that lasts longer than it probably should, considering we're at school. "So what do you think?" she asks, a bit out of breath.

My heart races too, but I get that she isn't talking about the kiss. "Definitely not Ebola or a heart attack."

"Yeah. But what?"

A group of freshman girls push past us. One knocks my elbow and turns back to apologize. I hardly notice. I'm picturing the cafeteria in my head. Jason writhing on the floor. Matty, oblivious as the source of all the tension, flapping his hands. Tom stepping back with an oddly detached expression on his face.

We were gathering our stuff and getting up to leave when Tom leaned over and whispered something to Jason: "You don't deserve him."

Did I hear him right? Last year when we leapt headfirst into the middle of a mysterious death and subsequent kidnapping, I was thrilled that it brought Virginia and me back together, but it also nearly got us killed. Still, I know her well enough to understand she's already thinking we should investigate. I chew a thumbnail and say in a weighty tone, "And so it begins again."

CHAPTER FOUR

Virginia

I force myself to put all thoughts of Jason and his seizure aside as I work through my afternoon classes. Honors English, AP calculus, and computer applications. Computer apps isn't required. I only took it because I thought Katie and I would be in it together. The first day of school we found out hers meets second hour, which sucks because it means we don't have a single class together.

When the last bell rings, I make my way to the library on the second floor. Most of it has been renovated with new computers and a huge, floor-to-ceiling window offering a gorgeous view of the Chugach Mountains, snow-peaked all year long.

Along one wall on the left are four conference rooms. Big Bear. Little Bear. Big Moose. Little Moose. Each holds a table and four straight-back plastic chairs, with clear glass between the rooms and library and a solid gray wall in back. Our old librarian called them A, B, C, and D. Mrs. Donovan, who was new last year, changed the names. Don't ask me why she didn't choose four different animals since the rooms are all the same size, but I appreciate her effort to personalize them. She's instituted several other improvements I really like. Bean bag chairs in front of the stacks. A couple of comfy couches under the window she must have brought from home. And a "help yourself" coffee corner with a new Keurig that's often out of coffee by late afternoon.

Today, however, is an exception. Seeing a box of coffee pods and paper cups, I rub my hands together happily and make a beeline for the machine. A Keurig is no substitute for one of Caseo's caramel mocha lattes, but a hot drink should keep me awake while I watch Shanice work through her math problems.

I stick a hazelnut pod in the machine and press the button just as a melodic voice behind me says, "Fifty cents a cup."

I spin around to find Mrs. Donovan holding out an empty glass jar. "I thought it was free."

"Sorry. Not anymore. I can't afford to keep it stocked. I bought twelve boxes at Bed Bath & Beyond last Wednesday. They were gone by Friday. You can pay me tomorrow if you don't have cash today. It's the honor system."

If it's the honor system, why are you holding out a jar?

Mrs. Donovan is young and pretty, with brown eyes that are almost too big for her face. I've never seen her wear an outfit twice. Matty says her GG Marmont mini bucket handbag retails for nine hundred bucks. She's got a bunch of other purses too. Still, I get that she shouldn't have to supply coffee to North's entire student population. Some kids pop in two or three times a day for a cup. That's got to get old.

I drop a couple of bucks in the cup, and she tries to hand one back. "Keep it," I say. "It's not my first time here."

"Well, okay. If you insist." Her pretty face brightens.

"My friend Yoon-hi Park signed out Little Bear for tutoring. I'm taking her place," I tell her. Steam rises from the paper cup when I pull it away from the machine.

"Great. Then you're here for Shanice. She's waiting for you."

It used to be you had to show your student ID to use a conference room, which seemed kind of silly to me. It's not like people off the streets are going to wander in for meetings. The new system is another of Mrs. Donovan's improvements. Now you just tell her that you're here.

I take my coffee to the second room from the right where a purple backpack with a WNBA logo is propped against the wall on the floor. Figuring Shanice has slipped out to use the restroom, I set my stuff on the table and wait for the coffee to cool, trying not to think about Jason's bloody tissue. I focus on Katie kissing my fingers instead.

My god, just thinking about her makes me happy. We fell in love the summer before eighth grade. Then, when her dad found out that her mom was cheating on him with Denise, the indigenous Alaskan woman who lived next door to them, he moved Katie and her mother out of state believing that would solve his problem. It didn't. Due to a misunderstanding involving Katie and me, he fired a bullet into her mom's face, taking out one of her eyes. He's in prison now and I hope he stays there forever. Katie was completely traumatized by the event. It took us a while to work through it, her mother even longer.

My coffee is drinkable by the time Shanice enters the library from the hall, followed by Tally who heads toward Mrs. Donovan and the coffee corner.

"Hey. Virginia, right?" I nod. Shanice takes a seat and glances in their direction. "Do you know her?"

"Who? Tally or Mrs. Donovan?"

She snorts a breath like the answer should be obvious. "The girl. Tally. What's her last name, and is she one of us?"

I didn't know Shanice was *one of us*, but my gaydar is practically nonexistent. Take Tom, for example. No frayed-hem booty shorts for him. Tom dresses like every other guy at North who isn't Matty. Jeans. T-shirts. Hiking boots. There's a certain softness to his face and the way he styles his floppy hair, but I doubt I would have noticed any of that if he didn't date Matty. Shanice is short and athletic with broad shoulders and muscular legs with slender ankles like an Olympic sprinter. The braided dreads that hang down her back appear to be all hers, and she's got chiseled cheekbones like they were carved from a statue.

"Tally Carter. Seventeen. Has lived in Anchorage all her life. Used to work at Caseo's, still performs there, and yes, definitely a lesbian," I recite. "Assuming that's what you mean."

"Single?" Shanice studies Tally with an almost predatory expression.

"As far as I know."

"Didn't you two used to see each other?"

It seems she's done her homework. "A while ago. Listen, you've paid for an hour of pre-calc tutoring. We can talk trigonometry or I can make an introduction. Your choice."

She snorts again like I've said something either funny or offensive, and then stretches a long arm behind her and drags her backpack across the carpet to the chair. "Teach me the law of cosines. I've got a test tomorrow."

We settle into measuring lengths of the sides of a triangle, but out of the corner of my eye, I watch Tally with Mrs. Donovan. They move to a computer. Tally takes a seat in front of it. Mrs. Donovan leans over her shoulder, smiling, and I glance again at Shanice.

I'm not jealous. I want Tally to be happy. But Shanice, with her irritating snorts, has put me off.

"You're not from around here, are you?" I take a sip of coffee that isn't as tasty as I'd hoped. A little cardboardy. I should have picked a different flavor.

Shanice looks up from her calculations. "Not originally. Is that a problem?"

"Of course not. I'm simply making conversation."

"On my dime?"

She's got a point. "Sorry. I just..." *I just what?* I can feel the tips of my ears burning. "Tally's my friend," I blurt. "I feel protective of her."

"And you think I'm going to hurt her just because I asked about her?" Shanice sits back, flipping a dreadlock over one shoulder. "I don't know what the deal is between you two, but take it from me, I'm not the hurting type. I'm a straightforward, cut through the bullshit kind of gal. You want to know something about me, just ask. And I'll do the same. Fair?"

"Fair." I'm not sure why I find her intimidating. Maybe it's the no-bullshit thing. She exudes it, like an exotic perfume. "Do you want to start, or should I?"

"I will. Are you in love with Tally Carter?"

"No. She's a friend, like I said. I'm with Katie McRanes."

"Right. I know her."

"You do?"

"Artist. Curly dark hair. Super cute dimples. Smart, but not in your face about it, if you know what I mean."

The heat in my ears meets a rush coming up my neck. Not in your face about it—I'm guessing she means me. Did I seem impatient when I pointed out the law of cosines printed at the top of her paper? "My turn?"

"Go ahead."

"Well, where are you from?"

"I grew up in the Philippines. My father was a lieutenant at Clark Air Base on Luzon Island. After he passed, my mom and I moved to Talkeetna. She's a chef. She worked for a tour boat business. When it folded this summer, we came here. I excel in English, PE, and art. I suck at math and science."

"Talkeetna Flatboat Tours?" I say, feeling my eyebrows inch up my forehead. How much of a coincidence would that be?

"Yeah. What about it?"

"Then you know Jason Gonzalez? His dad owned the company."

"Yeah. So what?" She curls her upper lip.

"I just…" Oh hell, here I go again. I want to state for the record that I normally get along with others. Most people like me. Not Shanice apparently.

Realizing I need to start over, I say, "I think we got off on the wrong foot. If it's my fault, I'm sorry."

"Forget it."

She waves my apology away, but I continue anyway. "Please. Let me make this right. I'm not going to charge you for this session, and in the future if you'd rather work with Yoon-hi instead of me, it won't hurt my feelings. Also, if you and Tally decide to hang, hook up, or whatever, it's all good with me."

"All good with you," she mocks, which makes me want to take everything back. She folds her lips into her mouth, one under the other. "Meaning you won't dis me to her or stand in my way?"

What is it with this girl? "Right. And the reason I asked about Jason is he used to date my friend Matty Brown."

"Yeah, I know. What a turd."

"Matty?" I'm so startled I nearly knock over my cup of coffee. I grab it before it falls.

"Jason." *Keep up*, her expression tells me. "I heard he had a seizure in the cafeteria today. I'll believe it when I see it. Bet it was faked. He's such a drama queen…Oh, hang on." Her backpack is singing one of my favorite Lizzo songs.

She zips it open, pulls out her phone, listens for a moment, then says, "All right, then," and hangs up. "Well, how 'bout that. Not faked, after all. That was my mom. Jason Gonzalez? Still a turd by the way, although his dad's even worse. He died twenty minutes ago. ER doc said the cause of death was rat poison."

CHAPTER FIVE

Katie

I'm on my way home from walking Virginia's adopted pit bulls, George and Abe, around University Lake when Virginia calls to tell me about her tutoring session with Shanice Kennedy. I have to pull off to the side of the road I'm laughing so hard.

"She's definitely an acquired taste," I say when she finishes with how Shanice called her in-your-face-smart, which doesn't take a genius to figure out isn't a compliment.

"If that's Klingon for scary, hardnosed bitch, I agree."

"And that's because you think she doesn't like you?"

"See? I knew you'd understand." She chuckles for a second, and then her tone turns serious. "I just got home from school. Where are you?"

"Still on O'Malley, just past C Street. What's up?"

"Nothing really. Any chance you can come back here?"

I frown into my phone. "If you need me to, of course. But it's my turn to fix dinner, and I'm already running late. What's going on?"

A moose strolls across the road in front of me, and I have to resist the urge to take a picture of it, like the lady in the car that stopped beside me is doing.

Virginia inhales a noisy breath. "Shanice got a phone call from her mother. Did you know her mom worked for Jason's father in Talkeetna?"

"No. But I guess it doesn't surprise me. I know her mom's a cook and that they moved to Anchorage from Talkeetna in August, just like Jason and his dad. In fact, she mentioned that they both worked for a wilderness outfit."

Talkeetna is a cute, touristy little town between Anchorage and Denali. Every summer the locals decorate wooden moose scattered up and down the main drag, but the real attraction is the three rivers that converge outside of downtown. Several boating companies offer day trips that include nature hikes and cookouts.

"How well do you know her?" Virginia asks.

The moose in front of me moves on and so does the car beside me, the noise from the engine rumbling as it drives away. "Not that well. We take art together and sit at the same table. Occasionally, we talk. Come now, babe. What's this about?"

"Okay." She sucks another breath. "Just this. Call me crazy, but Shanice despised Jason and now he's dead from what the doctors say was rat poison. That's why her mother called. I've been looking it up, Katie, and the symptoms fit. Strychnine, a common ingredient in rodenticides, causes spasms ten to fifteen minutes after ingesting. It can also cause liver failure. Remember how his skin turned yellow? That's a sign of liver failure. Death can occur as early as two to three hours after consuming even relatively small amounts."

It's my turn to take a few deep breaths. "Jason's really dead? Holy shit."

"I know. It's horrible. Hey, listen, don't restaurants keep rat poison? Do you know where Shanice's mom works now?"

"I don't. Why?"

"Because. Restaurants. Rat poison. Access to the murder weapon. Shanice's mother must have lost her job when Jason's dad's company went bankrupt. That makes people pretty unhappy, right? I'm not saying they killed him either separately or together, just that it bears checking out."

"Huh," I reply, because I can't think of anything else. In my mind, it's a pretty big leap to think someone would poison someone else over lost employment. Shanice doesn't even sit with us at lunch, but I don't say so out loud. Virginia's got good instincts about these things. "Do you want me to come back to your house?"

She hesitates. "I guess not. I can tell from your tone that I need to give this more thought. But thanks for the offer anyway. I think I'll check on Matty."

I haven't even considered how Matty might be taking this. He may not have heard. "Are you sure?"

"Sure, I'm sure. Call me later?"

"You got it. Love you."

"Love you too." We hang up. It's corny that we end our phone conversations with "I love you," but I don't care. My mom may be incapable of expressing emotion and affection, but Virginia gives it freely.

As I start the car, my thoughts return to Jason. I'm not sure what I was expecting when the EMTs took him away, or how I feel about it now. Part of me would like to take back all the unkind thoughts I had about him. When Marisol, the girl who got pushed down the stairs at school last fall, died, it was the same sort of thing. She ridiculed me relentlessly when we were neighbors, but I never thought she deserved all the hateful things people said about her later. Virginia's brother, Pete, dates her sister, Camila, and I hope for her sake that Camila stays off social media. A guy last spring set up a Facebook page selling "Ding Dong, the Witch is Dead" T-shirts popularized by our school newspaper's new editor-in-chief, Lilly Kahale. Lily wore the shirt as part of a costume and swore it had nothing to do with Marisol. Most people didn't believe it. And once Mrs. Foster found out about it, she made him take the page down.

I pull into my apartment building's graveled parking lot, shut off the engine, and listen to the ping-ping-clonking sounds my car makes. Evie, as I affectionately call her, is fifteen years old. Her primary color is rust, and her tires are as smooth as bowling balls. I'd love to get a new car, but I can't afford one on my Cinemark Theater paychecks, and I don't want to ask my mom because she and Denise are saving up to buy a house. I pat the hood and tell Evie she's a good girl, like I would with Virginia's dogs, who are really my dogs too, and head upstairs.

As soon as I unlock the door, I can tell something's wrong. Mom's got on her eye patch, which she rarely wears inside the house. She sits beside Denise, holding hands. When I drop my keys in a bowl inside the door, Mom springs to her feet to give me a hug. Weird. Like I said, she's not one for physical contact.

"Um, sorry I'm late," I say.

"No, honey, we're sorry!" Mom squeezes me tight. Too tight.

I pull away, wanting her to stop. "About what? Wait, is this about Jason? You already heard?"

"Jason who?"

"A guy at school. The one who got suspended last week." My mind reels with unrelated thoughts. "He—never mind. Did something happen? Where's Josh?"

Denise takes over and guides me to a chair. "He's in his room. Katie, you'd better sit down. We need to tell you something."

Uh-oh. I have a bad feeling about this. She hands me a letter from the Washington State Department of Corrections, an internal organization called the End of Sentence Review Committee. I flip through the pages, unable to make heads or tails of most of it, except for the last page that says my father's prison release day is Saturday. Just a few days away.

My throat goes dry and I think I might throw up. My dear old dad was sentenced to ten years at Airway Heights Correction Center in Spokane for shooting Mom, which he swore was an accident. He's served only two years of his time.

"I don't get it." I choke the words out as I hand the letter back.

"It's a SAVIN notification, Statewide Automatic Victim Information and Notification that lets victims know of a convicted criminal's impending release. Your father, Katie, filed an appeal claiming an officer lied about the evidence."

"How? What evidence?"

"I don't know. Apparently, it was pretty bad. The officer has a history of doing it and now all his cases are up for review. Long story short, your father found himself a top-notch lawyer, and his sentence was reduced. It's nothing to worry about right now. We'll just need to think through our next steps carefully."

My mother can't seem to meet my gaze and Denise shoots her an anxious look I don't fully understand. "Anyway, in the meantime, I thought I'd pick up a Moose's Tooth pizza so no one has to cook. How does that sound?"

Normally, it would sound great. I'm a decent cook, but I don't enjoy it. I nod and fake a smile and somehow make it to my room. My heart has worked its way into my throat. My stomach churning, I flop down on my bed, but immediately jump up to vomit in the wastebasket. My throat hurts and there's a bad taste in my mouth.

Dad shot Mom. How can they possibly let him out?

I grab my laptop and look up reasons why criminal appeals are granted. Legal error, juror or judge misconduct, ineffective counsel. I don't see anything about police officers perjuring themselves, but what do I know?

I hid in my bedroom the night Mom and Dad fought. I still cringe thinking about it. If I'd stepped out and told the truth, could I have stopped him? What did Denise mean about thinking through our next steps carefully? We're twenty-four hundred miles away from him. Aren't we safe?

I'd planned to look up information about rat poison, but I can't think about that now. What if Dad comes after us? Nine months ago, I got a call from Airway Heights. I refused at the time to take it. Maybe I should have.

A soft knock sounds at my door, and when I don't answer, Denise opens it a crack and pokes her head inside my room. "Okay if I come in?"

She's a small, dark woman with long brown hair. A biologist with the Alaska Fish and Wildlife Center. She's smart and caring and I don't know what Mom and I would do without her.

"Please tell me we aren't going into hiding." I beckon her inside.

She takes a seat at the foot of my bed. "That's one option. Your mom thinks we'd be better off in Fairbanks or possibly Elim, where I grew up."

No! I want to scream, but manage, "You still have family there?"

She regards me with her serious dark eyes. "Most of the people who live there are my family. Nome might be a better bet. It's bigger and not that far from Elim. Pretty cold and dark in winter. The summers aren't half bad."

No! She's making the move sound permanent. "How cold? How dark?"

"Now?" She tilts her head to think about it. "I guess it's not all that different from here in the fall. Single digits during the day in winter. Maybe three and a half hours of sunlight."

"Do they have schools and stores?"

She pats my leg. "Of course they have a school. And several stores. The Bering Tea and Coffee Shop is nice, although I haven't been there in quite some time."

No! A tea company, is that it? It feels like she's deliberately trying to scare me. And if she thinks I'm leaving Virginia again, she's got another thing coming. No way am I going to move to Nome or even Fairbanks, which is a decent-size city, though much smaller than Anchorage. She might as well suggest we pack our bags for Mars.

"You said that's one option." I swallow. "What are the others?"

"Personally, I'd like to wait and see how this plays out. I've got a little money put aside, and I'm trying to persuade your mom to let me hire a private detective. Someone to keep an eye on your father for a couple of weeks when he gets out. Just to see where he goes."

"You mean like if he buys a plane ticket for Anchorage?"

"Exactly."

I consider that. He can always drive through Canada or take a ferry. But for that he'd probably need a passport. Are ex-cons entitled to keep their passports? Crap, there's so much I don't know. "Wait. If he's on probation, he won't be allowed to leave the state. Isn't that right?"

"Honey. I don't know. The information sheet said he'd be on parole. And I don't think that's as strict. What I'd like is your help keeping your mother calm. I like living here in Anchorage as I'm sure you do. Help me, if you can, to convince her not to overreact—"

I jump up from the bed. "Hire a PI. Got it! I'm in."

CHAPTER SIX

Virginia

It's my brother Reggie's thirteenth birthday, and my mom insists I stay home long enough to have dinner with the family. We sing "Happy Birthday" and clap when he makes a wish and blows out his birthday candles, but all anybody can talk about is Jason's death.

"Eileen Foster is beside herself." Dad pushes back his plate and shakes his head at Mom's offer of a second piece of strawberry ice cream cake. "This is the second death at North in less than a year. She blames herself. But what could she have done differently? She's afraid the school board will ask for her resignation."

Mom picks at the vanilla frosting on a corner of the cake. "That hardly seems fair."

Pete, who is also home for the occasion, sticks a big bite in his mouth and talks with his mouth full. "Is it possible this Jason kid brought the poison from home?"

"You mean a suicide?" I turn to Mom who has worked as a store detective since Reggie was born but used to be with the Anchorage Police Department. "Why would somebody deliberately eat rat poison?"

She shakes her head. "They wouldn't. Peter, swallow your food before you talk, please. It would be a terrible way to go. Rodenticides are basically anticoagulants, which simply put, means blood thinners. They work by preventing the body from recycling vitamin K. We had a case my first year undercover, a gang member who tried to kill his boss. He didn't die, but I never saw anyone so horribly sick. For days, all he could do—"

"Carol." Dad gestures at Reggie who has dropped his fork and is looking wide-eyed at Mom.

"Oh! Sorry. Sorry. My point is only that it can happen accidentally in a warehouse or a kitchen, but there are plenty of faster and less painful ways to die. Are you ready to open your presents, Reggie?"

Reggie grins, showing food between his teeth. "You bet I am."

My mom is amazing. I'm always impressed by all the things she knows. Her explanation jives with what I read on the Internet earlier. Children and pets sometimes eat the stuff accidentally if it's left out where they can get it, because supposedly it tastes good. Apparently, it comes in flavors like chocolate, cheese, and peanut butter. I also know there's a simple blood test to measure clotting times, which is probably how the ER doctor figured out so quickly what was wrong with Jason.

Mom gets up from the table and comes back with a gold gift bag containing two new flannel shirts and an Under Armour ski mask, which I can tell from Reggie's expression are not amazing. Dad gives him a Jones Hovercraft snowboard with the price tag from REI still on it. This clearly is amazing. Reggie thanks them and looks at Pete and me. "Well?"

"Well, what?" says Pete.

"Did you buy me a present?"

"I'm your brother. That's my present."

"Same here," I add. "Being your sister is my present."

"This isn't funny." Reggie visibly swallows.

"It's not?" Pete can barely keep from laughing.

I think it's a little mean, considering we spent the first half of his birthday dinner talking about Jason's death, but I play my part because that's what we agreed on. The joke was Pete's idea, of course.

"Tell you what. I've got a couple of bike clips I guess I could part with. Let me go see if I can find them," Pete says, after letting Reggie stew a minute.

"He can have my old helmet, too. It's in my closet," I call after him as he heads through the living room back to the bedrooms. The dogs go with him, their long nails clicking on the hardwood floor. Despite Katie telling him not to, Pete feeds them table scraps, so it's hardly a surprise that they follow him everywhere he goes. I don't think they've fully recovered from nearly starving to death outside at their last home.

A couple of seconds later, Pete comes back with a brown paper bag that he drops on the table in front of Reggie. "Sorry, kid. It's been a busy week. This is all I could manage."

All *we* could manage, I want to say, but that would probably sound churlish. And to be fair, Pete did pay for most of the gift.

Reggie stares at the bag suspiciously (with good reason— Pete gave him a package of pine cones last year, also a joke), but when he opens it, he squeals with delight. "You remembered. I love it!"

How could we not remember? Reggie has been talking about the new Destructor VR game since he came back from coding camp last spring. It's an all-in-one headset with a gift card for one of the games. If I know Reggie, he'll play it a couple of weeks, then take it apart to find out how it works. The kid is a tech genius. Last year, he installed household cameras at one of our neighbors' houses.

I help Mom carry the dishes to the kitchen, and then tell her I'm off to see Matty. She gives me a hug. "Tell him…oh, I don't know…tell him I'm sorry for his loss." She knows Matty's history. His boyfriends tend not to stick around very long, but this is the first time one has died.

"I will, Mom. Thanks." I text Matty on the way out to my car. *Want some company?*

Please. Tom's here. He had to talk to the police.

That can't be good. *Twenty minutes. Leaving now.*

I turn on the car radio and listen to an aught station Pete turned me on to a few weeks ago. When Rihanna starts singing, "Shut Up and Drive," I pump up the volume and sing along. Sure, call me a nerd. I own it. I'm also in serious need of an upbeat tune.

When I get to Matty's house, he leads me to the kitchen table where I find Tom slumped on a stool, white-knuckling a ceramic mug.

"Hey," he says glumly.

"Hey, yourself. How's it going?"

"Wanna know the truth? Like shit, thanks for asking. Cops invited me and my folks to the station for a friendly chat. What they really wanted was info on the fight I had last week with Jason. He started it. You guys remember, don't you? Do you know he died from rat poison?"

"I heard," I say blandly. Matty nods, looking almost as miserable as Tom.

"Yeah, well, get this." He pushes the cup aside. "They also wanted to know if Dad's golf course keeps rat poison."

"Do they?" Matty asks.

"Shit, Matty. Whose side are you on? Of course, they do. It's for those ugly little voles that tunnel underground and mess up turf. Dad has to use the heavy-duty commercial stuff, which they said is extremely toxic. They practically accused him of giving it to me to poison Jason. Virginia, Matty says you and Katie might be able to help me 'cause you're good at figuring stuff out."

Matty hands me a tea bag and a mug of hot water, then sits down at the table next to Tom. "Virginia and Katie figured out who killed Marisol."

"Last year. I remember. You guys had your own detecting business for a while. What happened to that?"

I dunk the bag into the water. "Nothing really." *Life.*

"Yeah, well, I don't want to impose or anything, but I swear on a stack of Bibles I didn't put anything in Jason's food. I was as shocked as everybody else when his seizure started. And plus, when was I going to do it? You guys were sitting right there with me. Me and Matty figure it must have happened earlier when his lunch was in the refrigerator. Or hell, I don't know…maybe he did it himself. Or one of his parents did it. Or he dropped his lunchbox in the cafeteria and his food fell on the floor. Don't school kitchens use rat poisons?"

"Probably," I say. "Did you mention any of that to the police?"

"No way. I didn't want them to think I had my alibi all prepared or whatever. That would make me look more guilty. Besides, Dad told me to keep quiet and let him do the talking. Mom just sat there crying. She's been through so much with his MS diagnosis. I'm not sure she could handle it if something happened to me."

It's an interesting way of putting it, something happening to him.

Matty rubs Tom's back. Tom leans into him, then jerks away with a guilty look when Matty's mother walks into the kitchen. She gives me a big smile. "Oh, Virginia. Good to see you. I didn't know you were here. Matty, honey, did you offer her a piece of pie?"

Mrs. Brown is famous for her pies. She supplies them in bulk to every North High fundraiser. I particularly like her sweet potato pie with homemade crust, but I thank her and explain that I just had a couple of pieces of ice cream cake.

"Okay, if you kids need anything let me know. I'll be in the living room." She helps herself to a piece of what looks like apple pie from the refrigerator, casts a quick glance at her son, and departs. Tom visibly relaxes, and Matty gets up and heads for the teapot, his lips dragged down with hurt.

"Tom," I say carefully because I know it's not my business. "Are you out?"

He curls back on his stool. "What do you mean?"

Oh, come on. "Do you think Matty's mother doesn't know you're gay? And what about your parents, do they know you two are dating?"

"No! You got it wrong." He stops, and then starts again more slowly. "It's not what you think. Matty knows I care for him, but my dad's been sick. And Mom wouldn't understand. And anyway, I don't think my preference, or whatever you want to call it, has anything to do with Jason's death. I don't want to make things harder for my parents, at least not right now. You get it, don't you, Matty?"

"Sure." Matty lays a hand on Tom's shoulder.

A tear rolls down Tom's cheek, and he offers his boyfriend a grateful smile.

But it's Matty I feel sorry for. He deserves someone who loves him without reservation. He's kind and loyal and a remarkable person.

"I'll talk to Katie. We'll ask around and see if we can pick up any additional information," I say, giving Tom a long hard look, trying to convey how wrong I think he is for how he's treating my friend. I finish my tea and say good night. If Tom thinks he's fooling Mrs. Brown, he's mistaken. Matty came out to his parents when he was little, and his mom is super smart.

Matty sets my mug in the sink and follows me to the door.

"Seriously?" I say, when we're far enough from the kitchen that I don't think Tom can hear us.

"I know," he frets. "I know. But I really like him, and not everybody is as okay with all this as my parents." He gestures to his unconventional clothes: his pink satin blouse, his velveteen kitten heels and his tight, faux leather pants.

I get it. I'm not exactly butch but I don't make any pretense of being anything other than what I am. Matty and I are lucky. Katie knows a guy from work whose parents kicked him out of the house when he told them he was gay. "You know what you need?" I say.

"My own Katie?"

I laugh. "Yeah, that." I'm *very* lucky. "I think you need a night at Misconceptions, just the two of us. You and me. Nobody else and no drama. We can make fun of Cher's new wig. The one you told me about? You don't have to get so wound up in Tom's problems, you know."

"I'll think about it," he says unconvincingly. "In the meantime, maybe you can talk to your mom, see if she can persuade her cop friends to give Tom some space?"

I open my mouth to tell him that's not going to happen, but before I can say it, he adds, "I don't mean she has to pull strings or anything, but maybe she could put in a good word for him. Ask them not to jump to conclusions?"

"I'll try." In reality, it's not an avenue worth exploring. Dad coaches several sports at North and knows Tom from the cross-country ski team, but I doubt my mother has ever spoken more than two words to the guy. And more importantly, she doesn't like to use her connections for personal gain.

I punch him gently in the chest. "Buck up, my friend. Things will work out. You'll see." It sounds lame even to my ears. "See you at school tomorrow?"

His carefully plucked brows knit together. "Yeah. See you."

CHAPTER SEVEN

Katie

The next morning Virginia and I meet in the school parking lot before first hour. She hands me a cruller and a cup of coffee, which instantly cheers me up. "You got up early just to get me this?"

We kiss just as we do every morning, and then I dive into the cruller, which has real blueberries and is crunchy like a scone. I didn't have much of an appetite last night, not after hearing the news Mom and Denise sprung on me. I barely touched the pizza and spent the better part of the evening reading everything I could find on Dad's court case. It wasn't much.

"Not too early. Caseo's doesn't open until seven." Virginia pries the lid off a second cup she's kept for herself. "You seemed kind of down when we talked last night. Is everything okay?"

There's no good way to say it. "My father's getting out of prison."

"What? No! You just found out?"

"Yesterday when I got home from taking the dogs out for their walk. He filed an appeal and won." I take a seat on the rear bumper of her car.

"That motherfucker," Virginia rants, pacing back and forth in the narrow confines between our vehicles. "I can't believe it. Why didn't you tell me? How is that possible? He's a monster. I thought he got ten years."

"He did." Her fury makes me feel a little better, like I'm not alone. I wasn't up to talking about it last night, but I'm ready now.

I tell her what I learned, glossing over the part of how I confronted Mom in the kitchen after Denise left my room. "Didn't you get any notice of this before?" I asked her. No answer. "Shouldn't we have been allowed to testify or something?" Still no answer. I know now from my research that she probably did get notified, and likely several times. But typical Mom, why bother to explain when you're used to holding everything inside?

"A private detective. That seems like a good idea," Virginia says, calming down somewhat when I finish. "What happens if he does come here?"

"Then we run, I guess. Denise said Nome or Fairbanks." Last night I was scared and had even convinced myself that Dad would come and try to kill us. This morning I felt better until Mom popped by my room to say we'd never be safe as long as he was out.

Seriously, Mom? What am I supposed to do with that?

"Fairbanks isn't bad, but Nome? That's nuts." Virginia set her cup on the bumper of my car. "The only time that town is livable is during the Iditarod. Plus, there are like twenty houses, two stores, and three roads. None of the roads go anywhere."

"You've been there?"

"Once. It was freaking cold and the snow blew so hard I couldn't see my hand in front of my face. Teachers have to use a rope to get from their lodgings to school. Look. Here's what's going to happen. We'll let Denise do her thing, and then if your father does come back to Alaska and your mom and Denise decide to go into hiding, you'll come live with me."

I wish. She makes it sound so easy. But that's Virginia. She never met a problem she couldn't beat down with sheer determination. "My father knows you," I say quietly. "He could find me at your house."

And hurt your family. I'd never forgive myself if anything happened to one of the Eatons. Virginia's mom is tough, but I'm guessing that my dad, the prison convict, is a whole lot tougher. He's also vicious when he drinks.

Virginia tosses her head and pours the last dregs of her coffee on the ground. "Okay, fine. Then I'll come with you. And don't say no because we're not in eighth grade anymore. We're old enough to make our own decisions now."

The last time we were separated, Virginia and I lost contact with each other for more than two years. I take her hand. "I won't say no because I won't be without you again." I'm not sure how it's going to work, but I can't stand feeling powerless.

"Good." This time when she kisses me there's more heat between us. Her lips are soft and full, and her hand finds its way under my shirt. It's probably a good thing Matty's SUV pulls in next to her car. Otherwise, I'm pretty sure we'd be late for first hour.

The three of us head to the building, and then I remember my backpack in the car. "Go on. I'll catch up," I tell them.

I jog back and snag my backpack from Evie's back seat. When I turn around, a silver BMW glides around the totem pole in the circular drive and stops. Tally gets out of the passenger seat and waves brightly at the driver, our very own librarian, Mrs. Donovan.

Okay. Now that's interesting.

CHAPTER EIGHT

Virginia

It's been over seventeen hours since we got news of Jason's death. Now, of course, the school's rumor mill is in full swing with the most outrageous theory being that Jason was microdosing strychnine in preparation for some crazy gay orgy.

North has an average-size gay population and most students are pretty accepting of us, but when a guy I don't know pauses near my locker and says to his friend, "What is it with those freaks?" I'm ready to get up in his face until it occurs to me I might be a tad paranoid. For all I know he's talking about the UAA men's cross-country running team. Three of their star athletes have been academically disqualified from participating in next week's event, which is also big news this morning.

I should spend my energy worrying about Katie's father instead. How could they let him out? He was found guilty of shooting her mom. That part was undisputed. Some issue with a cop who lied on the stand. Shouldn't that mean a new trial, not an early release?

My phone buzzes in my pocket, and I pull it out.

Cafeteria closed. Police have hall entrance blocked off, Yoon-hi texts.

Ugh. They're probably searching for the source of the poison. It makes Jason's death feel more real. *How long?*

No way to tell. We can eat lunch in the library, the auditorium, or outside. Free pizza.

Cool, I write. *I vote outside.*

Sounds good. See you in a sec.

Some schools have an open lunch policy where seniors can eat off campus as long as they return on time for afternoon classes. Mrs. Foster tried it the year Pete and Camila were seniors. There were three fender benders in the parking lot the first week with kids rushing back because they were running late, so that was the end of that. Thank you, Pete and friends.

I text Katie, who's coming from the other side of the building, to let her know we're meeting outside, and then I send a similar text to Matty, Tom, and Tally. Yoon-hi walks up just as Mrs. Foster steps out of her office with an older woman in a navy pantsuit and Officers Hess and Dietrich, two cops I'm not particularly fond of. I got to know them last year when Marisol died.

"Foster has been relieved of her duties pending an investigation into conditions in the cafeteria," Yoon-hi tells me dryly, following my gaze down the hall.

"How do you know that?"

"I overheard Mrs. Pugh tell Mrs. Hicks. Something about missing a health inspection at the beginning of the year. Since then, several kids have gotten sick and they don't know if it's related. The new AP from East is taking over for the time being. They've asked Mrs. Pugh to assist him."

I guess that makes sense. Mrs. Pugh, my honors English teacher last year, has been at North longer than any other teacher. And our current assistant principal is out on maternity leave.

Mrs. Foster holds her head high and walks out the front door with the woman in the pantsuit. Hess and Dietrich start off in the direction of the cafeteria. Mom's right. It isn't fair that

Mrs. Foster is in trouble, but I guess as principal she's expected to bear responsibility when something goes wrong.

Yoon-hi and I reach the double glass doors just as Shanice Kennedy comes running up behind us, her flip-flops slapping the floor. She barely glances at me but asks Yoon-hi if she has time to meet her after school for tutoring. *Go for it*, I think. What do I care? I stand off to the side as they make arrangements, then Yoon-hi and I head outside. A cold wind has blown up, making me wish I'd grabbed the jacket in my locker.

"I don't think Shanice likes me," I say, pulling my shirt collar around my throat as we get in line for pizza behind a couple of freshman boys.

Yoon-hi shrugs. "She's different. I wouldn't let it bother you."

"It doesn't." I shrug back. "I just don't know why."

"Mm. Did she give you her cut-through-the-bullshit speech?"

"She did!" I feel vindicated. "You, too?"

"The first time we met. Standard fare, I'm guessing. She also knows I'm straight."

"Well, I don't know what that has to do with anything."

"Maybe nothing. I'm just saying I wouldn't let it get to you."

Mrs. Lorner, the cafeteria worker who witnessed Tom's and Jason's fight, is handing out paper plates at the first of three long folding tables set up in a row. The two freshman boys in front of us make a grab for the same plate, then shove each other and pretend to fight over it as if there aren't a hundred other identical paper plates sitting on the table.

"Knock it off," I tell them. Mrs. Lorner gives me a smile. I turn back to Yoon-hi. "What does being gay or straight have to do with it?"

"Like I said, probably nothing, except she doesn't see me as competition for Tally."

"You're kidding. She mentioned Tally to you, too? Yesterday she acted like she didn't know Tally's name."

Yoon-hi shakes her head. "I don't know what to tell you."

It's obviously insignificant to her, but it makes me even more curious about Shanice. "Her mom used to work for Jason's dad. Any chance…Ow!"

One of the boys, a kid with a pimply face, seizes a whole box of pizza from the table, and then steps back on my toes when the other one tries to snatch it from him. They're both laughing like it's the funniest thing they've ever done.

"That's it! Give me the box," I yell, hopping up and down on one foot. Pimply Face hands it over reluctantly and I return it to the table. "Now, you"—I gesture to his dorky buddy—"You get one piece, and one piece only. Get it now, then grab yourself a napkin, and get out of line."

"I don't think you can do that," Pimply Face tries to argue.

"The hell I can't. Go to the end of the line. Go on." I motion him to move past the last group who are all the way back at the doors.

"This place sucks." He stomps away, muttering something about how I'm not the boss.

"And be more polite when you get up here again," I shout after him. Out of the corner of my eye, I catch Katie waving at me from the steps. I wave back, but figure I'll be pushing it if I suggest she cut in front of the dozen or so people standing between us.

"Um, can I have a bottle of water?" the dorky buddy asks when I reach for my slice. The pizzas are extra large and cut into six massive slices so I don't think I'm being unfair by only allowing him a single piece.

"Go ahead."

He takes one from the end of the last table and hurries away.

Yoon-hi and I each pick up a water bottle, then step aside to wait for Katie and Matty, who has joined her. Tally and Tom are nowhere in sight.

"Damn, girl. I guess you told him," Yoon-hi deadpans, her gaze locked on Pimply Face, who is no longer at the end of the line because others have come out of the building.

"He nearly broke my toes," I grumble. My little toe smarts, but I'll recover. What I won't stand for is stupid freshman boys being disrespectful to adults. Mrs. Lorner doesn't deserve it, and it makes me think of Jason when he told her she was embarrassing herself by asking him to clean up his mess.

The corners of Yoon-hi's mouth twitch. "Hold this," she says, adding an exaggerated, "Please." She hands me her water bottle so she can nibble at a corner of her pepperoni pizza. "You were about to ask me something?"

"Yeah. Do you have any idea where Shanice's mother works?"

"Actually, I do. That restaurant near the train depot. Soba's."

"The Japanese place?"

"Right." Yoon-hi's inflection and the pause that follows is just long enough to make me wonder if Shanice mentioned the restaurant to her because she thinks Yoon-hi is Japanese.

It doesn't feel right to ask it though, so instead I say, "She's a chef there?"

"That's my understanding. Her name is Gailene." Her voice remains flat, indicating it's the end of discussion as far as she's concerned.

Yoon-hi is one of the nicest people I know. And when she isn't exercising a very droll sense of humor, she works in many small ways to make people around her feel more at ease. So it infuriates me when others don't bother to find out she's Korean. And what's worse, Shanice won't know that she offended her because Yoon-hi will likely never tell her.

Katie and Matty join us a minute later. Despite the chilly breeze, it appears that most students have chosen to eat outside. It means there's no place to sit except in the grass or around the concrete base of our school's Tlingit totem pole. It's as wide as an average tree trunk with a slanted ledge just big enough for our butts. Not uncomfortable, but it puts us all facing different directions.

"Where's Tom?" Katie asks Matty.

"Dunno. Where's Tally?" he asks me.

"Dunno." I'm imitating him as a joke, but he doesn't seem to get it. Or maybe he's choosing not to. The four of us munch noisily on our slices without talking. It's awkward and not just because of the way we're seated, but because something intangible has come between us. I'm not sure what it is, but things have changed since last year when we worked together as a team figuring out who killed Marisol.

When did it happen? Not today, I think. The small but seismic shift in our group's dynamics must have started the day Jason reenrolled at North, or perhaps it was before that, when Matty started dating Tom. I try to put a finger on why I feel uncomfortable.

Is it because Tally isn't with us, or because she hardly participates in group discussions anymore? Or is it because Jason's gone? Surely, it doesn't have anything to do with Shanice who irritates me to no end. I feel as if a tinted lens has dropped over my eyes, obscuring my vision.

The breeze picks up and blows Matty's empty, greasy paper plate out of his hand. It glides to the ground, then pinwheels over and over all the way to the parking lot, dancing like a broken kite.

I get up to chase it down, then stop as Katie's fingers close tentatively around my wrist. "It's his plate. Let him get it," she whispers.

Matty glances at me with a puzzled, tight-lipped expression, then goes after it himself when I sit back down.

For once, I can't read Katie's face when she says, "We need to talk."

CHAPTER NINE

Katie

"Let's go inside. It's too windy out here," I yell to Virginia, over the roaring sounds around us.

Yoon-hi and Matty dash in ahead of us, and Virginia hurries after me to the double glass doors at the building's front entrance. Everybody is racing to get inside as small branches from nearby birch trees break loose and whip them in the face.

Then just as quickly as the wind blew up, it stops, so we stay outside.

"Did I do something wrong?" Virginia asks when I draw her aside.

I step back, startled. "Of course not. Why would you think that?"

She rubs the back of her neck and stares across the grass, littered with paper plates and napkins and empty water bottles. "I don't know. I just feel…off."

"Sick?"

"No, just out of sorts, I guess. I find myself wondering if any of our friends could have had it in enough for Jason to want to hurt him. Silly, right? Anyway, is everything okay?"

"My father left me a message." I play it for her, shaking off my own peculiar sense of dread. Last December when Dad phoned from prison, his calls came collect to our landline. He must have found himself a phone since, although I have no idea how he got my cell number.

"Katie. I don't know if you heard that I've earned an early release from prison. I'd really like to talk to you. You have to know how much I love you. And I know you feel the same. Will you call me back? If I don't hear from you, I'll try you again on Saturday. You owe me."

You owe me? Shit. I owe him what? It sounds like a threat. The call came in this morning during second period, and I've already listened to it twice, my head painfully throbbing at the mere sound of his voice. Fear inches up my spine.

"Do you have any fond memories at all of your father?" asked the counselor who was assigned to my case three years ago.

Of course I do. When I was little, I could hardly wait for him to come home from work. He used to swing me around in circles until I'd practically throw up with giggles. On weekends, we'd go for walks with him telling tall tales of his own childhood that often started, "When I was a little girl…" I was probably three or four before I understood it was a joke. He'd tell me I was special and that I reminded him of himself. That idea makes me sick to my stomach now.

Suddenly I become aware of Virginia eyeing me with a curious look. "What?" I say.

"I asked you how you felt about the message."

"You're kidding, right? Are you my therapist now? What do you think? It makes me want to flush my phone down the toilet!"

I hear the snappishness in my tone. I understand what she means about feeling out of sorts. All this crap with Jason and now my father is wearing on me. "I'm sorry," I say. "You didn't deserve that. It's just my father's message is creeping me out. The 'owe me' part."

She nods. "Creepy. Do you know what it means?"

"Maybe that he wouldn't let his attorney question me at his trial. At the time I thought he might have been trying to protect me. Since then I've started to wonder if it was part of a bigger, long-term strategy having to do with his early release."

"But you don't know?"

"I don't. And I can't think of any way to find out without asking him and I'm not going to do that."

"Good. I'm glad to hear that. Good." She bobs her chin and goes back to gazing distractedly at the mess on the stairs and lawn. "Katie, why didn't you want me to go after Matty's plate?"

Her question takes me by surprise. Are we back to Matty already? I start to tell her I don't know, but actually, I do. I hesitate, not sure if she's open to hearing it. "Do you want me to be honest?"

"Of course." She takes my hand. "Always."

"Okay. Don't be mad, but sometimes I think you do too much for him. I mean, I know you love him and the two of you have been through a lot together. But sometimes I think he uses you. You take care of him when he ought to take care of himself."

"I don't get it." She frowns, loosening her grip on my fingers.

God, what have I started? But I force myself to go on. "Like, when he lost his job at Misconceptions. You were over at his house every night for more than a week. He's a big boy. He should be able to handle a little adversity. He's already planning on performing there again when school is out."

"I know."

"Do you? How about when Tom was talking about his father and Matty snapped at you just for asking about his illness. Having MS is not the end of the world. Tom said so himself. You've got to admit Matty's been kind of bitchy to you recently. It's not your fault he couldn't make a decision."

"I see." The skin in the outer corners of her eyes contracts, giving her an edgy look. I wait. Have I said too much? "Does this mean you don't want to help figure out who killed Jason?"

Where the hell did she get that? "No, Virginia. I'm not saying that at all. Look, I don't want to fight with you. I love you. Can we forget we had this conversation?"

She tips her head back and forth. "I love you, too. So yes. And by the way, Yoon-hi told me Shanice's mother works at

Soba's. I thought I'd head over there tonight and see if she's there. Do you want to go with me?"

It must be something in the air. I don't understand her obsession with Shanice Kennedy. All this because Shanice didn't fall instantly in love with her like everybody else? Like me?

So what if Mrs. Kennedy worked for Jason's father and ended up on the unemployment line for a bit? She's obviously working now. If you ask me, Tom is a much more viable suspect. He sat with us at lunch. He could have slipped something into Jason's food when no one else was looking. He's the one who whispered Jason didn't deserve Matty, which I told Virginia on the phone last night. Has she forgotten that already?

I blow a breath through my lips, figuring okay, if that's what it takes to make my girlfriend happy, it won't hurt to eliminate the Kennedys as suspects. "Sure," I say. "Let's do it."

The bell rings. Since I'm an office aide after lunch, I don't have to worry about tardies, but I don't want Virginia arriving late to class. She has big college plans, and I don't want anything I do getting in the way of that. I lean in to give her a hug.

She holds me stiffly and then we separate.

We'll work it out, I tell myself. We always do. We go inside and I head for the office to meet the new temporary principal, whom I instantly dislike.

"I'm Mr. Sullivan. No relation," he tells me, shaking my hand briskly when Mrs. Pugh introduces us. It takes me a minute to figure out he's probably referring to Sullivan Arena, Anchorage's indoor stadium where North holds its graduation ceremony every spring. Also, some former city mayor. This Sullivan is young and thin with a light fringe around his ears and a few dark hairs sprouting like weeds on top. I'm getting a gay vibe from him, but I can't pin down exactly why.

What I do get loud and clear is that he doesn't like seeing me stand around doing nothing or using the admin assistants' computers. Normally, when there are no errands to run or papers to be copied or any other scut work left over from the morning, I work on one of my art projects. My most recent is a picture of my father after he shot a zebra on an African safari.

I found it after Mom threw it out, and I scanned it in art. Now I'm using Photoshop to switch the zebra's head with Dad's so that the zebra is holding a hunting rifle and Dad is lying on the ground with a bullet in his chest. I call it *The Upside Down*, after the alternate but parallel dimension from a Netflix show called *Stranger Things.*

Mr. Sullivan walks by, catches a glimpse of the screen, and pauses. He wrinkles his nose and hugs his skinny arms around his waist like he's cold. "Is that homework, Katie?"

"Yes."

More nose wrinkling. "I taught computer graphics for two years before I went into administration. My students had to get my approval for each and every project."

This tells me two things about him. One, he didn't teach long before his students probably chased him out. And two, he doesn't care for my interpretation of shooting defenseless animals.

I'm grateful my art teacher doesn't censor my work. Mrs. Pugh looks over from the counter, lifts a brow, and gives her head a tiny shake. Last year I didn't like her much, but I find I'm warming to her now.

"Isn't there something more productive Katie can do?" Sullivan asks her.

To which she gives him one of her trademark sour smiles. "I'll find something."

He goes back into Mrs. Foster's office, and she comes over to take a look at my screen. "Any chance you could put a smile on the zebra's face when you finish the transposition?"

I'm practically in love with her now. "Liquify filter. I'll try that first. After school, I mean. Um, should I grab a mop and shine the floor?"

This time I get the sourpuss smile. "Don't push it."

She glances around the office and settles on the quad screen surveillance monitor on the wall behind a desk. The scenes constantly switch from classrooms to halls to the cafeteria to the auditorium to the library to the gym. My first couple of weeks I watched it all the time, hoping to catch a glimpse of vandals painting graffiti or fights breaking out in the halls. I've given that up because it's mostly boring stuff.

"Why don't you see if the cafeteria people could use your help?" She points to a live feed of Mrs. Lorner and Lindley Crowe throwing empty pizza boxes in the trash.

"You want me to go into the cafeteria?"

"I don't see why not. Just stay out of the way of the police and keep away from the food prep area unless Miss Jamie tells you it's okay."

I close out Photoshop and drop my project into my Google Classroom folder, wishing I could think of a way to get Virginia out of class. She'd love the chance to snoop around a crime scene. But I'll have to check this one out on my own.

It turns out it's not all that exciting watching forensic guys scour the six-foot-wide student refrigerator and crawl around on the floor, so when Lindley vanishes down a hall and Mrs. Lorner asks me to come outside with her, I do. The bright sun itches my back. It must be thirty degrees hotter than normal, an odd contrast to the earlier wind. We gather and toss away trash scattered clear out to the parking lot, and she thanks me about a million times for helping her.

"You're welcome. I don't mind at all."

"My, my. Such a dear little thing you are, aren't you?" she exclaims in a warbly voice.

I'm not sure how I'm supposed to answer that. *Um, thanks?* So I don't. Then, instead of going back inside, she turns over a plastic milk crate by the door and pulls a pack of cigarettes from a front apron pocket. "Bad habit, kiddo. It's a one-way ticket to hell." She hunches her back, resting baggy arms on hefty knees and lighting up with a cheap blue plastic lighter. "We're not supposed to smoke on school property, but you won't tell, will you?"

I assure her that I won't.

She bobs her head a couple of times and blows a perfect smoke ring. "When I was your age everybody smoked, but not because we didn't know better because we did. We thought we were cool. You don't smoke, do you?"

"No, ma'am."

"Good. Glad to hear it. Promise me you never will."

"Okay," I say. "I promise." It's an easy promise to make because who wants tiny fissures around their mouth where lipstick bleeds like hers? "I have my own bad habits," I confess, showing her the thumbnail I started working on last night. I used to bite my nails to the quick when I was little. Today the nail looks ugly and jagged. It hurts, but I can't seem to leave it alone.

She puts her fingertips to mine to see it up close. "Ick. But at least it's fixable and free. My habit costs a couple hundred bucks a month. Now why is a pretty young thing like you doing that? Some sort of new diet, maybe? Nails instead of food?"

I cough out a laugh. "No diet. I got bad news last night." She looks at me expectantly, and I wish I hadn't brought it up. "My father, he lives in another state. I don't see him much. I don't want to. But he might come for a visit."

"Your parents are divorced?"

"Almost. It's in the works. Dad's in prison, and he's getting out. He shot my mother in the face. She's gay. I'm gay. I'm not sure it matters to him about me, but god, he was furious when he found out about her. Mom thinks he's coming to kill us. Her partner is hiring a private detective to watch him."

Holy shit, why am I'm telling this to a stranger? I cover my mouth and back away, nearly bumping into the filthy yellow dumpster behind me. The stink of rotting food is overwhelming. It glistens with grease and sweat. "I don't know why I said all that. I'm not normally so—"

"Forthcoming?" she finishes for me.

"Yeah. I mean, I've had therapy and everything. I guess I'm feeling nervous and scared." Not to mention, crazy.

She grinds out the cigarette butt, then stands, scrutinizing me through her thick, magnifying glasses. Her eyes are slightly crossed. "Kiddo. Please tell me your name again. I'm sorry. I'm not very good with names."

"Katie. My name is Katie McRanes."

"Oh, my goodness, what a pretty name. I have a niece called Katie who lives just around the corner from me. She's a pretty little thing like you. Listen, kiddo, I'm going to tell you something, and I hope you'll believe me." She pauses, her gnarled fingers fumbling in her apron pocket.

"Okay," I prompt.

"First, you have every right to bite those nails of yours. Your daddy sounds like an awful man. But I can tell just by looking at you, you're smart. You'll work it out. And I think you've got good friends who'll help."

"I do." I figure she must have noticed my friends when Mrs. Foster called her into her office with us last week after Tom and Jason's fight. I wait another second and when she doesn't continue, I tell her thanks and start to reach for the crusty door handle behind her that leads back through the kitchen.

"Oh, I'm not done. Not yet." She locates another cigarette, lights it, and squints through the haze. "It's Katie, is it?"

"Um. That's right."

"So listen to me, Katie. Here's the part you may not believe. My husband was a biochemist. Worked for that big lab. I forget what it's called. Eco Bio Something? No matter, it does have a name. My Escobar was smart, but even he didn't always believe me when I told him I could predict the future. He'd laugh when I'd say something was about to happen. But then, you know what? When it did, I'd remind him about animals lying down in fields so they won't fall. Did you notice the wind today and how dreadfully hot it is now?"

"Yeah."

"Of course you did, because something's going to happen. And when it does, you won't have to worry about that horrible daddy of yours any longer. So bite your nails if you must, but I promise you everything is going to work out. You and that skinny girl of yours will be fine. I promise."

Animals that lie down so they won't fall? I can feel my eyes rounding in disbelief. Apparently, I'm not the only one who's crazy. "Okay. Well, thank you." I step around her and grab the door handle.

"No, kiddo. Thank you. And remember what I said. It's coming," she calls after me as the door swings slowly shut behind me.

I head back across the cafeteria, duck under the yellow crime tape, and slip out into the hall. It's not until I reach a water fountain that I stop, take a long drink, and lean my head against a locker.

Then I can't help myself. I laugh so hard, tears come to my eyes. I can't help but think Mrs. Lorner is right. Everything will be okay. Because for the first time since Jason fell off his stool, I'm not worried, nervous, or scared. Instead I got a crazy lady on my side who tells me everything will be just fine.

CHAPTER TEN

Virginia

Katie and I decide to go shopping after school for dog toys at Alaska Mill and Feed. It's a couple of blocks from the harbor and built to resemble an old country barn. Not the kind of store you'd find in most downtowns, just fun and kind of kitschy. They carry everything from Crocs to plastic flamingos to pet food and supplies. George and Abe chew through their toys like puppies and are always in need of more. Besides, we figure we can use a break from all the other stuff that's going on.

"We can go to Soba's and talk to Mrs. Kennedy afterward. It's just a couple of blocks away," I say.

"Great," Katie grumbles.

I can feel my eyebrows pinch together. Why is she so certain Shanice has nothing to do with Jason's death? It feels like she won't give the idea a chance. Before I can ask, we step outside and see Mom and Dad standing in the school's circle drive. Katie's mom and Denise are with them. Denise's red Jeep is in the visitor lot parked beside my mother's recently restored Volkswagen bug.

"This can't be good." I halt.

Katie licks her lips. "There goes shopping."

Mom lifts a hand as we draw closer. "Hey, you two. Officer Hess asked that we bring you down to the police station when school was out, and we thought it might be a good idea if we all went together."

It's probably her suggestion, a way to make Katie's mother feel more at ease. I'm not sure it's working. Mrs. McRanes is wearing her black eye patch. Sweat trickles down the right side of her bullet-scarred cheek below it, and she stands with her knees locked, as if expecting to be punched.

Dad must notice as well because he says to Denise, "I hate to ask, but would you mind if I ride with you? My wife's car is pretty small, and Virginia hates feeling cramped in the rear seat."

It's true, but I think he's just trying to do his part to make a difficult situation slightly better.

Denise says, "No problem," and guides Katie's mother to the Jeep with a hand in the small of her back. Dad, in his gold-and-purple tennis shorts and too-white shoes and socks, folds his long legs into the back seat next to Katie.

"Being summoned to the police station like this is normal?" I ask Mom, climbing in on the passenger side of her car and double-checking to make sure I'm buckled in. She's a good driver, but Pete recently souped up the engine by replacing the car's factory exhaust system with something high performance and occasionally she has a heavy foot. He wants to work on my car next.

She presses in the clutch and shifts, spinning the new power steering wheel with one finger and zipping around a line of drivers waiting at the stop sign. A guy from my computer apps class flips her off.

"You're witnesses to Jason's last moments in the cafeteria," she replies, whipping around another corner and frowning at a truck spewing black smoke in front of us. "Officers Hess and Dietrich have some questions, and they know better than to talk to you without your dad and me. You're not nervous, are you, sweetheart?"

I heave a theatrical sigh. "I'll try not to faint."

She chuckles but is all business as she tells me what to expect. Questions. Cameras. Notes. Possibly a follow-up. We paid a visit to the police station when Marisol was murdered, but back then I was volunteering information.

The VW alternately purrs and sputters down the New Seward Highway, with Mom moving in and out of the traffic as she talks about not responding to innuendos, or suggestions that I might want to change my story if details appear inconsistent. I'm to give her a nudge or nod if I'm uncomfortable with what they're asking. "Saying you don't remember is fine," she tells me. "Whatever you do, don't make anything up."

"I wasn't planning to." I tug the seatbelt digging in my neck and gulp, realizing this may be harder than I thought.

By the time the multi-story glass building that houses the downtown police station comes into sight, I'm starting to feel anxious. She jerks to a stop at a parking meter on the street and waits for Denise to catch up.

I let out a breath. "You drive too fast."

"You think so?" She shuts off the engine, hangs on to the steering wheel at ten and two, and drums her thumbs. An old woman pushing a shopping cart of flattened cardboard boxes and empty soda cans crosses in front of us, glaring at Mom through the windshield.

When Denise's Jeep pulls in behind us, my father jumps out and slips his credit card into the machine, and then does the same with the one in front of us.

"You didn't need to do that," Denise says gratefully, helping Katie's mom out of the car.

"Do what?" He winks. We head inside.

Yoon-hi and Matty are already there with their parents, sitting in a row of plastic chairs along a wall. "Well, this is fun. Who brought snacks?" Yoon-hi jokes as I take a seat beside her.

Matty leans in front of her and says, "Tally just left. Tom is with them now."

Poor Tom. It's the second time in twenty-four hours he's had to talk to the cops. When he comes out a couple of minutes later with a man in a forest green McKinley Golf Course polo shirt (probably his father) and another in a black, custom-tailored suit (probably his lawyer), he looks right past us and walks out without a word.

Poor Matty.

Officer Hess sticks his head out the door Tom and his dad just came out of and invites me and my parents inside.

"Good luck," Katie whispers.

"Cakewalk," I whisper back.

Five chairs surround a plain white table inside the interview room. My parents and I sit on one side of the table, Officers Hess and Dietrich on the other. Last year I attempted to do some social media research on them but found out little, other than Joe Hess is divorced and Sam Dietrich has a wife and two young children. They were patrol officers until a year and a half ago.

Dietrich, the older of the two, fingers a droopy moustache, and after politely acknowledging my parents' presence and Mom's time on the force, explains that this is not a custodial interrogation. Meaning I'm free to leave when I want and am not required to answer any questions. He also says the interview will be recorded, pointing to a small video camera in an upper corner of the room.

"Got it." I push down a lump in my throat.

"Now then," he begins. "Please tell us in your own words, Miss Eaton, what occurred yesterday at lunch, beginning with in what positions you were all sitting at the table."

I cross, then uncross my legs and lean forward in my chair. "Okay. So, Matty was in what you'd probably call the middle seat, with Tom on his left and me on his right. Katie was next to me." Each table holds twelve stools, six on each side, but I figure he already knows that.

"And just to be clear, it's Matthew Brown you're talking about?"

I nod.

"Please indicate your answer with yes or no." Dietrich motions over his shoulder at the camera.

"Oh, right. I mean, yes. Matthew Brown. Tom, I guess it's probably Thomas." *How do I not know this?* "Thomas Glass. And Katherine McRanes. We were all on one side of the table."

"Facing which direction? Hall or cafeteria?"

"Cafeteria. I could see directly to the lunch lines. Yoon-hi Park sat across from me, and Tally…Natalie Carter, that is… was next to her across from Katie."

"Fine. And again, just to be clear, Mr. Brown and Mr. Glass were facing *into* the cafeteria?"

"Yeah. And so were Katie and me."

"Excellent." He bobs his head enthusiastically like I've just scored big at the high school quiz bowl. "Now please tell us what happened once Jason Gonzalez joined you from the kitchen. Had everyone else finished eating?"

"That's correct," I say, with a quick glance at Mom who smiles back reassuringly. Dad pats my knee. "Jason walked over and sat beside Yoon-hi who was across from Matty. He opened his lunchbox and started in about how—"

"Can you describe his lunchbox and what was inside it?" Officer Hess cuts in. Dietrich swivels his head, giving him a look I don't understand.

"Sure." I cross my legs again. "It's one of those rectangular metal boxes kids have in elementary school. Twilight, Sparkle, and Rainbow Dash on the outside—"

"What's that now?" Hess picks up a pen from an otherwise empty table.

"You know. *My Little Pony* characters from the cartoon series?"

Apparently he doesn't know and probably thinks it's immature for a high school student to carry a little kid's lunchbox, to which I would agree. He asks for clarification, makes a note, then gestures to me to continue. "You were saying?"

"You mean about what was inside his lunchbox?"

"Yes."

"Okay, well, Jason always had the same thing for lunch." I explain about the meat and cheese sandwiches and his can of Diet Coke.

Hess sits back and taps the pen against his upper teeth as Dietrich asks how the food was wrapped and if the can was already open when Jason sat down.

"Plastic wrap like always, and tight all the way under the plate as far as I could tell. I don't think he opened his soda right away."

"Good," says Dietrich. "Very good. Now at any time after the moment Jason sat down was there a distraction? A point when one or more of you might have gotten up, or looked away from the table?"

I can see where he's heading. "You mean when one of us might have dumped rat poison on his food?" Mom nudges me under the table, but I don't think I'm saying anything the officers haven't thought of.

"Right," says Dietrich in his encouraging way.

"No. I don't think so. So, the poison wasn't in the can?"

Neither of them answers that, which was what frustrated me so much nine months ago. They wanted to know things but weren't willing to share any information with me. Now that I think about it, however, I realize the poison had to be in Jason's food. How else could it have happened? The can wasn't opened until later. And ten minutes after eating, his seizures started.

"Let's move on to the conversation that took place when Jason sat down. Who spoke first?" says Hess. He's shaved his overly long sideburns since the last time we talked, but he still reminds me of a werewolf. Must be his oversized canines.

I glance at a brown spot on the ceiling to collect my thoughts. "Jason did. He thanked us sarcastically for not waiting for him, his usual stuff. Then he told Tom he'd had quite the week. No, wait. I think he said that first. And it felt like he was trying to provoke Tom into a fight like the one they had last Wednesday."

They have to know about the fight because Tom said they asked him about it yesterday. I wait, expecting them to want my take on it, but instead Hess says, "Is Mr. Glass easily provoked?"

Oops. This is probably what Mom meant about innuendos. "I don't know him that well," I answer cautiously for Matty's sake. "What I can say is that Jason had a way about him. He was snarky."

"Snarky?"

"You know. Snide. Insincere. Often making cutting remarks that the rest of us tried to ignore." Mom nudges me under the table harder, and this time I understand I may have said too much.

"Do you all keep your lunches in the student refrigerator?" Dietrich takes over again.

"Not every day. Yesterday, I left my lunch in my locker. It was a peanut butter and jelly sandwich and didn't need to stay cold. Sometimes I eat from one of the à la carte lines. I hardly ever have the full, hot lunch." Just trying to be helpful here. I fake a sweet smile.

"What about Mr. Brown and Mr. Glass?"

I open my mouth, but Mom beats me to it. "Hadn't you better ask them?" Her tone is firm but polite.

Dietrich gives his moustache a tug and changes tacks again. "What can you tell me about Mr. Brown's relationship with Thomas Glass and Jason Gonzalez?"

"Again—" Mom cuts in.

He frowns. "I'm merely asking for your daughter's opinion, ma'am. But fine. We'll leave it. So, Jason Gonzales sat down next to Miss Park and attempted to provoke another argument with Mr. Glass?"

I sit back in my chair. "I don't think I said that." *At least not exactly. And actually it was Tom who provoked Jason last week.*

"We can play it back for you, if you like." Hess curls his upper lip and drops the pen on the table like he's caught me in a horrible lie.

I wave a hand. "It isn't necessary. How much longer is this going to take?" My voice is whiny like a kid who's missed a nap. Shoot, I thought I would be better at this.

"Just another couple of minutes." Dietrich gives Hess another look. "Now, then. When Jason, Mr. Gonzalez, started seizing, Miss Park and Miss Carter got up and left the table. Is that correct?"

"Yes. They went to get Mrs. Foster, our security guard, and nurse."

"And you ran around the table. To do what?"

I'm guessing they must have watched North's surveillance feed. I'm not sure how much the camera caught. "To see if there was anything I could do for him. He was lying on the floor. His whole body shook like his bones were going to snap. I wanted to help." Hess smirks. I really don't like this guy. "I know CPR," I say defensively.

Dietrich reaches for his upper lip. "I believe you. And I also know that Miss McRanes went through Jason's backpack."

"She was looking for medication—"

"Yes. I believe that as well. What I'd like to know is why Mr. Brown stood back and did nothing and why Mr. Glass told the deceased he didn't deserve him."

This really throws me. They clearly know nothing about Matty. "Matty screamed. I'm sure he wanted to do something, but he was too upset."

Last year one of the performers at the drag bar Misconceptions fell off the stage in the middle of a show. Matty was ashamed that customers rushed to help while he stood by feeling paralyzed.

"And Mr. Glass?"

"You'd better ask him," I say, taking my cue from Mom.

Dad pats my knee again, and Mom glances at the time on her phone. "I believe that's enough for now," she says. "If you want anything more from Virginia, you know where to find her. Understanding, of course, that we are not giving you permission to talk to her without us. Ever." She lifts the corners of her lips, but her eyes stay flat.

Dietrich sniffs. "Of course. Thank you all for coming in today. We'll be in touch." He stands and shakes our hands. Hess does the same.

I'm already replaying the interview in my head as we walk out. The things I should have said and didn't. The thoughts I should have kept to myself. I'm glad I didn't mention my suspicions about Shanice. They would have thought me an idiot when suspicions are all I have.

When we reach the lobby, I see Katie sitting in a chair all by herself, biting a nail.

"You're next, Miss McRanes." Hess comes out behind us.

I jump at the sound of his voice and turn to Mom. "Can you go in with her?"

"I'm sorry, Mrs. Eaton. Are you an attorney?" Hess puts on a phony smile.

Mom turns, her mouth set in a hard line. "I'm an interested party, Officer Hess. And so long as this is not a custodial interrogation, it's their right to have me join them." She addresses Katie's family: "If you want me."

"We'd love it," Katie's mom and Denise reply in unison.

"Of course," Hess mutters with a peevish look.

Katie puckers her lips at me in a silent kiss, and they all head into the interview room. Dad joins the other parents by the outside door, leaving me alone with Matty and Yoon-hi.

"How'd it go?" Matty falls back into a chair, stretching his long, thick legs out in front of him.

I stare at him in astonishment, noting for the first time that he's wearing jeans and a purple-and-gold North Anchorage High School sweatshirt. No makeup. I can't remember the last time I saw him dressed so conservatively. "Not bad. I survived. You slumming it?"

"This old thing?" His gaze drops to the shirt.

"You should wear it on Halloween and go as straight," Yoon-hi deadpans.

He shakes his head grimly. "Dress to impress. Mom's idea." He dips his chin at the door closing behind Katie's mother. "Do you think your mother will go in with us too?"

"Definitely," I say. "Just ask her." I know she will, no matter how late she has to stay. It's just the way my mother is.

The three of us stand there for a moment, then I murmur, "Love you guys," not sure how they'll take it. As a group, we're not that lovey-dovey.

There's a long pause before Matty answers, "Back atcha, girlfriend."

"Same here," Yoon-hi echoes, leaning in for a quick peck on my cheek.

I put my fingers to my face in surprise. "What was that for?"

Yoon-hi rolls her eyes, but I can see she's trying not to laugh. "Oh, please. You didn't know I had a thing for you? Are you that obtuse? Come on, we're all in this together, right? One for all, and all for one?"

"Yeah." Matty bobs his head. "Text later?"

I grin. "You got it." Then I join my dad to go outside.

CHAPTER ELEVEN

Katie

Officer Dietrich asks me a dozen different ways if I noticed anyone get up from the table or put something in Jason's food. No. No. No, and no, I answer. We spend a lot of time on how Jason's food was wrapped and if it looked like anyone had tampered with it. Tight, and not that I could tell, I say. I'm beginning to feel bored.

How about the student refrigerator? Did I see anyone lingering there? Anybody carrying in anything that looked suspicious? And on which shelf was the *My Little Pony* lunchbox? I have no idea, I say to every question, reminding them the fridge sits on the other side of a wall, not visible from our table, no matter which direction we were facing.

There's probably security footage of it, I say. "Have you seen it?"

"Of course." Hess makes a note.

"Tell me what you observed about Jason's relationship with Matthew Brown and Thomas Glass." Dietrich pulls hard on the corner of his moustache.

Virginia's mother puts a hand on the arm of my chair and looks him dead in the eye. "You're kidding, right?" I'm not sure what that's about.

Then Hess takes over, and it's more of the same. Who said what to whom, and did I hear Tom tell Jason that Jason didn't deserve Matty? Which must mean someone else heard it too since I haven't mentioned it to them. "Yeah. Right before Jason started to convulse," I reply.

He leans back in his rolling chair and taps a ballpoint pen against his teeth, a look on his face as if to say we're finally getting somewhere. "And how did Jason react?"

I steal a glance at Mom. She's handling all this pretty well, everything considered. She's got her hands tucked tightly between her knees, but her left eye is focused and she isn't fussing with her eye patch.

She was still in the hospital with a shattered cheekbone the first time the cops stopped by to ask me about the night Dad shot her. I get that they were just trying to do their jobs, but it kind of felt like they were accusing her of setting Dad off. As if her being gay and having an affair with Denise was naturally sufficient to provoke him to such violence. My mom has never been all that stable, but by the time the trial was over she was a basket case. It's understandable that she distrusts the legal system now and wants to flee, especially since my father, with eight years left on his sentence, is getting out.

"What did Jason say when Mr. Glass told him he didn't deserve Mr. Brown?" Officer Hess repeats, his tone bordering on impatience.

I sit back, imitating his posture and tap my thumb against my teeth. "I'm trying to remember. I'm not sure Jason heard him."

"I see." He sets the pen carefully on the table. "Do you consider yourself a reliable witness, Miss McRanes?"

"What?" Mrs. Eaton and I say simultaneously. I'm puzzled. She's upset.

Hess's eyes dart to his partner. "All I'm saying is that given your past trauma—"

"Stop it! That's enough!" Virginia's mother shoots to her feet. "We're leaving now. Let's go." She practically shoves me out the door.

Officer Dietrich trails after us, offering her a sheepish look. "I'm terribly sorry, Carol. That was completely uncalled for. Joe and I, we're both feeling frustrated with the slow progress on this case. I'm sure you understand—"

"No. I don't. Katie isn't a suspect. She didn't have anything to do with this. If you expect cooperation from these kids, you need to treat them with respect. Joe, I understand. But you have more experience, Sam. You ought to know better. I'm surprised and disappointed with you. If I hear of anything like this happening with the others, you can bet I'm going to file a complaint with your superior."

Her voice rises as she speaks. Two women dressed in skimpy skirts at the counter, glance around and titter behind their hands.

"Actually, would you mind going in with us, Mrs. Eaton?" Matty steps forward from the row of chairs.

"I'd be happy to, honey." She breaks eye contact with Dietrich and addresses Denise and Mom and me. "Are you guys okay? I'm sorry the tone in there turned unprofessional. APD works hard to maintain good public relations with the community. That was unexpected."

Not for me, it wasn't. I was caught off guard by Officer Hess's question, but what he asked didn't seem that bad to me. I imagine they've looked into all our backgrounds. It would have taken them no time at all to uncover my family's sordid history.

Denise assures her that we're fine. Mrs. Eaton gives me a fiercer hug than I probably deserve, and we thank her several times before heading out.

Denise drops me at school to pick up my car, and when I get back to the apartment, I head for my room and call Virginia.

"Your mom was terrific. You should have heard her lay into Dietrich. Hess was an asshole, although I did sort of mock him. Your mom's going to stay and sit in on Matty and Yoon-hi's interviews."

Hearing a familiar squeaking sound, I picture Virginia collapsing on her bed. "Good. I told them she would. Hess and

Dietrich are both assholes in my opinion. So, who do you think killed Jason? Any ideas?"

I hesitate. I wish she wouldn't ask because I don't want to feed into her fixation with Shanice. "I don't know. Probably Tom. Maybe someone else." Like Matty. I don't really believe Virginia's best friend would hurt someone, but I'd be stupid not to realize Hess and Dietrich view him as a suspect.

Voices and canned TV laughter fill the silence on her end, then her bedsprings squeak again. "Would you rather wait and go to Soba's another time?"

Relief flushes through me. "Would you mind? That'd be great. I'm exhausted. How about tomorrow night? No, wait. That won't work. We're supposed to go hear Tally sing at Caseo's. Did you know she plays guitar? Can't miss that. How about Thursday night?"

Virginia huffs a breath. "Fine. I'm going tonight. Get some rest. We'll talk tomorrow."

She abruptly disconnects, leaving me staring at the phone. *Why didn't you just say you were going to go tonight with or without me?* She's angry with me, but I don't know why. No, I don't think Shanice or her mother had anything to do with Jason's death, but I told Virginia that I'd go. It feels like she's cutting me off.

I don't get it. I don't get it at all.

CHAPTER TWELVE

Virginia

It's nearly the dogs' dinnertime so I feed them before heading out. When I step outside, the sky has taken on an ombre cast. Indigo above our roof fades into cornflower that turns translucent closer to the grass. There's a filmy haze where the colors blend together. It's weird, given that the sun won't set for a couple of hours.

The strangeness is compounded by a bull moose lying in our neighbors' yard. Their calico cat crouches a couple of feet in front of it. Most small animals are scared to death of moose. They won't go anywhere near them, but the cat doesn't seem afraid at all. It inches closer as the moose shakes its dewlap as if inviting it to share a twiggy shrub. I snap a picture with my phone and start to send it to Katie.

No, forget it. She won't care. She's too tired or busy doing *whatever*. She obviously doesn't take my theory about Shanice Kennedy being a suspect seriously. A voice in my head reminds me that Katie's got other things to worry about. But I can't shake the feeling that something's not right between us. Surely she knows I'd never let her father hurt her. I'd put myself between her and his bullet.

A chill races up my spine.

Holy crap. Where did that come from? Katie and her father's bullet. An image briefly fills my brain of her dad standing with a gun in the doorway of a darkened house. It's so vivid a shriek escapes my lips.

The last time I saw him was four years ago, a handsome man with dark hair and dimples just like Katie's. The Paul McRanes I knew talked too loud and laughed too much. Still, he was more personable than her mom. I never saw him for the spiteful psychopath he turned out to be.

The picture leaves my brain and the moose glances over as if to say, "Chill, Virginia. Now you're just making stuff up." The cat runs off, and it goes back to chomping on a twig.

I wiggle my shoulders to release the tension, then get in my car and head south on O'Malley toward Ship Creek, all the while working to convince myself that Katie still loves me and that just because she doesn't agree with everything I say doesn't mean there's something wrong between us. That her son of a bitch psycho father has better things to do in his post-prison life than come here and kill her. And that my imagination is working overtime due to the strange weather we had today. Wind. Heat. An eerie ombre sky straight out of *The Dead Can't Talk*, the student film that started all the trouble we had last fall before Christmas.

By the time I pull into Soba's gravel parking lot, it occurs to me that if Shanice is here, it might be a good idea to have company. Because, well, because the girl kind of scares me. She's short, but with those knotty shoulders and ropy calves, she could likely pound me into the ground. I'm fairly athletic but I've never been a fighter.

I text Yoon-hi and Matty. Wait a couple of minutes but get no answer from either. Right. They're probably still at the police station.

There's an online site where you can look up inspection reports for food facilities, and earlier I learned that Soba's has had numerous health code violations. They were closed for a week last year when mice droppings were discovered in a food prep area. Hmm. Mice droppings. Rat poison. Maybe I should have mentioned that to Katie.

There's no way I'm going to have dinner here even though a sign out front says the restaurant is under new management. It ends up not being an option anyway when I go inside and a woman in a bright red kimono and a cheap black wig asks me if I have a reservation. She sounds like she's from Texas.

"Do yah have a reservation?" *'Cause you cain't eat here if yah don't.* (Okay, I added the last part myself, but it was definitely implied.)

Despite the crappy wig, she's so pretty I find myself stammering. "Um, no, sorry. I just wanted to find out if the mother of a friend of mine is here tonight. Gailene Kennedy, I think her name is? I believe she works in the, um, kitchen?"

The hostess offers me a charming smile. "Not tonight, honey. Tuesdays and Wednesdays are her days off. Would yah like me to tell her y'all stopped by?"

"That's okay. I'll come back another night."

"Have a pleasant evening," she calls after me as I head for my car. I'm partly glad I don't have to talk to Shanice's mom when I haven't even thought about what I'm going to say. But I'm also frustrated because I would have loved to tell Katie that Shanice and her mom really are good suspects. But are they? Just because Shanice expressed dislike for Jason and she and I didn't hit it off? I'm starting to wonder if I'm losing my mind.

When I get home, Mom is fixing dinner. I set the table, and she talks about the color of the sky, then tells me that Officers Hess and Dietrich have been taken off Jason's case.

I'm happy to hear it. In case I haven't made it clear, I don't like either one of them. "What happened?" I ask, fishing in a drawer for knives and forks.

"Nothing really," she replies. "Their supervisor simply felt a more experienced point of view was needed. They've been replaced by Detective Sandra Rosen, an old friend of mine from my academy days. Oh, look." She points at the TV in our family room. "There she is now."

An attractive Black woman with glasses and gray hair shaved close to her head stands in front of rolling hills of lush green grass with the corner of what looks like a shed off to the left. Beside her is a female reporter from one of our local news stations. Rosen leans into the reporter's microphone. "We're not naming any suspects. At this point we're simply trying to trace the source of the poison."

"But you are talking to students, specifically the ones who ate lunch with the victim?"

Rosen gives her a patient smile. "As I said before, I'm not free to comment on it at this time. What I will say is that what happened yesterday afternoon was a terrible tragedy. A bright young man is dead. APD intends to leave no stone unturned in our quest for answers."

"Of course. And is it true the victim had a heart condition?"

"No comment."

The camera zooms in on the reporter. "The police request anyone with information about the case call their hotline." She glances at her phone. "Also, the father of the victim, Mr. Michael Gonzalez, has set up a GoFundMe page for those who'd like to help with funeral costs. The information is available on our website."

I can feel my pulse hammering the soft tissue below my eye. Detective Rosen is obviously at McKinley Golf Course, where Tom's father works. Recalling my promise to Matty, I follow my mother back into the kitchen.

"Mom, if someone thought she might know something relevant to the case but has no proof, would you recommend that person call the hotline?"

She gives me a long look as she sets last night's leftovers on the table. Turkey meatloaf, Reggie's birthday dinner request every year. "Sweetheart. What is it you think you know?"

I twist my fingers in a cat's paw knot. "Just that lots of people who don't eat lunch with us use that refrigerator. And if the police are focusing their investigation on just our group, they could be missing someone else who might have a motive."

"Such as?"

"Someone else." I unknot my hands and let them hang at my sides.

"Virginia, sit." She motions to the kitchen island and takes a seat beside me. "Now, start at the beginning, please. Who are we talking about?"

The twitching under my eye increases. I'm practically winking at my mother. "There's this girl, Shanice Kennedy. She's new to North. When I was tutoring her yesterday, she got a call from her mother letting her know that Jason was dead. It's how I found out about it too. From her, I mean. Anyway, Shanice called Jason a turd. She didn't even pretend to care that he'd suffered a horrible, painful death, because her mother used to work for his father as a cook in Talkeetna and when his business folded, she lost her job. Now she—her mother, that is—works at Soba's. By the railroad station? They've had plenty of health code violations, and I'd put money on it that they use rat poison in the kitchen. I know it's not a lot to go on, but haven't you always told me to trust my instincts? And right now they're screaming at me that this shouldn't be ignored. If your friend doesn't know about it, how can she investigate?"

My words rush together and for an instant I feel as if I'm drowning in a sea of conjecture. Does any of this make sense?

Mom reaches for my hands, once again twisting in my lap. "Honey, calm down. I know you want to protect your friends."

"I do. But that's not why I'm telling you this. You didn't hear Shanice. Nobody did but me. Look, doesn't it at least bear looking into?"

"Okay. Okay. I get it. Would it make you feel any better if I talked to Sandy Rosen?"

"Would you?" I'm so thankful, tears fill my eyes.

"Yes, of course I will. I'll call her after dinner." Mom hesitates. "But I hope you don't mind me saying that I don't understand why you're so worked up over this. Is everything okay between you and Katie? Hess and Dietrich never suspected either one of you, if that's what you're worried about. And as for Matty, I'll make sure Sandy knows how much your father and I respect his family. In fact, I was with him and his mother when she came into the interview room. No one who's ever met that boy would think—"

"Detective Rosen, your friend, is at Tom's father's golf course. Didn't you see it? They're probably searching the maintenance shed for rat poison. Tom says they have it."

"Oka-ay." She draws out the word as if to give me a chance to better explain myself. I wish I could. "Sweetie. I don't know Tom as well. But you do understand that we have to let the police do their jobs—"

"Katie's dad is getting out of prison," I interrupt again.

"I know."

A hiccup catches in my throat. "Christ, you know but you haven't said anything?"

"I figured she'd tell you herself."

"Oh, really. You *figured*, did you?"

I'm about to really lay into her, but something in her expression slows me down. She lets go of my hands and settles back as her eyebrows squeeze together with a familiar expression of concern. Dad suggested I see a trauma counselor after Marisol's death. I had no interest in it, and Mom supported me, outvoting him. I'm a little worried she might regret that now.

I unknot my fingers and imitate her stance. Can't have her thinking I've lost my marbles, even if I have. "She did tell me. Her mom and Denise are concerned he might show up here when he gets out. I told Katie she could come stay with us if it happens. Is that okay with you?" I make my voice sound casual.

Mom's eyebrows slowly relax. "Yes. Of course. You probably know that Denise has hired someone to keep an eye on things in Washington. I told them to let me know if there's anything I can do to help."

"Good idea," I say, because it probably is. "Should I call Dad and Reggie in for dinner?"

"Yes, please."

My knees shake as I slide off the stool. I take a few deep breaths. When we all sit down at the table, I slide my phone out of my pocket and send a text to Katie. *Shouldn't have gone to Soba's without you. Sorry.*

"You know I can see you," Reggie says with a mouthful of food, peering at my lap.

I give him a *shut the hell up* look. Dinner is family time, meaning Dad isn't supposed to check tennis scores from other high school teams, Reggie can't go on and on with boring stats about zillionaire game developers, and I can't text my girlfriend.

"You're as bad as Pete," I hiss. I say it because he's talking with his mouth full, but I can see from his face he thinks it's because Pete is always up in my business.

"I'm not going to tell." He eyes me with a wounded look.

"See that you don't and I'll play that stupid Destructor game with you after dinner."

"Deal."

"What are you two whispering about?" Dad reaches for the mashed potatoes in the center of the table.

"Nothing." Reggie sticks his tongue out still thick with meatloaf. "Virginia just agreed to let me whoop her ass with my new game."

Dad gives me a sympathetic look. "Ah. Good luck with that."

CHAPTER THIRTEEN

Katie

The texts start coming in eight-to-ten-minute intervals just after I drop my school clothes in the laundry hamper and slip into my nightshirt.

I'm sorry, says the first. It makes me want to puke.

Then: *It wasn't my fault.*

And after that: *Did you know she hit me first?*

And finally: *You owe me.* Yeah, that one again.

Three guesses who they're from. I feel like throwing my phone out the window. But what good will that do? Then I won't have a phone. I block the number and shut the damn thing off before Dad tries to feed me more bullshit about how Mom's the bad parent and her depraved sex partner, Denise, is only after our money.

I think to myself: Hold up a second, Dad. Do you realize we don't have any money because of you? I drive a fifteen-year-old Corolla that begs to be put in her grave. Denise is spending her paycheck trying to keep us safe. And Mom can't even work. She volunteers at Clare House three days a week. I went with her once and helped her separate donated clothes to hand out to women and their children in need of emergency sheltering. God, I hope that won't be us.

I work on my AK History assignment for a while: Identify why Alaska, the forty-ninth state, is unique. Uh, gee. Let me think on that. Because it's colder than shit nine months out of the year? Because it basically sits by itself, a peninsula to Canada and not really part of the rest of the country? Because it's the largest state by area, but one of the smallest by population?

What the hell does my teacher want? Why Alaskans are better than everyone else? A lot of people here think that way. They're hardier than Texans, more loyal than New Yorkers, smarter than most everybody else. I like the class, but tonight the assignment is bugging the crap out of me.

It's not due until Friday so I close out my Google Doc and search for Shanice Kennedy on Instagram, wondering again why Virginia has it in for her. She's actually an introvert whose expression is often kind of sad when she thinks no one's watching her.

It takes me a while to find her because I don't see a profile pic, but her name is distinctive enough that when I come across a cover photo of water, mountains, and a man with his arm wrapped around the shoulder of an attractive Black woman on a boat, I pause and zoom in.

The boat has a blue awning and the words "Talkeetna Flatboat Tours" in cursive on the side. The man looks like Jason only older with the same beady eyes and smirky mouth. Does that mean the woman is Shanice's mother? I remember Jason saying one day at lunch that his parents were recently divorced and he had an older brother who had gone to live with the mom. There's no way to tell anything more because there are no posts or comments, and evidently Shanice doesn't do friends. In fact, it appears that she rarely uses the account.

Now what? Thinking of Virginia's theory about restaurants and rat poison, I try a search on what kind of businesses use rodenticides and quickly learn the answer is that any business with a rat problem would purchase it. Well, duh. I also learn that rodenticide baits are permitted by federal regulations inside of all common food handling facilities, including restaurants, cafeterias, and supermarkets. The EPA has set major restrictions on commercial use and a license or certificate to handle the really toxic stuff is required. It's a two-billion-dollar global business.

An odd little fact pops up: some Pentecostal preachers ingest strychnine, a key ingredient in certain formulas, to demonstrate their faith. The updated version of handling snakes, I suppose.

Hang on. This sparks a memory of the first day of school, nearly a month ago, when I was working in the office and a guy in a cowboy hat came strolling in. Said he'd been sent by his Spanish teacher for disrespecting other students.

It takes an exceptional student to get kicked out of class the very first day, which is a half day that teachers usually spend going over rules, explaining how they grade, and then organizing some kind of activity to help kids get to know each other. This guy had an odd kind of strut, like a country music cowboy.

"Lord help me but you're pretty," he said, leaning both elbows on the counter.

"Not happening," I informed him in my best *leave me alone* voice.

He was clearly full of himself in his bell-bottom jeans, checkered Oxford shirt with button pockets, and a big silver belt buckle embossed with a bison.

I directed him to a chair to wait for Mrs. Foster. He couldn't sit still, bobbing his head and tapping the toes of his pointy boots to a beat only he could hear.

"What does disrespecting mean to you, Miss Office Aide? Having a good time? Having a little fun with a guy wearing a high pony?" he asked me.

Mrs. Foster came out of her office, took one look at him, and told me to find Pastor Reed's phone number for her. That's how I found out his name was Dillon and his father was minister at Lord First Pentecostal Church. Dillon came to the office twice more that week and then withdrew from North.

It's probably nothing, but it makes me curious now. Jason wore a high ponytail and took Spanish after lunch. And Amy

Meeks, my chemistry lab partner last year, dated a guy named Dillon Reed.

Amy and I were pretty close for a couple of months. She was new to North like me, and we bonded over deadbeat dads. It was a while before I realized she had a drinking problem. She kept coming to class with bloodshot eyes and was barely able to keep her head up off the desk. We parted on good terms at the end of the second semester, but I haven't talked to her since.

No time like the present to reconnect. I send her a DM: *Hey.*

What's up? she replies half an hour later.

Not much. You still date Dillon Reed?

Nope.

So, that's the end of that. I start to shut my laptop when another message comes in. *Why?*

No reason. Heard he withdrew from North.

Withdrew, ha! Then: *You okay?*

I squint at the screen for several seconds. Is she telling me Dillon got expelled? It wouldn't surprise me. He wasn't stopping by for a chat with Mrs. Foster because they shared a love of country music. And why is Amy asking if I'm okay? Is she referring to my father? Hers was dating college girls last I heard.

Fine, I answer. *You?*

Same. So the douchebag juiced?

Huh? I send back a couple of question marks.

Lunch yesterday? Hope he wasn't a friend of yours. Heard you sat with him. Anything I can do?

Oh, she's talking about Jason. Douchebag, guess it fits. I'd feel disloyal to Matty telling her my true thoughts, so I reply: *All good here. Let's get together sometime.*

It's the kind of throwaway remark you say when you're ready to end a conversation. But her response comes back fast. *How about Saturday night? Party at my place. Mom's out of town. Bring your friends.*

A party with a bunch of drunks doesn't sound appealing. It's highly doubtful that I'll mention it to the others, but I say thanks and tell her that we'll try to make it. Then I reopen my

Google Doc. Can't work on my art project because I don't have Photoshop at home as it's ridiculously expensive. Might as well have another go at why Alaska is unique.

For me, the answer's simple. It's because Virginia is here.

CHAPTER FOURTEEN

Virginia

The next day Katie and I meet up by the totem pole before school. The weather is back to normal. Cloudy, cool, dismal.

"Hey. Good morning. I texted you last night," I say casually, as if it's no big deal that she didn't get back to me.

Katie looks even more gorgeous than usual today with her hair pulled back in a covered paisley headband. She's wearing her black yoga pants, the ones her butt fills so nicely.

It's unusual she didn't call me, but I'm almost certain it doesn't mean anything. We love each other. I know it's true, but I can't forget how we snapped at each other yesterday. And why the hell did I go to Soba's without her?

Katie pats a jacket pocket. "Sorry. I shut my phone off. Did you talk to Shanice's mother?"

"I didn't. Turns out Tuesdays and Wednesdays are her days off. I've got to go to Whittier for the NHS service thing tomorrow. We can try again when I get back, or, I don't know, maybe skip it. I told Mom what Shanice said in the library about Jason. She didn't think it meant much, but she offered to talk to the new detective assigned to his case. You know, honestly, the more I think about it, the more I think she's right. God." I sigh and run my fingers through my hair. "Feel free to tell me I'm losing my mind."

A group of cheerleaders moves past us, chatting about this Friday's football game. Evidently we need to win this one before the big Homecoming game next week. I like to cross-country ski and bike, but I don't follow fall sports except for tennis because my dad coaches it.

Katie zips and unzips her jacket as we head up the front walk to the building. "See, here's the thing, Virginia. I don't think you're crazy. It's possible Shanice's mother was having an affair with Jason's father."

My ears perk up. "Oh, really? Tell me more."

"Later," she replies, pointing to her own ear when we get inside. The halls are bustling with locker doors slamming and kids shouting at one another. It's too loud to have a conversation.

Our interim principal, Mr. Sullivan, stands outside the front office, his back curved like an old man, his toothpick arms wrapped around his waist. He's wearing a business suit with high-water pants and sleeves that fall an inch short of his wrists. It looks like he's trying to tell two guys throwing a baseball back and forth to cut it out, but they're ignoring him.

We scoot around a couple of juniors at the bulletin board discussing an assignment, and I hear a voice calling my name. I glance around. A second later, something sharp hits my spine.

"You bitch! Why are you determined to ruin my life?" Shanice yells as I stumble forward and catch myself on the edge of the water fountain. I manage to hit the lever and shoot a stream of water in my face.

"I got a visit from the cops last night." Shanice snarls like a rabid dog. "They've confiscated my computer *and* my phone. How am I supposed to do my assignments? Thanks a lot, you stupid cunt."

At least I think that's what she says. It takes me a second to process why she's mad at me. Oh, right. Mom spoke with Detective Rosen. Adrenaline courses through me. I swipe the water from my eyes with the back of my hand and lift my fists in a disgraceful attempt to get ready for a fight.

Thankfully, Katie steps between us. "Shanice. Get a grip. What's wrong with you? Virginia didn't do anything to you."

"The hell she didn't! Some bitch-ass cop named Rosen showed up at my door and accused me of messing with Jason and his dad. And now my mom's about to get fired. They've closed her restaurant to look for rat poison, and Mike's put out a restraining order on both of us."

Ouch. I've got to admit that's a lot. "Why *do* you hate them?" I ask, thinking I'm not going to pass up a chance to question her just because I earned myself a face full of water and nearly got my teeth busted out.

Shanice takes a step forward as I back up. "Seriously? You're even dumber than you look. Delores thinks my mom broke up their marriage. And you know what? Mike left her candy ass anyway. Then he cut Mom loose. How easy do you think it is to get a job when a business goes under and you got some fucking liar saying you stole their money and her asshole husband?"

This is what I get from that: Mike is Jason's father. I may have heard that on the news last night. Delores is his mother. Gailene, Shanice's mom, is the "other" woman. And the parting of ways among them was somewhat less than friendly.

Mr. Sullivan gets wind of the yelling and heads our way. Other students have stopped their conversations to stare. One of the cheerleaders takes out her phone and points it in our direction. Everybody's eating this up. Meanwhile, Shanice wants to hit me so badly, she's quivering. She starts telling me all the ways she's going to kill me, beginning with burying me alive (a particular fear of mine) when behind her, Tally and Yoon-hi appear.

Tally looks from one to the other of us and offers an uncertain smile. "Hey, guys. What's going on?"

I'm not sure if it's Mr. Sullivan's imminent arrival or Tally's pretty smile that settles Shanice. "Hey, how's it going?" she says to Tally almost sweetly, then swivels back to jab a finger in my face. "This isn't over, bitch!"

Throughout the rest of the morning I keep looking up to find people gawking at me. Is the video of our encounter already on the Internet? I can almost hear the whispers. *There goes the narc, Virginia Eaton. Did you hear she almost got her ass kicked by a girl half her size? If it hadn't been for Mr. Sullivan, she'd be dead meat.*

Of course I'm embarrassed, but not so much that my curiosity about Shanice hasn't been re-piqued. An affair between her mom and Jason's dad? Stolen money? Was that what Katie was going to tell me about before school?

I finish the last question on my physics test and hand it in a half second before the bell rings. When I get to the cafeteria, I see Katie helping Mrs. Lorner break down cardboard bread boxes at the hoagie line. She must have gotten out of her last class early. They stack the flattened cardboard under the counter. My eyes rove the room and settle on the student refrigerator, which has been moved out to the other side of the wall where everybody can see it. Other than that, everything seems back to normal, which is weird all by itself. I take a seat at our usual table, waiting for Katie to finish up.

Tally joins me first. "Do you think anyone's ever going to use that again?" She inclines her head in the direction of the fridge that students seem to be avoiding.

"Eventually." I shrug. "Maybe not this year."

"I think Miss Jamie should put money in it for us to find every day, like a treasure hunt. That'll make people forget."

"It's a thought. What did you bring for lunch?"

"Ramen. You?"

"PB and J."

"Right, your favorite." *Not really, but it doesn't matter.* "Virginia—"

"Tally—" We both speak at the same time, then chuckle awkwardly before lapsing into another brief silence.

She opens her lunch sack and sets a plastic spoon and cup of noodles on the table. "Do you want to tell me what that was about this morning? Who that girl is and why she wanted to rip you a new one?"

"Shanice Kennedy." I tell her about Shanice's mother working for Jason's father and my whole poison-being-available-in-the-restaurant theory, then confess to snitching on Shanice to my mom. I'm not sure how Shanice found out it was me that prompted the visit from Detective Rosen, but it doesn't matter now.

"Wow. Really?" Tally says when I finish.

Okay, maybe not as riveting as the Bear Brooks murder podcast I listened to a couple of weeks ago, but not the reaction I'm expecting either. "Nope. Just kidding."

This is why we didn't make it as a couple; we don't communicate. And of course there's Katie. "Shanice likes you," I say as Tally goes silent again.

She plucks at the lid on her carton without opening it. "Really? Well, she's cute."

It's my turn. *Seriously? The girl assaulted me this morning! Have you heard a single word I've said?* "Absolutely," I say dryly. "And the best part is that's exactly what she says about you. Personally I don't go for the beat your face in type, but you two might just get along."

I put down my sandwich and look her straight in the eye. "What the hell is going on with you, Tally? You hardly ever come to lunch anymore, and when you're here, your mind is somewhere else."

She stops playing with her cup of noodles and puts them back in the sack. "That's not fair. You're just jealous because I've found someone else. And what does it matter anyway? You and Katie. You and Matty. Matty and Tom. I'm left out of everything. I'm the last to know things. I've invited you to hear me sing at Caseo's a hundred times. You're always busy. All of you."

Again, not what I'm expecting, but I can kind of see her point. Tally and I broke up weeks before Katie and I got back together, but we stopped hanging out shortly after. "If by a hundred you mean twice, then okay, you're right. I'm sorry. I do want to hear you sing. I promise I'll be there tonight. But can't you tell me who it is you text all of the time? Who's your secret someone?"

She crushes the top of her brown paper bag and shoves back her stool. "Jesus, Virginia. Why do you care? So you guys can laugh about it? Forget I mentioned it. I'm out of here."

She stomps out of the cafeteria, bumping into Matty who's coming in. He grabs her by the arm and tries to talk to her. She shakes him off and keeps going.

He goes up to the pizza à la carte and comes back with three steaming slices of pepperoni, and a milkshake. I ought to ask how Tom is doing since on Wednesday they often come in together, but I'm sick of all the drama. Tally. Tom. What's going on with us? It almost makes me miss Jason. At least when he was around, we weren't turning on each other.

"We need to go to Caseo's tonight," I say when Matty sits down next to me. "Tally is feeling unappreciated."

He takes a noisy slurp from his milkshake, then folds a slice of pizza and stuffs it in his mouth. Matty is an emotional eater. The diet he's always trying to start probably went out the window the day Jason showed up at our table. He chews and talks, reaching for the milkshake like it's a canister of oxygen he can't do without.

"Not sure I can. I want to be available in case Tom calls. He stayed home from school today. Last night the cops raided McKinley's. His dad had a relapse."

"I'm sorry." I keep it to myself that I saw Detective Rosen at the golf course on TV last night because I don't want to pick at that particular scab. My dad's second cousin has MS. Her feet go numb and every now and then she has trouble seeing. A couple of years ago she moved to Arizona, saying Alaska was too cold for her.

Yoon-hi comes in and heads for the refrigerator, grabbing her lunch from an otherwise empty shelf inside before joining us at the table.

"I will not be a slave to foolish rhetoric about haunted refrigerators," she pronounces when Matty and I give her a look. We talk about my blowup with Shanice, and then I ask her if she's available to go to Caseo's.

"Sorry. I've got to hand in my AP English paper before our field trip," she replies.

"Please try, won't you? Tally thinks we don't care about her."

"That's ridiculous. If you ask me, she's feeling guilty for getting cozy with Mrs. Donovan. Be interesting to see if *she* shows up."

"Mrs. Donovan, the librarian?" Matty and I ogle each other.

"Don't tell me you haven't noticed. Tally's with her every afternoon after school."

"I saw her getting out of Mrs. Donovan's car yesterday morning," Katie says, taking a seat beside me and unwrapping a ham and cheddar hoagie.

"Did Mrs. Lorner give you that?" Matty gestures to the sandwich hungrily.

"Mrs. Donovan, the librarian?" I repeat, refusing to be sidetracked.

Katie turns to Matty. "You can have half. She says they always have plenty left over." And to me: "Yes, Mrs. Donovan. The rich, young, and very pretty librarian."

Matty leans in front of me to help himself to the larger section of the sandwich. "Holy shit, Katie. Don't tell me you're doing the nasty with the old lady." He picks off the lettuce and flicks it on his tray before taking an enormous bite.

Katie throws a napkin at him. "That's disgusting."

He laughs. "Aw, come on. I think she's sexy. Varicose veins. Crepey skin. Love that husky voice."

Katie sits back, visibly upset. "Stop it, Matty. I mean it. She's sweet and lonely and too old to put up with crap from high school students. I like her."

As if hearing her name, Mrs. Lorner glances at us from the serving line and blinks through her thick, smudged glasses. I can see her unfashionably red lipstick smeared across her teeth.

Matty lifts his big shoulders, clearly wanting to give Katie more crap about nutty Mrs. Lorner, but he lets it go, instead saying, "So, do we think Tally and our rich, young, and very pretty librarian are getting it on?"

"No," I say.

"Maybe," says Katie.

Yoon-hi shakes her head, her choppy black hair falling back in place. "I don't know and I don't really care."

I care. Tally isn't known for making good decisions, but I've got to believe she has more sense than that. And surely Mrs. Donovan wouldn't risk her career by being intimate with a high school student. In middle school when it came out that our vocal music teacher was having sex with a high school senior, he went to jail.

"I saw her once with Jason," Yoon-hi says, surprising us again. "She—she was giving him a hug."

Katie takes a drink from her water bottle. "She, Mrs. Donovan?" she stutters, snorting water out her nose.

"No way!" I yelp. "Mrs. Donovan with Tally *and* Jason?"

"When?" Matty stares at her in disbelief.

"Beginning of the year in the library. Nobody else was around. It was peculiar. Not exactly sexual, but you know, strange."

"Did he hug her back?" Matty drops the hoagie on his plate.

"I'm not sure."

"You're not sure?" he snaps. "That's complete bullshit, Park. All of it. What I don't get is why you're lying."

"I'm not." Yoon-hi's voice is small and hurt.

"Did you get a picture of it?"

"I didn't know I'd need one."

"Exactly. Because it isn't true. You must have misseen it."

It's a moment before she speaks. "You're probably right." She catches her bottom lip in her teeth, her voice smaller still.

Katie releases a low, uncomfortable breath beside me. Matty and Yoon-hi arguing is practically unheard of. Matty isn't confrontational. And Yoon-hi just says what she means. It's one of the things I like most about her. I don't think she's lying. There's got to be a rational explanation for Mrs. Donovan embracing Jason. On the other hand, I can't think of any reason Tally and Mrs. Donovan would be coming to school together.

"Did you tell the cops about Mrs. Donovan and Jason?" Katie asks Yoon-hi.

She nods. "Detective Rosen." Which means my mom probably knows too. For some reason, this upsets me almost as much as everything else.

"You gotta be wrong," Matty says again.

"Probably." She stares at the table.

We try to make small talk after that. Katie talks about her Photoshop art project. I bore everybody with way too much detail about the formula for kinetic energy from my physics quiz, and Matty and Yoon-hi don't speak at all. By the time the bell rings, Yoon-hi still hasn't touched her lunch and Matty has half a hoagie and two slices of pizza left on his tray.

CHAPTER FIFTEEN

Katie

Oh my god, could lunch have been any more awkward? I know I should feel sorry for everybody else, but I have my own problems, mainly a text from Denise saying Dad called our apartment landline again. *Has he tried to get hold of you?* she asks.

I don't answer because if she knew he had, she'd tell my mother. And then Mom wouldn't want to wait until the weekend to get the hell out of Anchorage. We'd be on our way to Fairbanks or Nome, or Elim—wherever that is—which would mean Goodbye Virginia, maybe forever. So instead I have to pretend that everything is normal and that I'm not freaking out. The worst part is I can't tell Virginia because she'd try to fix it. And this situation can't be fixed, at least not by her.

When I get to the office, Mrs. Pugh sends me off to a teacher's room to hand him some papers he left in the copier. I find Mr. Sullivan standing at the counter like he's waiting for me when I get back. He drums his birdlike fingers on the paper cutter.

"Katie. I want to talk to you about that art assignment you were working on. Do you think it's appropriate to mock hunters?"

It's a picture of my father! "Only those who kill for sport." I try to sound calm.

"I disagree. God gave man dominion over animals. Do you know what that means?"

No, because I'm an idiot. No, wait. That's you. "I think I can figure it out."

"It means man is supreme because we were made in the good Lord's image. Therefore, we can do no wrong in His eyes. I've had a talk with your art teacher and she's agreed to let you do a different project."

"Is that right." I don't need to look in a mirror to tell my cheeks are on fire. Can adults push religion on students in a public school?

"You'll have an extra day, and you won't lose points for turning it in late. Personally I think a nice collage of native fauna—"

"Did you teach art?" I gaze longingly at the paper cutter where his fingers have come to rest.

"Computer graphics. I also owned my own business for three and a half years."

I don't give a shit about his business. "Did your students like you?"

His arms circle his chest. "I'm not sure what you're inferring."

"I think you mean implying." *Dumbass.* "What I'm saying is that two years of teaching doesn't make you an expert. And if a single student ever told you they liked you or that you were any good—"

"Katie!" Mrs. Pugh cuts in, her eyes going wide like cue balls. She slips up beside me, blocking Sullivan from my view. "I forgot to tell you Mrs. Lorner asked if you could help out in the cafeteria again. You don't mind, do you?"

"I'm not done here!" I want to shout. But I get that she's doing me a favor by saving me from getting suspended for blowing up at our new principal. I force my lips into a curl that hopefully resembles a smile. "I'd be happy to help."

"Think about what I said," Sullivan calls after me as I walk out of the office. With my back to him, he can't see me giving him the finger.

When I reach the cafeteria, I see Miss Jamie counting money at the register on the far side of the room. Lindley Crowe, the guy Jason argued with on Monday, is wiping down tables a few feet away. "Is Mrs. Lorner around?" I ask him.

His gaze darts to my face, then back to the table, and he goes on wiping. Big back and forth motions, getting way too much soap and water on the table. I wait a minute and then finally realize he isn't going to answer. Is every man in this school a dick? I cross the cafeteria and head outside.

Mrs. Lorner is sitting on her crate on the steps. She tries to hide her cigarette. Smoke floats up and she sees me eyeing it. "Oops! You caught me."

"Hi, Mrs. Lorner. You needed help?"

"With smoking?" She hacks into a fist.

Some of the tension leaves my neck as I laugh out loud at that. "Mrs. Pugh said you asked for me. Do you want to dump the cardboard?"

The green recycle bin is next to the rusty yellow dumpster. I glance around, looking for the cardboard boxes we flattened before lunch and see them peeking out the top of the dumpster. "You don't recycle?" I probably sound judgy. We recycle everything we can at home.

"It's full." She pouts defensively. "Why are you here?"

"Because Mrs. Pugh said you needed my assistance. Sorry to bother you." Crazy old lady. I spin back to the door.

"No." She starts to stand. Her knees creak and her flabby face creases in pain. "Don't go, kiddo. Kate, right?"

"Katie."

"Ha. See, I remembered, and I'm the one who should be sorry about hiding out here to have a smoke. You probably think I'm lazy. But the recycle bin really is full, and well, I guess I am a little lazy. I'm actually glad to see you. And thank you for your help at lunch. See, I remembered that, too. Did you like the hoagie? Come sit with me and tell me what's going on with that awful daddy of yours."

Which is how I find myself divulging all the stuff I've been keeping from everyone else. Why not? Talking about my father with her is like therapy, and she won't remember most of it tomorrow.

"Your daddy really said, 'She hit me first,' as if that makes it okay to shoot your poor mama in the face?" Mrs. Lorner, my new, slightly batty friend is clearly outraged when I tell her about the texts Dad sent last night.

"He did. As if she deserved what she got! It's always about him. No one else matters. And if I tell my mom's fiancée, Denise, we'll have to leave Anchorage. I don't want to do that. I can't leave Virginia. Or Matty. Or Yoon-hi and Tally, either. I love them all. And I adore Virginia's family. This is the first time I've had friends who actually like me."

It's true, but the confession is also embarrassing. We do still like each other, don't we? God, Matty and Yoon-hi. I still can't believe Matty called Yoon-hi a liar.

I sink slowly to the concrete stoop, which is stained with baked-on food and something blue that looks like paint or gum. "What did you mean about animals falling down?"

Mrs. Lorner lights another cigarette, squeezing one eye shut to see through the smoke. "Animals falling down?"

"Yesterday you said you could predict things."

"Oh, that. Didn't I tell you? We're going to have an earthquake. The signs are all around us. Wind and heat. The color of the sky. Tempers flaring out of control. Tell me what's going on in the investigation of that young man's death."

She's right about tempers. Alaska has its share of earthquakes, some devastating like the one in 1964 that wiped out several Native villages. Yet I'm pretty sure no one can predict when one is coming, so I let it go. "You mean Jason?"

"Right. Jason. I'm sorry I'm not very good with names, but I remember yours. Katie." She gives me her cross-eyed, smudgy glasses smile.

I take off my headband and scratch the top of my head. I've been trying to leave my thumbnail alone and I wore a glove to bed last night. Today I'm back at it, finding a loose cuticle and pulling at it with my teeth.

"All I know is that he died from eating rat poison. I heard he had a heart condition, which might have made him more susceptible, I guess. Anyway, Mrs. Foster's been suspended because they think it happened in the cafeteria to his food. She skipped a health inspection and possibly some other kids got sick a week or so ago. Anyway, the guy who took her place, Mr. Sullivan, is a jerk." I start to talk about Sullivan's stupid suggestions for my art project but cut myself off. I hate to have Mrs. Lorner think that all I ever do is complain.

She chuckles, then hacks a smoky cough. "Kiddo, don't be silly. We're friends, aren't we? Friends tell each other things. Like I'm going to tell you that I don't like Mr. High-and-Mighty Sullivan either, complaining about your art. What does he know about art? And that young man, Jason. He wasn't always the most thoughtful either. Still, I'm sorry that he's dead. Do you think Mr. Sullivan might have poisoned him?"

I can't tell if she's joking. The cuticle comes away from my thumb, which instantly wells with blood. "Probably not. He was at another school when it happened. Yesterday was his first day here."

"Oh. Well, then. It must have been somebody else." She hands me a smelly tissue from her apron pocket.

While she finishes off another cigarette, I persuade her to let me put the cardboard in the recycle bin. It's full, but I finally get it shoved down the side between a couple of gallon-size milk cartons and a plastic salad box.

I think about what she said as we go inside to help Lindley finish wiping down the tables. Mr. Sullivan poisoning Jason? It's highly doubtful, and yet he's now in charge at North. It's a fast leap to the top for a new AP.

CHAPTER SIXTEEN

Virginia

I need to get to the bottom of this thing with Tally before my head explodes, but when I text her to meet me in front of the bulletin board after school, she doesn't answer so I go upstairs to the library.

Mrs. Donovan is flipping through a magazine at the checkout desk, and I can see Yoon-hi and Shanice in the Little Bear conference room. It's all I can do not to charge in and have it out with Shanice. I'm still embarrassed about our altercation in the hall this morning. I stand outside the library, shifting from one foot to the other for a minute, then head down to Mrs. Hicks's room, thinking it'll give me a chance to cool off.

The NHS sponsor and I have a complicated relationship, meaning she's always trying to get me to work harder and be a superstar like my brother Pete. The problem is I don't tend to have Pete's "thirst for an academic challenge" as she calls it. I turned in my NHS application last spring and was accepted right away, but in her eyes I was already a year late, which makes me a disappointment. Still, I like her, and it's easy to see she likes me, despite my lack of ambition. I'm definitely going to college, but I don't have to be valedictorian or student council president, I've told her. I want to enjoy my senior year.

"What's up?" I say, sliding on top of a student desk under one of those "Believe in Yourself" posters.

Mrs. Hicks glances up from a stack of papers on her desk. "The sky. The stars. The sun."

"Brilliant. You should be an academic."

"I was thinking that myself. What can I do for you, Virginia?" She tosses her red pen on her calendar blotter. I don't need to see it up close to know it's full of neatly penciled-in engagements. Meetings with students. Coffee dates with other teachers. Dinner dates with her husband and their friends. The woman is on practically every teacher committee in the district.

"Why do people lie?" I kick the chair in front of me, mainly because I'm restless, but also because I figure it annoys her.

"To makes themselves look better. To hide a secret. To avoid hurting someone else's feelings. To sidestep embarrassment. Should I go on?"

"There's more?"

"What's this about?"

"A friend who's hiding a secret. Should I confront her?"

"Well, that depends. Are you prepared to hear the answer? And will bringing it up jeopardize your friendship?"

Well, shoot. "Maybe you should have been a psychologist."

"I had to go where the money was, teaching high school."

Ha. She's hilarious. "What if more than one friend is lying? What if everyone you know is keeping secrets?"

"Then it's simple. Find yourself a cave in the woods and go live by yourself. We all have secrets, Virginia. Some important. Some not. No, I take that back. They're all important to the person keeping them. For example, I'm trying to hide the fact that I have fifty tests to grade this afternoon because I don't want to hurt your feelings by telling you to go away." She looks meaningfully at the stack of papers in front of her.

I cross my ankles and make my swinging feet go still. Suddenly I'm not sure why I stopped by to see her, or more accurately, if I really know what I'm doing. And yet now that I am here, I might as well say what's on my mind. "How well do you know our new librarian Mrs. Donovan?"

Mrs. Hicks glimpses out the window and then looks back, tilting her head at the door in thought. Two students walk by, talking about the Homecoming dance. "Now there's an interesting question," she says once they're out of sight. "I'd call Erin Donovan a work friend. She's competent and enthusiastic. She cares about kids."

All true, I think. And I don't want to spread rumors about our rich, young, and very pretty librarian based solely on the fact that Katie saw Tally getting out of her car and Yoon-hi caught her with her arms wrapped around Jason Gonzalez. "You and your husband don't actively socialize with her and her husband? Outside of school, I mean?" I'm trying to be subtle, but I wouldn't be surprised if Mrs. Hicks sees right through me.

"I don't because she's busy. Or perhaps I should say her husband's busy. She's also several years younger than I am. He's a few years older. Tell me what it is you think you know." She sits forward, pushing the papers aside.

Telling her about Tally and Mrs. Donovan would be a betrayal of our friendship, but I don't feel the same about Jason because he's past caring. "Someone saw her embracing Jason Gonzalez. It's probably nothing."

Mrs. Hicks relaxes and her face goes smooth. "It is nothing. And it's no secret either. Erin's husband is a cardiologist. They both know the family well. He was Jason's doctor."

"You said he's older?"

"Quite a bit. Is that important?"

I think about that. "No, I guess not. Okay. Well, thanks," I say with some relief.

"Don't mention it. All right if I go back to grading papers now?"

"Be my guest. Do I need to check in with you tomorrow morning before the Whittier trip?"

"I don't think so. I trust you, Virginia."

I think she means she trusts Yoon-hi who isn't the slacker I am. It's our NHS service day, which involves chaperoning eighth graders from Reggie's class on a boat trip around Prince William Sound. I say goodbye and head home to get an assignment done.

A couple of hours later I find myself sitting across from Katie at Caseo's, filling her in on the conversation with Mrs. Hicks. She frowns and chews a nail. "That's Jason's mystery solved, but it doesn't explain what Tally was doing in Mrs. Donovan's car yesterday morning. Or the texts between them."

"I know, but I couldn't think of a good way to ask."

Katie nods and sips her smoothie. She's got her black ballet flats propped up on the chair across from her. I've put my backpack on the other one. We're saving seats for Matty and Yoon-hi in case they change their minds. When I texted Yoon-hi, asking her to put her argument with Matty aside for Tally's sake, her answer was one word: *No.*

Matty was more explicit: *I need a break. Yoon-hi is a liar.*

I don't understand it. Is he mad because Yoon-hi knew something about Jason that he didn't? Surely he doesn't still think she fabricated the story after I called and explained that Dr. Donovan was Jason's cardiologist, adding how patients and their doctors, even their doctors' families, can grow close. Dad's cousin, the one who has MS, still talks to her doctor in Alaska. She used to have his whole family over for dinner. And Mrs. Donovan is a warmhearted person; you can tell that within a minute or two of conversation with her. Why else would she want to supply our student body with coffee and a machine she purchased with her own money?

"Don't care," Matty answered and hung up on me when I finished.

The new barista who goes to Service High School brings me a hot chai tea. I'm chilled tonight. I can't seem to warm up. Hope I'm not coming down with something.

"I think I figured out how Shanice knew you were the one who sent Detective Rosen after her," Katie says thoughtfully.

"Detective Rosen probably told her."

"I doubt it. It would have been unprofessional of Rosen to say anything to the Kennedys. I'm guessing Shanice and her mother put it together themselves after your visit to Soba's. The hostess must have mentioned it."

"Oh. You're probably right."

"Virginia, is everything okay? You're not upset with me about anything, are you?"

I reach over and take her hand. "Absolutely not. I thought you were mad at me."

"I'm not. Mrs. Lorner says things are off because we're going to have an earthquake."

I laugh out loud at that. "She must be psychic. Look, you want to bag this thing with Tally and go back to your car and make out?"

She gives me a sexy wink. "Let's."

We grab our stuff and start to get up just as Tally walks around from behind the bar wearing an acoustic guitar on a leather strap around her neck. She wraps her laced-up hiking boots around the base of the stool and nods a thanks to the barista, who sets a bottle of water on the floor beside her. Our eyes meet. I smile; she doesn't. Katie and I sit back down.

"I'd like to dedicate my first number to someone I used to call a friend." She strums three chords, and I know exactly what she's going to sing. "Adia" by Sarah McLachlan.

The song is about a failed friendship. It has haunting lyrics with the kind of melody that stays with you long after. Tears prick my eyeballs when it's over. Katie leans over and whispers, "Oh my god. Tally is still in love with you."

Please, no. Tally and I never loved each other.

She starts another song that I don't know. It's a little more upbeat. A second later, her gaze pivots toward the door and her eyes light up as Mrs. Donovan steps inside and gives her a three-finger wave. Katie and I exchange shocked expressions because, yeah, we thought Mrs. Donovan might show up, but I was hoping we were wrong. I wanted to be wrong. Teachers aren't supposed to carry on with students. They're supposed to know better.

When the song ends, Mrs. Donovan steers around the other tables, murmuring, "Sorry. Just let me get out of your way. Oh, dear. Was that your foot?" She pauses next to ours. "Hi, girls. Mind if I join you?"

"Sure. No problem." Katie scrambles to get her feet off the chair in front of her, and I spill my tea, grabbing my backpack from the other. Mrs. Donovan goes to the bar to get napkins, and Tally eyes us with a look of pure fury, like we're ruining her set on purpose.

"For my last number, I'd like to sing…"

It's another Sarah McLachlan tune. I don't hear much of it because I'm fixated on Mrs. Donovan setting her nine-hundred-dollar handbag on a chair and blotting my shirt with a fistful of brown paper napkins. My heart is thumping about a mile a minute, but I try to be cool as I say, "Thanks. I got it. You don't have to do that. Seriously, please stop."

Katie knocks my knee under the table, a silent warning telling me to chill.

The audience of maybe thirty people applaud when Tally gets up. She sets her guitar in a corner, picks up the water bottle, and comes over to join us. Mrs. Donovan moves her handbag to her lap. "Natalie Carter, that was wonderful. Thank you for inviting me. You're very talented. I had no idea."

"That I could sing? I told you I could." Tally beams. She runs her fingers across her scalp, fluffing up her hair. "Thanks for coming, *Erin*. Can I buy you a cup of coffee?" I'm pretty sure she calls her Erin for our benefit. She acts like we aren't there.

Katie disregards all that. "Hey, Tally." She gives the table a shove, threatening to spill the drinks again.

"Oh, hey. Katie. Virginia." Major pause as Tally unscrews the cap and tips the water bottle to her lips. "Glad you guys could make it." She doesn't sound glad. She sounds resentful.

Meanwhile, Mrs. Donovan gushes on about the performance, talking about how Tally channeled one of her favorite singers, some indie artist named Layla James, and how she didn't know Tally was such an accomplished musician. Guitar? Wow! You sing and play at the same time? Amazing! She says she should buy Tally a cup of coffee, not the other way around.

When they finally sort out who's paying, Mrs. Donovan heads to the bar to order and Tally turns back to me. "It isn't what you think."

I start to ask what it is she thinks I think, but Katie is faster. "Meaning you're not having an affair with Mrs. Donovan?"

"She's my friend. Believe it or not, I used to have friends. Not that you'd know anything about that." Tally scowls.

If I didn't know better, I'd think she was doing an excellent job of redirecting the idea of a personal relationship with Mrs. Donovan into a personal attack on Katie. But subtext isn't Tally's thing. "Why were you in her car yesterday morning?" I ask, scooting my chair closer to the table in order to keep my voice low and still be heard. The next performer is scheduled to come on in five minutes, and the audience is chattering away.

"Shit, Virginia. For your information my car broke down, and Erin gave me a ride. Okay? If you don't believe me, ask my sister. Here. Call her if you want." She thrusts out her phone.

Tally's ancient Land Rover used to belong to an older sister who's away at college in Nebraska. I'm tempted to call Tally's bluff, but I can't picture having such a conversation with someone I've never met.

Mrs. Donovan comes back, looking flustered. She tugs at the collar on her blouse as if it's choking her and fiddles with the buttons underneath it. "The girl at the register said she'd bring your drink to the table in a minute. I've never been here before. It's…interesting."

I follow her gaze around the room, realizing she means "interesting" because most of the audience is comprised of women kissing one another and holding hands. There are a whole lot of short haircuts and plaid flannel shirts. I'm quickly revising my opinion about Mrs. Donovan's and Tally's relationship. The crush, I think, goes only one way.

We sit through a couple more sets, then Mrs. Donovan decides to be the adult by reminding us it's a school night. We wait for another intermission and all get up together. When we reach the front door, Mrs. Donovan gives Tally a friendly shoulder squeeze and tells her again that she's an awesome singer. "Invite me again sometime? Next time I'll have to bring my husband. He loves this kind of music."

Oh, her husband. Tally gives her a thin-lipped smile. "Sure."

"See you at school?"

"Yeah, see you."

Mrs. Donovan's stilettos make clicking sounds on the pavement as she peels off to a silver BMW parked a few feet from us.

I wait until she's driving away before turning back to Tally. "Girl, I think I owe you an apology."

She raises both her hands and gives us a double flip off. "Go to hell. Just go to fucking hell."

CHAPTER SEVENTEEN

Katie

Last night was a pleasant break from reality. Tally is truly talented, but the lovelorn glances she kept shooting at Mrs. Donovan were—I'm just going to say it—pathetic. I get Mrs. Donovan now. Young, attractive woman with a successful older *doctor* husband. No doubt she's a trophy wife with too much free time on her hands. Someone who doesn't recognize boundaries and was probably flattered by the attentions of a lovesick teenage girl. She probably didn't realize that Tally would be devastated if her affection wasn't reciprocated. I'm not even sure she got it last night, although it was obvious to everybody else at the table.

"That's just sad," I told Virginia after Tally took off in her car, tires squealing, like she could hardly wait to get away from us.

Virginia stared after her. "I know. Do you think I should say something? Maybe call her?"

My fingers played at her wrist. "Babe, you tried. Leave her alone for now. She'll get over it. Right now she's embarrassed."

I would be. I've never crushed on a teacher, not unless you count fourth grade. Mrs. Stockton, with her pink lipstick and Barbara Bush fluffy hair, filled my dreams at night. I hung around her desk every day at recess until she finally told me recess was her "me time" and to go outside and play. I got over it. She was like Medicare age or darn close to it.

It reminds me of Matty's stupid comment about Mrs. Lorner's varicose veins being sexy and his suggestion that I might want to feel her up. Sometimes that guy genuinely annoys me. *Get your mind out of the gutter, dude.* If Matty had only told Jason he was in love with Tom or vice versa maybe none of the other stuff would have happened.

Virginia and I were standing in Caseo's back parking lot with me wondering if she still had feelings for Tally when suddenly her eyes went wide and she grabbed me by the upper arms and kissed me. Romantic, sure. But abrupt. I glanced over my shoulder to see what she'd been looking at half a second earlier.

"Did you see a ghost?"

"Yeah. Jacob Marley. He told me I'd be visited by three spirits. I think you should spend the night with me."

I looked at her blankly. "Um, I don't want to interrupt your bedtime story, but you know I can't."

Mom has made it clear that despite this being my last year of high school I still have an eleven o'clock curfew on school nights. She doesn't ask what Virginia and I do on weekends. She's probably afraid I'll want to know what she and Denise do when I'm not there.

I drove Virginia home and we made out for a while in her driveway until the porch light flipped on, nearly blinding me, and her dad stuck his head out the door. "Everything all right out here, girls?"

Sometimes I feel like a cliché. Next thing you know I'll be hiding hickeys under my turtleneck sweaters. Maybe girl romances aren't that different from heterosexual ones. You still have to deal with parents. Even after her dad went back inside, Virginia held on to me. Her breath was cold on my neck. "Please stay. Or let me stay with you."

So tempting. "Once we graduate, okay?"

"Yeah. Okay. Just be careful."

"Right." I waited until she was safely inside the house before driving off.

The morning radio alarm comes on, forcing me from the cocooned warmth of my sheets and tattered quilt. I stand and stretch, avoiding a glimpse at my rat's-nest hair in the dresser mirror. Bedhead, yuck. It's why I shower in the morning. The humidity in Anchorage is truly terrible. A lot of the coastal area is a rainforest, which means humongous trees and lush vegetation. Also, oily skin and frizzy hair. I drag a pair of nearly clean jeans out of my closet. I'd like to wear my yoga pants again because I love the way Virginia stares at my butt, but Matty's likely to make fun of me by asking if I have only one pair of pants.

Just be careful. Virginia's warning flicks back into the outer reaches of my brain. I can't shake the feeling that I missed something. Just be careful? I'm always careful. I head for the hall bathroom just as Josh steps out of it. He's four now and beginning to talk like an adult. I muss his dark-brown hair. "Did you go pee-pee, Joshy?"

He gives me a look. "I went potty and I washed my hands. You should do that too, Katie." His daily reminder.

"Okay. I will." I shut the door behind me and notice that he's left the toilet seat up. Such a man. When I come out, Denise is standing barefoot in her nightgown in the hall. "You never answered my text." She's a good head shorter than I am, but with her hair tied up in a messy bun she looks taller than normal.

"You mean yesterday?"

"I don't mean to nag, Katie, but I feel it's important that we're all on the same page. Has your dad tried to contact you?"

"How would he get my phone number?" Not a lie, just a sidestep.

She nods to herself. "You're right. He probably couldn't. That makes sense. It's just…Come with me, will you?" I follow her back into my bedroom. She closes the door and whispers, "I don't want your mother to hear this yet. It's possible your father may be getting out of prison before Saturday."

"How can that happen?" My hands start shaking uncontrollably. I drop back down to the bed.

Denise lowers herself beside me. She takes my hands in hers and rubs her calloused thumbs across my knuckles. "Overcrowding at the prison. It's not definite. But honestly, I don't know why he would have to wait until Saturday anyway since he already won his appeal. Don't worry though. My guy's in place."

"Your guy? Who's that?" I can't help wondering if her guy is standing outside the prison gates watching for him. *Come on, lady. I need details!* I'm imagining a scene in a movie with a concrete yard and a chain link fence topped with rolled barbed wire and some sheriff type on the free side waiting patiently for my father so he can kindly direct him to a warmer climate as far away from us as possible.

Denise gives my fingers a squeeze, then folds her hands in her lap. "The PI's name is Brian Jessup, and he came highly recommended from a friend of a friend at work. He's got a contact in the warden's office who gives him updates.

"Listen, sweetheart," she goes on. "I'm sorry to worry you. But just to be on the safe side, it might be a good idea to have a bag packed with a few essentials. Your mom and I have done it. I've made up one for Josh. Will you do that for us?"

"What kind of essentials?" I look wildly around the room.

"Toiletries. A change of clothes. A coat and gloves. Cash, if you have it."

I swallow. "Have you decided where you'll go if Dad does come here?"

"Nome. I've bought four open airline tickets."

I pick at my sore cuticle. Leave it to Denise to be prepared. I should be grateful. Instead, I find myself feeling resentful. Of my father. Of Denise. Of Mom. Why do we have to do this?

Denise opens her mouth. "What do you mean where *you'll* go? Don't you mean where *we'll* go?"

"I don't." I chew my thumbnail. "I mean, god, Denise, I'm sorry. But I'm not going with you. I appreciate all you've done. But I'm staying here with Virginia."

She runs a hand down the front of her nightgown, her brown face etched with distress. "Okay, okay. I get it. Your mom isn't going to like it, but you're old enough to make your own decisions. When are you going to tell her?"

"Um. I was hoping you would do it for me."

She looks at me like I've slapped her. "I will not. This will kill her, Katie. Do you have any idea how much she depends on you? How much she loves you? You are her world. Every time I went to visit her in the hospital, you were all she ever talked about. How's Katie? Is Katie all right? Did that monster hurt her? Everything she does is about keeping you safe. I understand why you don't want to go, but you need to tell her. I will not be the one to break her heart."

I gaze at Denise in surprise. Are we talking about the same person? My mom who barely speaks to me? "Okay, I will. Sorry. I shouldn't have asked."

"No, you shouldn't have. And I urge you to think carefully before you make your final decision. It's not just her. Your father is likely dangerous. Prison changes people, you know? He's— never mind. I've probably said too much. Just know that your mother loves you."

She stands, awkwardly patting her thighs a couple of times, and leaves the room. I feel horrible for disappointing her.

Sure, I'll tell Mom, just not this morning. Today's the day she planned on formally applying for a job at a florist shop where she'll work in the back, accepting deliveries and arranging flowers. With her eye patch on, she doesn't look nearly as gruesome as she did at first, but she's still worried she'll scare away customers even though the owner has assured her it won't be a problem.

If Mom and Denise and Josh have to leave, they can start over. I can't. I don't want to. Will Mom really care?

I shower, dress, fix my hair, and grab a granola bar on the way out to my car. It squeals in protest as I twist the key and pump the gas. The engine finally turns over. I start to back out, then jerk to a halt as our building super steps out from behind the dumpster. He points at the back end of my car and turns his wrist, indicating I should roll the window down.

"Katie?" He leans into the car with ferocious coffee breath. "Did you know you have a taillight out?"

"What?"

He signals me to put the car in park and step out of the driver's seat to see for myself. There are bits and pieces of red plastic on the ground. Sure enough, the light is broken.

"You need to get this fixed," he gently scolds. "I'll sweep up the mess, but it's dangerous driving around with only one taillight. At night your car could be mistaken for a motorcycle and someone might get too close, trying to pass you. Will you take care of it right away?"

"Sure, Mr. Jacobi. I'll take care of it, I promise." Great. More money that I don't have to spend on the stupid car.

"Probably those kids with bicycles," he adds, squatting by my rear tire to tie his shoelace. "Brats threw a sparkler in the dumpster the other day. Could have set the whole thing on fire. I've seen the boy who lives in the apartment a couple of doors down from yours picking on his little brother. I've had it with him. I'm going to speak to his father tonight."

I'm edging back around the car because I don't want to be late for school. He notices and waves me on. "Go on now. Have a good day. You know, your mothers are so nice. I wish all my tenants were like them. See you later."

"Have a good day," I tell him.

Crap. A broken taillight, just my luck. It's early. What else can go wrong today?

CHAPTER EIGHTEEN

Virginia

The bus for Whittier should be here any minute. A few lockers down, Tom catches sight of me and whips around like he just remembered he left a wallet full of cash in the bathroom. He takes the steps to the second floor two at a time. Does he think I'm going to chase him? I keep an eye out for Shanice, not wanting a repeat performance of yesterday. Pete's repainting my car now, and Katie texted that she was running a little late, so Mom drove me to school this morning. I asked her if Detective Rosen had come across anything of interest when she visited the Kennedys.

"I don't know, honey. She doesn't confide in me because it's really none of my business."

Not mine either is what she was trying to tell me. I wanted her to understand how the situation is destroying our group. But I couldn't bring myself to say that Matty and Yoon-hi aren't speaking to each other, that Tally blames me for the fact that her relationship with Mrs. Donovan isn't working out, and that I'm seeing ghosts.

Last night, god, last night, I could have sworn I saw Katie's father in Caseo's parking lot. I'm definitely losing it. Mom's expression when she dropped me off told me she was worried about me too.

I spot Katie by her locker at the same time she sees me and feel a huge smile spread across my face. If she's here, then everything is okay. Surely there's no way her dad can get to her at school. I only wish she was going to Whittier with me and Yoon-hi.

When Katie and I were in eighth grade our class did the downtown planet walk. The Lightspeed Planet Trip is a scaled walk of the solar system beginning on Fifth Street with the sun and ending at Pluto in Kincaid Park about six-and-a-half hours away by foot. We didn't get back until school was out. It will probably be the same thing today since Whittier is over an hour away and we have to travel through a mountain tunnel that closes periodically throughout the day for the train. I'm looking forward to the cruise, although I've done it dozens of times when family and friends visit from the lower forty-eight.

Katie hands me a brown paper bag when I get to her locker. "What's this?" I peek inside.

"Lunch. Smoked salmon on saltines, dried mango chips, and apple cake. There's enough for Yoon-hi too, if you want to share. I thought you guys might enjoy something special."

My smile deepens. I trade her the cheese and pickle loaf sandwich from my collapsible travel cooler and set the paper bag in its place. "You're the best."

She leans in to kiss my cheek. "Don't you forget it. But I've got to be honest. I didn't make it. You can tell my mother you appreciated it later. Do you need a ride home after school?"

"Thanks, but we'll probably be back late. I'll catch a ride with Yoon-hi."

"Okay. Have fun."

I want to pull her into my arms and run my lips up and down her neck and collarbone until she moans with delight, but Mr. Sullivan is standing across the hall staring at us. His eyebrows twitch like an angry rabbit. "Katie, I've been giving more thought to your art project. Why don't you paint me nailed to a cross," I mimic him in a whisper. How dare the guy push his religious views on her?

She throws her head back and laughs that beautiful, deep, hearty sound I love. "You know what? I might just do it Let me see if I can think of a title for it. *Maybe Heaven Will Have to Wait?* Or, *I'm the Only One Who Doesn't Know I'm an Asshole?*"

"Ha. I like the second. Call me later?"

"You got it."

Silverview Middle School's yellow school bus pulls around the totem pole and a female teacher with a round blond bob and too-short bangs steps out to the sidewalk. I go outside and introduce myself. She checks my name off a printed list and thanks me for agreeing to be a chaperone.

The bus is full of noisy eighth-grade students, including my brother Reggie, who pretends he doesn't know me. I call out his name and blow him a kiss just to embarrass him, then take a seat near the front and wait for Yoon-hi. She comes out of the building a minute later, moving awkwardly in a clear plastic rain jacket with a bulky coat underneath and knee-high rubber boots. She boards the bus, lifts her chin, and starts to walk on by.

I grab her wrist. "Oh, come on. Please don't tell me you're pissed at me too." The day is going to be miserable if she won't talk to me.

"Not happy. Not pissed. Not anything," she grumps and slides down beside me, her rain jacket and the tail of her coat falling in my lap. "Just so you know, your friend Matty is a sekki."

My friend, not ours? "What's a sekki?"

The daughter of a South Korean diplomat, Yoon-hi was born in Peru, moved to New York when she was six, and spent her first two years of high school in Busan before coming to Alaska. She speaks four languages and has no accent, except on rare occasions when she gets upset. Then her R's can sound a little heavy. *Ferriend.*

"Sekki. Sekki. Wakey-wakey," she rhymes. "Son of a dog. Or bitch, whichever you prefer. I don't know how you stand him. And Tally. Don't get me started on that." She spins her hand, palm out in my face.

I cross my eyes and push it aside. "Are we trying out different languages now? You'll forgive me if I don't understand a single word you're saying." *Except that you and Matty are still fighting. And now you're mad at Tally too even though you're the one who didn't show up to Caseo's last night.*

The bus burps stinky smoke and rattles forward as a group of kids in back start singing a song about spinning bus wheels. They're loud and probably off-key on purpose. Yoon-hi glances back as if she'd like to tell them to shut up. She doesn't, though. Too polite.

She still sounds cross when she says, "I've never been to Whittier."

I shove her heavy coat off my lap. "Then you're in for a treat. And you're certainly dressed for it. You know what they say about the weather—"

"Always shittier in Whittier. Yeah, I heard." She pulls her phone from the inner recesses of her coat and checks the weather app. "Sunny for once. Better than here."

I'm pleased she's talking to me, but I'm not loving this funk. Reggie's teacher gives a history lesson on a megaphone, and for a few minutes I can barely hear myself think. Not that the bits of flotsam circling my brain are coherent.

All I've got is that I want Yoon-hi and Matty to be friends again, for Tally to stop all this crazy nonsense with Mrs. Donovan, and for Katie's father to disappear off the face of the earth. It doesn't seem too much to ask for.

We stop at West High School and pick up a couple of male students who are waiting out front. The Asian one nudges Yoon-hi's shoulder as he passes on his way to an empty seat a few rows back. She gives him a chin lift. "Adam."

"Adam? He's cute." I glance over my shoulder at him, a slender guy with shiny black hair.

"Don't." Yoon-hi pulls up Apple Music and shoves a pair of earbuds in her ears. Conversation closed.

It's a long and lonely drive to Whittier, not helped when Reggie starts throwing potato chips at my head. It's a while before I notice. I pick up one from my lap and stick it in my mouth. I'd like to throw the others back, but I'm supposed to be the adult here.

Luckily we don't have to wait long in Porter to drive into the tunnel, which is one of my favorite parts of the trip. The jagged rock along the sides appear to be chiseled out by hand. Dim lights along the upper walls glow like pockets of gold nuggets. The tunnel has an earthy scent, a little like mushrooms, or maybe more like dirty socks. I walked through it a couple of summers ago and decided it would be the perfect place to hunker down during the zombie apocalypse. There are tiny safe houses scattered along the route in case of accidents or earthquakes.

When we enter the tunnel and the bus goes dark, Yoon-hi sits up straight and rigid and drops her phone in her lap.

"The Anton Anderson Memorial Tunnel, longest tunnel in North America," I say at the same time as Reggie's teacher Mrs. Gaines announces it on her megaphone.

"How long?" Yoon-hi's polished nails dig into my thigh.

"Two-and-a-half miles, I think. Don't worry, there's plenty of fresh air being pushed through jet fan engines at both ends."

These are facts nearly every kid in south central Alaska can recite. Reggie and most of his friends have taken this trip as many times as I have. "Claustrophobic?" I ask, noting her face has turned ashen.

Yoon-hi gives her head a tiny shake. "Not at all. I just don't like small, dark places."

At least she feels well enough to joke. And she's in a better mood when we reach the other end. "Sorry I'm being such a bitch," she mutters when we get off the bus.

"Sekki wakey." I wink.

She tucks her earbuds and phone into a side pocket of her enormous coat.

Whittier is a town of about two hundred seventy residents. Most live in a fourteen-story building that resembles an ugly hotel. There are a few small shops, but no single-family homes to speak of because the winter weather is exceptionally wicked here, with sixty mile-an-hour winds often blowing day and night. The tunnel closes at midnight but the shops shut their doors much earlier. There's a semi-rustic inn with good views of the harbor, but you don't want to be stuck overnight in Whittier as there's nothing to do. The saving grace is the easy access to beautiful Prince William Sound.

Mrs. Gaines directs me, Yoon-hi, the Asian guy named Adam, and a Black guy I met at Model UN last spring, to the groups she wants us to supervise. I take my designated spot by a guard rail and inhale brisk salt air. Shiny rocks and tiny seashells crunch underfoot. Bubbles of brown foam lap the beach. The water beyond is a gorgeous midnight blue.

I have the kids whose last names begin with A through H. Yoon-hi has I through N. Being eighth graders, they bunch up in their own little groups and ignore our efforts to make them stand in lines. Yoon-hi and I end up together on the ramp facing small clanking sailboats that rise and fall with the wake from larger cruise ships.

Adam walks over and stands on the other side of Yoon-hi. When he says, "I was hoping I'd run into you," I'm a hundred percent certain he doesn't mean me.

"How've you been?" Yoon-hi rests both arms atop the railing and barely turns her head.

"Can't complain. You?"

"Same."

"Glad to hear it."

This is a conversation going nowhere fast. I give it a few more seconds in case one of them wants to say something more interesting, then lean around behind her, introduce myself, and ask how they know each other. Yoon-hi gives me a dirty look.

"Our fathers worked together." Adam tosses a wave of neat black hair off his forehead.

"Your dad's a diplomat?"

"Used to be. He works for Exxon Mobil in corporate planning now. This is Jeff," he says, introducing my Model UN acquaintance.

"We've met," I say.

Jeff steps closer and we reminisce for a couple of minutes about the half hour we spent together months ago at some downtown office. Jeff obviously has no more interest in me than

I have in him, but he's polite. My sole purpose in engaging him is to give Yoon-hi and Adam time to talk privately. My efforts are in vain, however, as they stumble through a brief discussion about homework and the differences between the AP physics courses at West and North.

Mrs. Gaines saves us from more awkward conversation by using her megaphone to tell everybody it's time to board the ship. I shepherd my group, including Reggie and his two best friends, to the gangway where a crewmember hands them each a clipboard with a couple of worksheets and a pencil on a string. From there, we shuffle to the interior lounge where the kids are instructed to find seats at the dining tables.

Normally these single-day cruises provide passengers with a hot meal, but to save money, teachers have instructed students to bring sack lunches. Over the intercom the captain informs them they can buy chips and candy at a snack bar at the rear of the ship and that when they go outside, they can leave their lunches and whatever snacks they purchase on the tables.

I hope this means someone employed on the ship will stay inside to keep an eye on things because if I know eighth graders, there will be a lot of food stealing going on. Reggie won't, but one of his friends is a trickster. He'll switch lunches and pilfer chocolate bars from others just because he can.

After that, the captain issues the standard warnings about no running, no standing on the railings, no throwing stuff off the ship, no throwing each other off the ship, no clogging toilets, and most importantly, to enjoy the scenery. "After all," he says, "this is a unique opportunity."

"I thought this would be fun but it feels like school," a girl with pigtails complains in a loud voice to a couple of her friends.

I step over and tap her on the shoulder. "Don't forget to complete your worksheets. There's a quiz tomorrow, and you'll be expected to hand them in."

"Really?" Her blond brows shoot up her forehead.

"Mrs. Gaines didn't tell you? Well, that's just irresponsible of her, don't you think?"

She looks wide-eyed at her friends and they each reluctantly retrieve the clipboards they've deposited at their feet.

Reggie rolls his eyes at me but keeps his mouth shut. He knows it's bullshit. Pete and I have told him all about our eighth-grade field trips, but he also understands from my look that the potato chips he threw at me earlier are going to wind up down the back of his shirt if he doesn't let me do my job. The worksheets are busy work and a way to try to keep know-it-alls like the girl from spoiling the trip for kids who might actually care.

I'm in line behind Yoon-hi and Adam when we file out to the deck so I hear him ask her if she wants to wear his wool knit cap.

"Is that a joke?" she snaps.

I understand why she thinks it. It's roasting inside the cabin. She's probably sweating in her heavy coat and rain jacket, not to mention her goofy rubber boots. But Adam rears back, startled. "No. It'll be much colder on the deck when we hit the open water."

"Oh." She blinks. "Well, no thank you, then." She gestures to a band of noisy kids headed for the bow. "I need to stay with my group. And you should probably stay with yours."

Wow. Way to shut the guy down, Yoon-hi. Adam would have to have a whole lot of self-confidence to come back from that.

Apparently he doesn't. He mumbles something about keeping an eye out for Dall's porpoises, adding that they look like baby orcas and often can be seen swimming under ships. He threads his way around a group of girls and disappears into the crowd.

I can't wait to hear Adam's and Yoon-hi's backstory, but I'm distracted by the alternating voices of the captain who is telling the history of the Sound and Mrs. Gaines calling out a kid who's busy untangling a life preserver from the ropes with the obvious intent of strangling one of his classmates. Gotta love eighth graders.

We cruise down Passage Canal toward Blackstone Bay, hearing how an oil tanker known as the Exxon Valdez nearly destroyed the Sound thirty-four years ago by spilling eleven million gallons of oil into the water, and how the glaciers we'll see shortly are receding due to climate change. We glide past adorable little otter rafts and small herds of sea lions barking aboard buoys, while small birds known as kittiwakes drop random clops of white poop overhead.

The bitterly cold wind picks up. I snag my beanie from a jacket pocket and pull it over my ears.

"That's the Tebenkof Glacier over there," I tell Yoon-hi a second before the captain announces it.

"It's incredible. The Sound is amazing," she concedes.

"I bet you've seen tons of cool stuff in the places you've lived before."

"Yeah, but each one is different. Listen, about Adam."

I wait, but she doesn't continue. I've been to Yoon-hi's house exactly once. It was stuffy and over-decorated with Korean art, most of it probably expensive. Her parents were courteous and formal. "I think I get it."

"How can you?" There's a note of wistfulness in her voice.

"Let me take a stab at it. He isn't Korean?"

"You can tell?"

I'd like to say yes, but I'm as oblivious to facial distinctions in other races as most other Caucasians. "No, but it's the only reason I can think of why you're snubbing him. Did you date?"

"We went to a movie a couple of months ago. I told my mother we were friends. She was fine with it until she caught us kissing. The very next day my father sat me down for the talk. Chinese are not our friends, he said. They are close to evil. Beijing is a bully. The same old stuff. You people think we're all alike, that our customs are all the same."

I stiffen. "You people?"

Yoon-hi flaps a hand. "You know what I mean. Non-Asians. You think all Asians are smart, polite, hardworking. I don't mean to offend you, Virginia. Tell me, am I wrong?"

I wish I could. But honestly, Yoon-hi is the only Asian I really know and that's exactly how I would have described her. She's been to my house dozens of times. Why don't I get invitations to hers?

"How about Americans? Would your parents be okay with you dating Jeff?"

"Who?"

"The guy who came with Adam."

She stares at the icy mass of a calving glacier in the distance. The crackle echoes across the water and a small boat leaves our ship to retrieve a block of the ice. Up close on shore, bird nests fill every crag. "What do you think? Adam. Jeff. It makes no difference to my parents. Anyway, didn't I tell you I'm crushing on Matty now? I've been leaving love notes in his lockers. I don't understand why he ignores me."

I release a grunt that I hope sounds like a chuckle. She said practically the same thing at the police station, that she had a thing for me. This time it feels like an old joke that needs to be retired. I shift to the starboard side of the ship to get out of the wind. Two girls crouch together on a cargo hatch, their heads bent together as if they're sharing a secret. I peer closer. They're actually filling out the worksheets. That was me and Katie a few years ago.

Yoon-hi follows me a moment later. "What happened last night at Caseo's? Did the rich, young, and very pretty librarian show up?"

What do you care? You couldn't be bothered to come. I stuff resentment down my throat. "She did. But it was pretty obvious she wasn't into Tally. She didn't seem to get that Tally thought it was a date."

"Figures. Tally is an idiot."

I stare at Yoon-hi in shock. "You're kidding, right? Tally's our friend."

"If you say so." She studies the shoreline for a second and then heads back inside.

CHAPTER NINETEEN

Katie

Every now and then things actually go my way. I ace a test. A teacher singles me out in class with praise. An interim principal is called to a meeting away from the building, leaving me free to work on my art project after lunch. It's that kind of morning.

I finish my zebra picture and complete the online rubric about what my piece should say to critics. Easy. "Animals should be armed against trophy hunters for a fair fight," I write. I give myself an A and turn the sucker in. With Mrs. Pugh out of the office as well, I check my phone.

No texts from Virginia. A bummer, although there's probably no cell service on the water. No texts from Dad, Mom, or Denise either. That's definitely good news. With eight minutes of free time before fourth hour starts, my thoughts turn to what Denise told me this morning. Mom said I was her world? I'd like to believe it, but it doesn't sound like her.

Back in Washington when I visited her in the hospital, we talked about school and whether the neighbor I was staying with was feeding me enough. Fruits? Vegetables? No processed meats? She quizzed me every day. We didn't discuss Dad or the shooting except when it came time to prepare for his trial. And even that was brief.

"Just tell the truth," she instructed.

Dad's text yesterday said she hit him first. I don't believe that either. But regardless, it wouldn't have mattered. There's no justification for shooting someone unless you're a zebra exercising self-defense.

The office door opens and I slide my phone into my pocket. Mrs. Pugh's a pretty okay person now, but last year you earned yourself a detention if you so much as thought about taking out your phone in her class.

It's not Mrs. Pugh at the door, however. Amy Meeks walks up to the counter. "Oh, hi! I didn't expect to see you here," she says. "Are you in trouble, or do you work here?"

"I'm an office aide. The pay stinks."

She laughs. "Mine, too. I'm Mr. Spurling's aide."

"Lucky you."

Mr. Spurling is considered by many as the single best teacher at North. It's widely known that his tests come straight out of the back of the textbook, and he spends most of every hour at his desk with his face hidden behind a newspaper. Kids say he'll talk sports on occasion because he also coaches football, but he mostly leaves them alone. That's my kind of class, but one Virginia would detest.

"Are you running an errand for him?" I ask.

"Yeah. Is Mrs. Pugh here? I'm supposed to tell her he needs a sub sixth hour, but under no circumstances is she to ask Mrs. Hicks because she always complains he doesn't leave enough lesson plans."

I hide a smile. Sounds just like Mrs. Hicks, which is probably why she's Virginia's favorite teacher. "Mrs. Pugh stepped out. I'll pass along your message."

Amy taps a finger on the counter and turns her gaze to the teacher photocopier in front of the mailboxes.

"Anything else?"

"Not really. But as long as I'm here, how would you feel about me making a few party flyers?"

"You got twenty bucks?"

"Not on me."

I chuckle at her startled expression. "Just kidding. But better hurry. Mrs. Pugh could be back any second."

Amy runs out and comes back with an orange piece of copy paper. "It doesn't have to be in color. Is a hundred too many?"

"It's fine." Nobody keeps count.

Teachers can be kind of wasteful anyway. I've seen some make twice that many before discovering some tiny error and starting over. We go over to the copier together and place the printed notice on the glass.

"Party starts at eight, or as soon as you can get there. We'll probably go all night." Amy presses the button to set the copier in motion. It's a noisy one, the sound reminding me of my Washington neighbor's CPAP, delivering oxygenated air so her airways wouldn't collapse while she was sleeping. I hated the sound then got used to it. It makes me think of Mom again and the weeks she spent in recovery.

I'm Mom's entire world? Damn. Why doesn't she say that to me? Should I pack a bag for Nome just in case?

"You are coming to my party, aren't you?" Amy interrupts my thoughts. "It's going to be a blowout."

"Maybe."

She flips her hair and pretends to pout. "Oh, come on, Katie. That sounds like a no. Don't say that. There'll be plenty of booze, I promise. I did say your whole crew was invited, didn't I? That dude Matty is a hoot."

Not always.

"My boy Dillon will be there," she adds slyly.

Why would I care about that? Unless…does she think I'm interested in him? "You invited your old boyfriend to your party?" The photocopier goes silent and I pass her the flyers.

She presses one back into my hands. "Sure. Why not? We're friends. His dad's whacked, but Dillon's always up for a good time."

Dillon's father is a Pentecostal preacher, I recall. I can't imagine what it would be like growing up with an uber-Christian father. Maybe not that bad, I guess. And obviously kids don't have to be like their parents. Look at me. God help me.

Realizing I need to set the record straight, I say, "Actually, the reason I messaged you the other night was because I met Dillon here in the office the first day of school. He'd been sent out of class for bullying another student. I'm wondering if it was Jason Gonzalez."

Amy's posture suddenly goes stiff. At the same time, she runs her tongue across her upper teeth as if she's got a bad taste in her mouth. Last fall she wore braces, then got them off before Christmas break. Her teeth are white and straight now, and I like the way her hair flows down her back like a movie star's. It's red and thick. Doesn't she get that if I was interested in anyone other than Virginia, it wouldn't be her former boyfriend?

"I sincerely hope you're not suggesting Dillon had anything to do with that bastard Jason's death," she growls.

"Of course not. I'm just curious. Believe me, I know as well as anyone that Jason had a way of getting under people's skin. Even the cafeteria workers. You should have heard the way he talked to them. He didn't have many friends."

"Many?" Her growl grows more pronounced. "You mean none, except you guys who ate lunch with him. Jeez, Katie. I get that you and Virginia figured out who killed Marisol and everything, but your little group, you're not crime fighters, you know? And honestly, I'm just going to say it. Everybody assumes it was one of you."

I feel my eyes grow wide. "Well, it wasn't."

"Sure. Fine. Keep telling yourself that. But let me ask you this. How well do you know each other? Because I can tell you that I know Dill pretty well. He's a sweetheart, and he didn't deserve to get expelled when Jason was the dick making fun of Dill's accent. But if you want to talk to him about it or whatever, ask him yourself. Be my guest. He goes to Grace Lord Charter off Debarr, like half a mile past the Fred Meyer there. God, I gotta say"—she blows a breath—"this really pisses me off."

That makes two of us. Before I was curious, now I'm ticked. I don't like her hostile attitude, especially considering I just let her use the copier for her stupid flyers.

Mrs. Pugh walks in and her eyes go immediately to the stack of papers in Amy's hand. I can see her working it out. "Amy? Did you need something?"

"Mr. Spurling needs a sub sixth hour," I say quickly before Amy gets us both in hot water. "I let Amy photocopy his lesson plans. Here. Don't forget this one." I shove the flyer she handed me earlier back on top of the stack and show her out to the hall.

"Sorry," she whispers once we're out of earshot.

I guess she's had enough time to cool down. I haven't. "Get real. You aren't either."

"Yeah. I am. Look, don't be mad. I shouldn't have said that about your friends. It's just that everything is so messed up. Dillon. Jason. You guys who sat with him. I don't get why you put up with him, but I am sorry if I've gotten you in trouble with Mrs. Pugh. Dill and me, we don't date anymore, but that doesn't mean I don't care about him. He's sweet. You'll see it once you get to know him. I mean, he's like totally ADD but harmless. And think about it. He got expelled the first week of school so he couldn't have poisoned Jason. Talk to him, if you want. I'll tell him to expect you."

"Maybe I will." I plant my feet a good ten inches apart and fold my arms across my chest, probably looking a lot like Mr. A-hole Sullivan.

Amy reaches out but stops just short of touching me. "Do," she says again as if she hasn't already made her point. "And please, will you come to my party? Dill's bringing vodka and I'm getting a keg. If nobody shows up, how lame will that be? Dumb to care, I know. But I really want it to be successful. It's my first big event since we moved to Anchorage. Here, please take the flyer."

"I'll think about it." Gracious. Yeah, that's me. I fold the paper and stuff it in a pocket.

The bell rings and she runs off. I wave to Mrs. Pugh from the hall to let her know I'm heading to class. As I head upstairs,

I spend a few seconds trying to figure out why Amy and I both got so upset. It only makes sense that other kids would suspect the people who ate lunch with Jason. After all, I have my doubts about Tom. So why did I get so pissed off?

CHAPTER TWENTY

Virginia

Fuck Yoon-hi. Fuck this crappy field trip. If Yoon-hi makes no bones about calling Tally an idiot, what is she saying about the rest of us behind our backs? I've never heard her talk this way. It's a side of her I definitely don't like. I keep Katie's special lunch to myself and eat it outside on the deck when we make the turnaround at Beloit. Normally I love smoked salmon, but this is pretty tasteless.

Most of the eighth graders go back inside to eat and for a minute or so it's just me and a flock of gulls diving for my food. I toss them a couple of crackers even though the captain has asked us not to feed them. A frigid gale whistles around me.

"I think you're supposed to be inside with us. Where did you get that?" Reggie yells over the roaring of the wind. He drops to the bench beside me and gestures to the plastic container in my lap.

"Katie." I hold it out for him to help himself, but he shakes his head.

"I'm seasick."

"Really? Not you. Are you serious?" My little brother has an iron stomach. I've seen him consume moldy cheese, wilting lettuce, and green grapes that have turned slimy.

"Nate started waving chocolate milk in my face. I thought I was going to barf so I came outside."

I wipe my sticky fingers on a paper napkin and hold the back of my hand to his forehead. Reggie make a gurgling sound in the back of his throat. He stands up and upchucks at my feet. Some of it blows back. I leap up, but it's too late. Chunks of vomit lands on the salmon.

"Oops." His hand goes to his mouth and comes back trailing saliva and pinkish bits like oatmeal.

"Gross! That's disgusting. You couldn't have turned away from the wind?"

We clean it up together, dabbing slime off our puffer jackets, then throw away the rest of my lunch and wipe down the wooden bench as best we can. "Do you feel better?" I ask him, taking a few steps to the bow to get away from the scent of puke.

"A little. Sorry. How come Yoon-hi isn't out here with you?"

How do I say because my sweet, normally well-mannered friend is being a jerk? I knew Yoon-hi didn't have a lot of respect for Tally's intellect, but usually she humors her. I settle on, "We had a disagreement."

"About that guy who got killed?"

"Not exactly. Don't you ever get mad at your friends?"

"All the time." Reggie sticks a finger in his mouth to dig more vomit from his teeth so he can look at it. "Yesterday, Nate knotted my shoelaces together in PE when I wasn't looking so I'd trip. The day before, Lance told this girl Simone that I liked her, but she shouldn't think about kissing me because I have a venereal disease. And guess what? I don't like her. He's the one who likes her. I mean she's got big tits. Like enormous, and I do like that. And sometimes you can see her nipples through her shirt. That's cool."

I hold up a hand to stop him before he talks about her other parts. "Reggie. Show respect. Don't talk about girls that way to me or anybody else, even your friends. It's disrespectful. Do you want Simone to talk about you like that?"

"She probably does." He grins.

"Well, even so. You shouldn't. Someday you're going to want a girl to like you."

"Or a boy?"

"Yes, or a boy. Regardless, I don't care what Nate and Lance do. But you've gotta be the bigger person. Anyway, I know you understand about friendships. Yoon-hi and I both got upset, but we'll get over it. No biggie. Are you going to be sick again?"

"Nah. Are you done lecturing me?"

I roll my eyes. Was I that immature when I was thirteen? Surely not. "For the time being. Let's go inside."

We head into the cabin as others pour out to the deck. Reggie joins his buddies at a table by a window. I stop to compliment the girl with pigtails and her friends on their worksheets and to tell another kid to stop spitting on the chunk of glacier ice that was brought aboard earlier. I remind myself not to accept any drinks made with it and search out Yoon-hi.

She's alone by the bar in back, gazing out a window. "Oh, I was just coming out to look for you. Mrs. Gaines gave me our service hour forms. Here's yours." She passes it across the table. "I've also been meaning to tell you that I got the scoop on Shanice Kennedy. Remember, you asked about her? She works at a vet's office, the one on Huffman Road by the grocery store not far from your house. And did you know Jason has an older brother? He lives in Willow with the mother."

"Okay." I slip the service hour form into a side pocket of my cooler.

Yoon-hi purses her lips, perplexed. "Well, you're welcome."

"Thanks."

We sit for a long time in silence, then the captain announces that we'll be docking shortly, and Mrs. Gaines reminds students not to leave any personal possessions on the ship. Yoon-hi, Adam, Jeff, and I check the tables after the kids get up and herd them back out to the bus.

I take the empty seat across the aisle from Yoon-hi and ask if she can give Reggie and me a ride home when we get back to North.

She shrugs out of her rain jacket and unwieldy coat. "Whatever you want."

CHAPTER TWENTY-ONE

Katie

With heavy traffic due to road construction, it's after three by the time I pull into the Grace Lord Charter School's circle drive. For a second I worry that I might have missed Dillon because the parking lot is deserted, save for a single car parked near the back. I get out and start for the door of a gothic-looking building just as two young women dressed in unfashionably long skirts come out chatting about some TV show they both watch. I'm about ask them what time their school gets out when I notice Dillon sitting by himself with his elbows on his knees on a nearby step.

"I was beginning to think you wouldn't show, Miss Office Aide." He gazes at me, expressionless.

I hesitate a second, then join him. "You talked to Amy."

"I did. I did," he says. His "I" sounds like "Ah," taking me back to the first day of school and his peculiar country accent. He's wearing pointy leather boots again, the belt with a silver bison buckle, a brown felt cowboy hat, and another checkered shirt, this one red and white. My head is singing an old George Strait song, and I almost have to slap myself to stop.

I sit a foot or so away and press my knees together, not sure how to begin. "So, the reason I wanted to speak with you, my girlfriend and I used to run a small and very amateur detective service at school. Which isn't important, except that one of the guys we eat lunch with us asked if we would look into Jason Gonzalez's death."

"Okay." Still no expression.

"First." I brush my palms down my jeans, feeling more and more nervous. "I just want to say that I imagine you heard Jason died from eating rat poison. I'm not accusing you of killing him. I only want to know if you have any insight into anyone who might have wanted to hurt him."

Dillon spits something brown and ugly on the sidewalk at my feet. "Anyone at North."

"Mm. Right." I draw my legs up underneath me, trying not to look to see if any of it hit my shoes.

"Sure. I get it. Good thing I got kicked out early then, what with my ol' man handling snakes and speaking in tongues and all that other weird ass spiritual crap. He's a crazy SOB, my ol' man, but what you need to know is that I ain't a chip off that ol' block. That's the expression, ain't it? Chip off the ol' block?"

"I think so." The women get into the car and drive off, leaving me alone with Dillon Reed, whom I find very strange. It's not just the accent. He isn't friendly like he was at North at the beginning of the year. What made me think questioning him without Virginia was a good idea?

He digs in his pocket for a can of chewing tobacco. "Thing is, Miss Office Aide, I got my own bad habits, and preaching gospel ain't one of them. Frankly, I drink too much, blaze too much, and I can't seem to keep lil Dilly in my pants." I blink in alarm as he motions to his junk.

"Couldn't even blame that sweet gal Amy for breaking up with me, what with lil Dilly having a mind of his own and all. But to answer your real question, Pony Boy and me did indeed get into it. The silly little snot. Remember back in grade school how a kid could get on your nerves by acting like he's better than you, and you just wanna punch him?"

Not really. "You punched Jason?" I say softly, not wanting to provoke him.

Dillon flashes shiny teeth. "I wanted to. Didn't say I did. I might have wanted to give him a taste of his own medicine. You ever milk a snake, Miss Office Aide?"

"Not recently." I swallow soundlessly. Maybe it's all the stuff going on with my father, but I wish I had a weapon for protection. A knife or bat. Not a gun, though. I hate those things.

"Good one. Not recently." Dillon checks me gently with his shoulder. He smiles, then but it fails to make its way up to his eyes. "You gotta be careful 'cause that ol' snake, given half a chance, will bite you. Happened to my daddy twice. Nearly did him in. Anyways, I'm here, and Pony Boy was there with you at North. So the moment never came my way. Now, that's not to say I couldn't find a body to do it for me. Still got a friend or two at North, you get my drift. Sweet Amy says the venom most likely come outta that big ice box in the cafeteria. Ain't that right?"

"I think so." I need to get out of here.

He sees my face and knocks my elbow. "Aw, come on, pretty girl. I'm just playing with you. You get that, don't you? Don't take me seriously. No one does. By the way, you going to my ol' girl's party Saturday night? It's gonna be fun. Promised I'd bring a couple of vodka handles. Other stuff. You gotta come. Say you will. Pretty please, Miss Office Aide?"

"I'll try." I stand and inch my way down the steps.

Dillon is still grinning. His smile looks real now, probably because he's laughing at me, knowing that I'm scared. "I'll take that as a yes, then. No snakes, guaranteed. We're gonna have fun."

I just bet. I race walk to my car. For once Evie's engine turns right over. She knows I'm frightened.

Dillon waves, and I force myself not to slam my foot too hard on the accelerator. In my head, I know he was deliberately messing with me the whole time we talked, but I am most definitely not going to that party.

CHAPTER TWENTY-TWO

Virginia

Katie's friend Amy Meeks is passing out party notices by the school's totem pole when Silverview's school bus lets Yoon-hi and Reggie and me off at North.

"Saturday night. No cover charge. Everybody's welcome," she shouts to football players leaving practice.

It's the first I've heard about a party and I eye her with surprise when she tells me Katie's going to be there. "She is. Just ask her."

I will later. I shove the party flyer next to the service hour form in my cooler and follow Yoon-hi to her car. She stops in front of our house just long enough to let us out, then speeds away. Clearly, she feels like I do, that we're strangers. How did we become friends when we barely know each other?

"Can I go to the party too?" asks Reggie.

"You're too young."

"No, I'm not."

"Okay, then you weren't invited." I press the four-digit code on the garage door keypad, which is our house numbers, how original. The door rolls up noisily, like the wheels need oiling.

Reggie draws back, hurt. "You don't have to be mean about it."

"Oh, come on. Since when is being honest mean? It's a high school party. There won't be anybody there your age." I put a hand to his forehead. "How do you feel? Are you still sick?"

"What do you care?" He runs into the house.

This is what I get for treating him like an adult. Jeez, one minute he and his friends are tying each other's shoelaces together, the next they're giggling over a girl's breasts. I follow him inside, grab a handful of trail mix from a kitchen cabinet, and check my phone. Nope, not a single text from Katie. Well, isn't that spectacular.

Abe and George pad down the hall and sit by my side, clearly hoping for a treat. Their long sharp nails dig into the kitchen floor. It's past time to trim them, but I hate doing it. I'm always afraid of cutting into the quick. George squeals like a baby and Abe gives me a look like I'm hurting him on purpose. That's when I get an idea. I call the Huffman Family Vet Clinic. "Do you take walk-ins for nail trims?"

"Dogs?"

"Yep."

"Sure do. Come on in."

"I'll be right there."

Thank goodness the receptionist didn't ask what kind of dogs. Some people think pit bulls are dangerous. George and Abe are anything but. Still, at sixty pounds apiece with massive jaws and a tendency to occasionally growl at strangers, they can seem a little scary. That's on the receptionist for not asking. I leash them using the nose harnesses Katie has been training them with and head back out the door.

We normally use another vet, but the place is clean and the man at the front desk is friendly, considering he scoots his chair as far away as he can get as George and Abe scrabble through the door. "Are these the nail trims?" he inquires in a high-pitched voice. I confirm it and assure him that George and Abe hardly ever bite. He says somebody will be with me in a minute and asks me to wait outside. I can hardly blame him. A Yorkie in a woman's lap is trying to climb inside her shirt.

"I was told to ask for Shanice Kennedy if she's available," I call over my shoulder as I drag the dogs outside. I have no idea if nail trims are a part of Shanice's job, but it's worth a shot.

I sit on a bench between the clinic and the Carr's Safeway next door. Shoppers grabbing grocery carts give me nervous smiles and the dogs a wide berth. Pretty soon Shanice comes out with heavy-duty nail clippers in one hand, a Dremel in the other.

"Hi, pups! Aren't you adorable." She drops to her knees on the sidewalk in front of them. "Come here, babies. Come on over. I won't hurt you."

They yank away from me to get to her, making little puppy yipping sounds and slobbering all over her face. "Wasn't sure if you wanted a clip or a grind." She looks up then, and recognizing me, her happy expression turning sour. "Oh, it's you. Are you stalking me?"

"What if I am? I never got a chance to respond to your stupid accusations." My tone is all bluff. It's obvious I won't be able to count on George and Abe to defend me since they've clearly fallen in love with Shanice. George twists his head around to lick her ears, while Abe tries to squeeze his body into her tiny lap.

She pets and cuddles them but offers me an unmistakable snort. "Fine. Nail trim first?"

"Go ahead." Might as well since we're here.

Shanice chooses the Dremel when I tell her I have no preference. She slips the clippers into the front pocket of her scrubs, and sits cross-legged on the ground, all the while persuading George to back off and Abe to stand still and hold out a paw.

"I wouldn't have pictured you the pitty type." She fingers the raised scars on George's back when she finishes the nail trim. The dogs lie quietly on either side of her. Abe has his head in her lap, loudly snoring.

"My first. I didn't do that to them, by the way. The scars, I mean. They're adopted. I haven't had them very long." I'm not sure why I feel the need to explain all this to her.

"How long?"

"Nine months."

"Well, they're obviously well-fed now." A dewy-eyed look overtakes Shanice's face. "Dogs aren't born hateful, you know? They're innocent like babies. It's how they're treated that forms their personalities. Every few years there's a new breed we're supposed to be afraid of. Dobermans. Rottweilers. German shepherds. I hate to think what might be next. You're lucky to have these two. I had a German shepherd in the Philippines. When my dad passed and we moved to Alaska, I had to give her up."

"That's terrible. Did you find a good home for her?" I hate stories like this.

"My ex-girlfriend took her. She sends me pictures of her every week. Her name is Pika. Do you want to see her?"

"Sure."

Shanice pulls out her phone and scrolls until she finds a photo that looks like the kind of dog on the Purina dry food bag we buy.

"She's beautiful." I'm getting a little misty-eyed myself. "Do you think you'll ever get back to see her?" I can't believe I'm actually feeling sorry for Shanice.

"I hope so. I miss her." Shanice puts away her phone.

I sit down on the sidewalk on the other side of Abe. It's time to get back to business. "Can we talk about Jason Gonzalez without you threatening me?"

"I guess." She strokes Abe's chunky paw, fingering the soft skin between his pads.

I gesture to the dogs. "Because one word from me and they'll take your face off."

The corners of her mouth twitch. "You want to know why I'm not sorry Jason's dead?"

"It's a good place to start."

"Jason's father, Mike, took advantage of my mom when she was at her most vulnerable. Dad had only been gone a couple of months when we moved here, and Mike immediately started hitting on her. It didn't matter that he was married or that she was recently widowed. I hated the way he used to sidle up to her at cookouts and press against her, saying shit like what a great cook she was and how warm and soft she felt against him. He knew she was lonely. He didn't even seem to care that people might see and tell his wife. I'm not saying Mom was completely innocent. But like I said, he started it. When eighteen hundred dollars went missing from the office register, Jason told his parents that my mom took it."

Did she? I clamp my teeth together before I say it out loud. Shanice seems to know it's coming anyway.

"Jason stole it, I'm sure of it. How else would you explain the Vespa he never had before and the cash he started flashing around at parties? I tried to tell his folks, but he insisted it came from tourist tips. Seriously, that much? He accused me of lying and even told his dad I had a thing for him. Anybody with half a brain would know that was bullshit. But Mike refused to hear it. His golden boy could do no wrong."

Golden boy, it's a good description. Jason could be charming when he tried. "I heard he has an older brother. Do you know him?" I ask.

A car pulls up next to the curb and a small Black woman climbs out.

"Yeah, Mike Junior. I never saw much of him, but he actually seemed okay. Lives with Mrs. Turd up in Willow. Mom? You're early." Shanice rises gracefully to her feet and dusts off her butt. "This is Virginia Eaton, the girl from school I was telling you about."

I half-expect Mrs. Kennedy to cuss me out. Instead, she comes around the car and holds out a hand. "Nice to meet you, Virginia. I'm so glad Shanice is making friends. By the way, I understand you visited Soba's. It's closed now, which you may have heard. Don't worry though, if you're the reason. The place was a mess. They needed to raise their standards."

I shut my mouth, realizing my jaw is hanging open. "Have you found another job?"

"Not yet. But something will turn up. It always does," she answers cheerfully.

Shanice holds the dogs' leashes while I go inside and pay for the nail trims. When I come out, Mrs. Kennedy is crouched beside them with her arms around their necks. A tear slides down her cheek. "They're so sweet. And named after two of my favorite presidents, how great is that? Shanice was just telling me you rescued them. I have to think there's a special place in heaven for people like you."

"Thanks." I gulp. That ought to make me proud. Instead I'm ashamed that I ratted her out to the police. "Hope to see you around," I say, urging George and Abe to their feet. They're reluctant to leave Shanice and her mom.

Shanice's mom pets them one last time. "You too, Virginia. Take care of these beautiful boys."

"Bye," says Shanice.

"Bye." I wave back as the dogs and I start off. Surreal. Well, damn. Now I like Shanice. She could still have killed Jason, but I'm not so sure anymore.

CHAPTER TWENTY-THREE

Katie

"Did you tell your mom you're not going to Nome?" Virginia asks when I pick her up the next morning.

"I'll send her a text today." But even as I say it, I know it's not the answer. A text? How lame is that? I should have talked to Mom last night and told her how I felt. It's not like I didn't have plenty of opportunity. I was home all night.

When I got back to my apartment after seeing Dillon, our building super stepped out of his apartment and handed me a roll of red duct tape. "For your taillight, until you have time to take it into the shop."

I was tempted to tell him I'd do it later, but he followed me back out, saying how car safety was too important. He doesn't get that I have other things to worry about. The whole situation regarding Dad's early release is beyond stressful. I spent most of the night pacing my bedroom, dresser to closet and back to my bed. Every little sound outside the building gave me jitters.

When we get to school, I see Mrs. Lorner unpacking boxes at the lunch counter. She'll understand, I think. She's a sympathetic listener even though she still can't remember my name. Yesterday when she called me Kathy, I didn't bother correcting her. What a funny old bird. I kiss Virginia goodbye and start to head into the cafeteria just as Mr. Sullivan steps in front of me.

"Hello, Katie. Do you have a minute? I'd like to speak to you in my office."

"Okay." I follow him back across the hall. Mrs. Pugh is nowhere in sight.

"Shut the door behind you, please, and have a seat." He drops into Mrs. Foster's chair and rocks back with a smug expression on his face.

He's made a few small changes to the room. Mrs. Foster's mug of pencils with the points facing up is gone. The African violet that used to sit on the corner of her desk is wilting on the window ledge behind him, and there's a stack of interior design magazines resting on the blotter alongside a ceramic jack-o'-lantern.

"Looks like you're settling in," I say conversationally when he doesn't speak.

"I am. No thanks to you." His tone is pleasant, so it takes his words a second to register.

"Excuse me?"

"You heard me. I tried to help you with your art project and instead of thanks I'm called to the superintendent's office and get my wrist slapped for speaking Christian in a public school." His skinny fingers form air quotes around *Christian*.

My spine curls in on itself. "I'm not sure what you're talking about."

He tilts his head, allowing the light from the window behind him to thread between the tiny hairs on the top of his head. The room has a sickening sweet scent like cheap perfume. "Let me give you a little history lesson, Katie. While it's true the US Supreme Court struck down school-sponsored prayer in the early 1960s, it doesn't mean adults, students too, shed their constitutional rights to private religious speech the minute they step inside a school building. Do you understand what I'm saying?"

"I think so." This time he's a little over my head.

"I'm not sure you do. Answer me this. Did I ask you to support my religious beliefs? Did I ask you to pray with me or give up *your* faith if you have one? Did I bully you into making you agree with me?"

I shake my head slowly to each question because no, he didn't. He just ticked me off with all that crap about man's dominion over animals when all I wanted to do was switch a zebra's head with my dad's.

"I'm confused," I say. "Do you think I reported you?" I'm perched on the edge of the chair. I want to lean back and at least look relaxed, but my feet are blocks of ice.

He swats the question away with a couple of his own. "Do you like it here at North? Do you enjoy canoodling with your girlfriend in the hall?"

Ugh. Did he really say that? Canoodling? Hello, Mr. A-hole. Welcome to the twenty-first century. We don't canoodle, smooch, or snoggle. We kiss and do other things I'm certainly not going to tell you about.

"I haven't done anything wrong," I begin, making no attempt to keep the self-righteousness from my tone. "If you're thinking of sending me somewhere else, I'm not going. North is a public high school."

Sullivan flips a wrist and gives me a fake sweet smile. "Oh, don't you worry about that. You're perfectly welcome here, but I'm changing your schedule. We don't need office aides. There's just not enough to do in here. Unfortunately, it's too late in the school year to enroll you in another class for credit, so you'll report to Mr. Spurling. He teaches history, I believe, and he's agreed to let you be his aide. You'll start today. I expect you to be on time, of course, and I'll be checking up on you periodically. That's all. You may go now. Have a delightful day."

I stand and stomp out. Point, match, Sullivan. I didn't see that coming. It's not that I mind the idea of sitting in Mr. Spurling's room. Amy's also an aide for him, and like I said, he's cool. But I feel like I've been fired for something that's not my fault. God, I can't stand the thought of Mr. Sullivan staying on as acting principal next semester. When will Mrs. Foster be back?

So what if she missed a stupid health inspection? I wonder how much he's poisoned the district office against her.

Mrs. Pugh is coming in just as I'm leaving. "Katie?" Her razor eyebrows slide together in a jagged line.

"What?" I snap.

She drops an oversize book bag on the counter. "You look upset."

"I am. You got me fired."

"What? No, I didn't."

"You didn't report Mr. Sullivan to the district office for talking Christian?"

"Well, yes. But just to let them know what he was up to. He had no right to ask you to change your art project. Where are you going now?"

"To Mr. Spurling's room. I'll be his aide from here on out."

"Oh, heavens no. That's a terrible idea." She puts a hand to her throat. "Don't worry, Katie. Give me a day, won't you? I'll get this figured out. You'll be back here Monday, Tuesday at the latest. I promise."

I'm barely listening because I'm so angry. "Forget it. Mr. Spurling is great. And you know what? I'm looking forward to a change in scenery. So thank you, Mrs. Pugh, for that. And please"—I pause, then mimic Sullivan's irritating singsong voice—"by all means, have a delightful day."

When I get out to the hall I immediately text Virginia who messages me back a couple of hours later. She's in the middle of an honors course, the only one in which she can sneak her phone out. *Canoodle? He really said that? No way.*

Way. I hate that guy. I punch hard on my phone.

Smug?

Exactly.

Wanna kick his balls at lunch?

Yes.

Okay, let's do it. See ya then.

I glance at the clock. Thirty-five more minutes until we'll meet up for lunch. It's a safe bet I won't still be full-on raging by then, just grumbly enough to keep complaining. I need everyone at our table to come up with Sullivan jokes to help take the sting out of my embarrassment.

Who gets fired from being an office aide? Answer: nobody. You've got to do something really dumb to get removed from that post, like letting Amy Meeks make flyers on the staff-only copier? Well, shit. That could do it. But this is Mrs. Pugh's fault. I mean, sure she was looking out for me. But all that means is it's my cushy job that's gone, not hers. I'll have no more visits with Mrs. Lorner after lunch and I won't hear any more of her crazy theories that somehow keep me sane.

And then another thought hits me. Is there still a lunch group? I haven't seen Tally since Caseo's. Matty's not speaking to any of the rest of us. Yoon-hi and Virginia bitched it out on their field trip yesterday. And Tom never really was one of us. He'll likely be arrested before the weekend because who else could have killed Jason? Unless Dillon somehow snuck back into the building or talked someone else into doing it for him…

There is one thing I can do. When the bell rings, I send a text to Mom. *Not going to Nome. Sorry.* My thumb hits send before I can rethink it, and I instantly regret it. I don't want to hurt her feelings. What's wrong with me? Should I go to Nome?

Virginia and I meet in the hall outside the cafeteria. There's no sign of the others. Our table is empty.

"We could go to the auditorium or the film club stairwell to canoodle," she says, giving me a sexy wink that yanks the breath right out of my lungs. "Do you know I had to look that word up? It's like embracing. Kissing. Caressing. I think I like it."

Before I can reply, a disembodied voice floats through the hall. "Virginia Eaton, Katie McRanes, Matty Brown, Tom Glass, Yoon-hi Park, and Tally Carter, please report to the front office now."

"Canoodle later?" Virginia laces her fingers through mine and gently squeezes. She's trying to make light of everything, though her voice is low and serious.

"Sure." I nod, thinking if we don't all wind up in jail, that is. I've got a bad feeling about this. I wish I could visit with Mrs.

Lorner first. I just want to see her friendly face. We spin around and head to the office.

Mr. Sullivan leans against the radiator in front of the window, his short pants exposing bony, hairy shins. He motions to seven chairs pulled up around the conference table as we enter.

Tom is the last to arrive. His normally coiffed hair looks greasy and disheveled. Whiteheads dot his neck and his wrinkled clothes look like he slept in them. "I have a lawyer. Do I need to call him?" he says, without looking at the rest of us.

Sullivan shuts the door behind him. "You don't. There's no need because I have good news for you. The police have found their guilty party, a cafeteria worker named Lindley Crowe."

"Lindley?" I can feel my eyes go wide with surprise.

Sullivan gazes at me sharply. "That's what I said. Now, every one of you, please tell your parents to quit calling me as this is no longer yours or their concern. That's it. You may go."

He flicks his skinny fingers toward the door. Slowly, we all get up. As we start to file out, an attractive Black woman in tan pants and a blue collared shirt steps past us; the cop, Detective Rosen, Virginia's mother's friend.

She looks at Sullivan. "What's going on?"

"Detective Rosen, you're a little late. I was just telling them the good news."

"What good news?" She frowns.

"That they're no longer suspects in Jason's murder. I told them what you said, that Mr. Crowe must have put the poison in his lunch."

"I never said that!"

"Sure, you did. You said you found evidence in his kitchen locker, and combined with the cafeteria surveillance footage of him going into the refrigerator that day, has to mean it's only a matter of time before you have him in custody. I'm sure their parents will be glad to hear it. I've got to say, if I get one more phone call—"

"Stop!" Rosen shouts. "Just stop! Sir, that was not your information to share." For the first time, Sullivan looks a shade less smug.

Detective Rosen turns to us. "Please, all of you, I'm sorry you heard that. It's not meant to be public knowledge, nor is anything definite. We're still in the early stages of this new lead. Good lord, what a mess. Please don't breathe a word of this to anyone. Promise me? Not to your teachers or your friends. Not on social media. Not to your dogs or cats, or in your sleep."

"Can I tell my dad?" Tom asks.

"Christ." She rubs her hands together like they hurt. "I guess I can't stop you from that. But that's all, do you understand? Please, each of you, tell me that you understand."

We go down the line each repeating what she's said. "Cross my heart, I won't tell a soul," I say when it comes to my turn.

"All right. I guess that will have to be good enough. Thank you. I'm so very very sorry."

CHAPTER TWENTY-FOUR

Virginia

I'm happy for Tom, of course, but I hope Sullivan is catching all kinds of shit for telling us what he obviously shouldn't. Mrs. Foster would've never made that kind of mistake. Through the glass, I can see Rosen leaning over Sullivan's desk, her posture stiff, as if she's still yelling at him. Meanwhile, when we reach the hall Tom collapses against a wall.

"It means I'm off the hook, right? Isn't that what he meant? She wouldn't have told him anything if there wasn't truth in it, right? God, I can't believe it's finally over. I feel like I'm waking up from a nightmare. I'd like to give Principal Sullivan a big fat kiss in thanks. Who the hell is Lindley Crowe?" He looks at Katie. "Should I know him?"

"The guy Jason was talking to before he had his seizure. He wipes down tables and takes out trash."

"Ha. You mean somebody else Jason managed to piss off."

"Yeah." She shrugs. "I guess."

I glance at her face and see her eyes dart down the hall toward the cafeteria.

"Well, I don't give a flying crap about some rando dude who takes out garbage," Tom adds. "You guys have no idea what it's like when people look at you like you're a monster. Even my parents. Maybe even you guys. What the hell. You know what, we should celebrate." He claps Matty on the back. "Let's go to Amy Meeks's party. All of us. What do you think, Matty Boy?"

Matty ducks his head. "Sure. Yeah. If that's what you want."

"Well, all right then. It's exactly what I want. Music. Booze. Friendly faces. No more dead man walking talk. You wouldn't believe all the Insta messages I've been getting from people I don't even know."

"Like what?" Yoon-hi asks.

"All kinds of crap about how I murdered my competition. As if. Wait until they hear this. They're gonna have to eat their words."

"But you know you can't post it until it's official, right?" I say, thinking of our promises to Rosen, but Tom isn't listening. He swivels his head in time to note Matty's unhappy expression and his euphoria fades.

"Dude. Jason wasn't my competition, was he? Be honest, man." For half a second I see a different Tom, a boy wracked with doubt.

Matty recovers quickly and puts an arm around Tom's waist. "Of course not. It's just that I've been thinking too."

"And?"

"We should definitely go to Amy's party. I'm all for it, but what if we did something special before that, just the six of us?"

"Like what?"

"Well, when Marisol was murdered last year Mrs. Foster arranged a memorial service for her here at school. I didn't go, but I heard it was really nice. Virginia went. It was cool, wasn't it? The jazz band played, and Marisol's family talked and said how much they loved her. Stuff like that. It doesn't seem like Mr. Sullivan's the type who's going to do that for Jason, so I was thinking maybe we could have a private service with just our group in Virginia's backyard."

What's this now? My backyard? What's wrong with yours? "You mean tonight?" I give him a look.

"Whatever you guys want," Katie says and takes off suddenly in the direction of the cafeteria.

Matty bumps me with an elbow. "Yeah, tonight. Why not? It's Friday, so no homework. We could have a fire in your backyard pit and each of us could say a few words about what Jason meant to us. It doesn't have to be religious, or you know, even that much about Jason. We could take turns talking about how this experience has affected us. It feels like we're all, I don't know, like different somehow. We used to be friends. But now, maybe not so much. Hell, if you think it's a bad idea, just forget it."

"I think it's a good idea," Yoon-hi says to my surprise. "And I do know what you mean about everything being different. Jason was…well, he had his good points." She's back to being diplomatic.

"I'm in." Tally sticks her hands in her pockets.

"Fine," I relent. "My backyard. But you guys bring the food."

"No problem." Matty turns to Tom who hasn't yet weighed in. "Hey, I get it if you don't want to come. You never really got to know Jason. There was a time when you guys might have liked each other."

It's all I can do not to burst out laughing at that. I doubt it very much, not with Matty unable to make up his mind who he wanted to be with.

Tom tilts his head, clearly dismayed, but aiming for a smile. "Sure. Whatever. If that's what *you* want. What time are you thinking?"

Matty and I look at each other in a silent consultation. "Seven?" I suggest.

We all agree on the time. Matty says he'll bring hot dogs. Tally offers to bring paper plates and napkins. Yoon-hi says she'll pick up water and soft drinks. Tom says he doesn't know what he'll bring, but he'll think of something. They scatter, and I go in search of Katie.

I find her in a prep room behind the kitchen with Mrs. Lorner who's saying, "This is Linney's locker. I watched a police officer, the one with the droopy moustache, taking everything out. They found an open package containing Cholecalciferol on the shelf. I'd show you but they asked me not to open it."

Katie motions me to join her by a metal table holding half a wheel of cheese, a bowl of lettuce, and a tray of sandwich buns. "That's okay. I don't need to see inside. But you mean Lindley, not Linney, don't you?"

Mrs. Lorner pushes her glasses up her nose. "Who?"

"What have I missed?" I say to Katie.

"Just that Mrs. Lorner was telling me she overhead Officer Dietrich say the cops received an anonymous tip suggesting they look in Lindley's locker, only now he's vanished. They don't know where he is."

"When was this?"

The old lady squints in my direction. "Who are you, dear?"

"I'm Virginia. We met last week."

"Virginia's my girlfriend. I told you about her," Katie adds.

"Oh, that's right. I'm sorry. I'm not very good with names. What did you ask me, kiddo?"

"Did Mr. Crowe come to work today?" It's clear I need to keep my questions simple and straightforward.

"You know, that's a very good question," she replies, fussing with her apron. "Now let me think. You know, I can't remember. Maybe yesterday. What day is it today?"

"Friday."

"Oh, then that's probably right. Yesterday. Oh, I just thought of something else. Would you like to hear it?"

"Yes." Katie and I both vigorously nod our heads.

"Do you want to go outside first? I could use a cigarette."

"No problem." We follow her out.

"You were saying?" Katie prompts once the cigarette is lit.

Mrs. Lorner gazes at her through a smoky haze. "About what?"

"Something else you were going to tell us about Lindley, I think?"

"Oh, right. Right. That's the man who poisoned the young fellow. I prefer not to speak ill of other people, but he wasn't polite. He didn't work very hard either."

I'm not sure which one she's talking about and I'm starting to feel restless. We haven't had lunch yet, and this constant explaining and reexplaining about who is who is taking too long. I don't know how Katie puts up with it. I raise my wrist, thinking to gesture her to move the story forward, but Katie takes me by the hand to stop me.

Mrs. Lorner takes another drag and gives me an appraising look. "You're pretty, young lady. Virginia, is it? But not as pretty as Kathy here. I hope you don't mind me saying that. You're too thin. Girls need a little meat around their chests, if you know what I mean, and you should think about cutting your hair."

Breathe in. Breathe out. Like I care about her opinion? "Yes, ma'am. I'll definitely do that. Thanks for the advice. So, you were saying about Lindley?" I do my best to be polite, keenly aware that Katie's chortling softly beside me.

"Oh, yes. What was it? He was in the Army. But he deserted and lied about it on his district employment application. Miss Jamie found out. She should have fired him. I'm not sure if that's important. Is it?"

"I don't know," I admit. "Did Officer Dietrich happen to mention if they have any idea where he is or how close they are to catching him?" I can almost predict her response. And I'm right.

"Who?"

It's all Katie can do to keep a straight face now. I don't blame her for laughing, and I'm really not offended that Mrs. Lorner thinks Katie is prettier than me because she's right. We ask her a couple more questions, then thank her for all her wonderful help and tell her we need to get going. Katie adds that she won't be able to see her for a couple of days because she's been assigned a new position after lunch. That seems to go right over Mrs. Lorner's head.

As we leave, she calls out, "Don't forget what I said about the animals, kiddo."

"I won't," Katie calls back. And to my questioning look: "Animals lying down? The earthquake?"

Why not, I tell myself. Why not a tornado too?

CHAPTER TWENTY-FIVE

Katie

After lunch I make my way to Mr. Spurling's room where I soon discover that being his aide isn't as much fun as I'd expected.

"I have two rules for student aides. Leave me alone and don't bother me," he grumbles at me from behind his newspaper when I introduce myself.

I don't bother trying to hide an eye roll because he isn't looking at me anyway. It turns out he has other rules I also don't care for, including no talking and no making noise of any kind. I take a seat as far away from him as I can get.

"Is this what it's like every day in here?" I whisper to Amy who shrugs and lays her head down on her desk. Sixty seconds later I glance again at her, noting saliva pooling in the corner of her mouth. I wish I could fall asleep that easily. I probably got less than an hour last night with all the stressing I've done thinking about my dad and now my mother, too. I shouldn't have sent that text.

Everybody else in Mr. Spurling's room spends the period on their phones. It's so boring I'm ready to gouge my eyes out. When the bell rings, I can't wait to get out of here. All of which makes me resent Mr. A-hole Sullivan even more. I really hope Mrs. Pugh comes through and gets me assigned back to the front office next week. Surely, Sullivan will be gone by then.

It's nearly dark by the time I make my way around the side of Virginia's house to the back gate. I'm the first one here, and the dogs race over to greet me, shoving their big heads under my hand, telling me they want to be petted. "Hi, boys. Good to see you too."

Virginia throws crumpled newspaper on logs in the fire pit and comes over with an unsettled expression on her face, saying she's worried Tom's going to post the info about Lindley on social media. Fortunately, he hasn't yet. "Do you think it's too late to cancel this?"

"The memorial service? I'm afraid so. Is everyone still coming?"

"As far as I know." She frowns and wipes a sleeve across her nose.

"Cheer up. It won't be bad," I say. "We'll eat and tell ghost stories. Tally can sing a song, then Matty will take a hundred selfies and say how much he loves us. I'd give the whole thing an hour, tops. By the way, you are skinny, but I like your hair just the way it is. Don't cut it." Her long brown hair is tied back in a ponytail tonight. Sun-streaked strands escape the sides, framing her narrow face. Mrs. Lorner is wrong about her. Virginia is perfect just the way she is.

"Thank you, Kathy," she grumbles around a smile.

I cup my hand around her butt. "I prefer kiddo."

She pulls me close. "Then kiddo, it is."

Matty makes his way through the backyard a minute later, followed by Tally, Yoon-hi, and Tom. I'm not particularly surprised to see Tom cradling a six-pack of beer under his jacket. He's earned it, but it's obvious he's had a few already. He stumbles and collapses into the closest lawn chair.

"Let's get this party started," he shouts, shoving a fist in the air.

Virginia squirts lighter fluid in the pit and strikes a match while Matty passes out flattened coat hangers speared with cheddar brats. Puffy clouds drop a mist obscuring the outer reaches of the fence. I snag a lawn chair and snap my fingers to the dogs. They come right over and settle at my side.

The fire roars, then settles back to a crackle and a pleasant woody scent as Matty begins. "Thank you all for coming tonight. I'd like to start by saying this past week has been one of the most difficult of my life. Who'd have thought five days ago we'd end up here without one of our own?" Tom releases an audible snort, then pops a can and takes a swig. Yoon-hi holds a coat hanger to the fire. Tally takes out her phone and fiddles with an earring.

"With that in mind, I want to acknowledge that even at the best of times I may not always be the easiest person to get along with. I can be selfish and inattentive to my friends. You guys know what I'm talking about, don't you? That's why I want to say you're the most important people in my world."

"Are you done?" Yoon-hi asks when he pauses. She's wrapped from head to toe in a scarf, wool cap, and heavy coat. Her pale face shines with sweat.

"For now. But I reserve the opportunity to speak again later. Who wants to go next?"

Tally's hand shoots up. "I will. I agree."

"With what?"

"With everything you said about being selfish. You are. But I'd also like to add that you've never once said I'm important to you."

"Oh my god, this is hilarious." Tom spits beer through his nose.

"It's not supposed to be." Matty sits back and blinks. "Look, Tally, if that's how you feel, I'm sorry. And I'm also sorry things didn't work out between you and Mrs. Donovan."

She thrusts out her jaw. "Who said they didn't?"

"Well, nobody. But come on. The woman's married and probably twice your age."

"Not twice," she snaps.

"Close enough," he mocks.

"Matty," Virginia interjects. "Is this really the way you want the evening to go? How about I take a turn?"

"Go ahead."

She sets her coat hanger with its half-browned brat on a tree stump. I have to grab the dogs' collars to keep them from lunging for it.

"First, I think we're all sorry if we've made Tally feel less than important. We do care about you, girl. But we also think you're making a mistake mooning over Mrs. Donovan."

"Damn you, Virginia. Damn all of you!" Tally leaps to her feet, knocking over the soda can beside her chair. "Mrs. Donovan— Erin—is a friend. I'm not *mooning* at her, whatever the hell that means. I never once said there was anything between us."

Flames from the fire reflect in Virginia's eyes. "Maybe not. But you certainly made us think it. How many texts have you sent her? Let me see your phone." She makes a move to snatch Tally's phone from her hand. Now I *am* surprised. This isn't like Virginia.

Tally stretches her arm out behind her, holding it out of reach. "Hell, no. Get the hell away from me!" she shouts.

George, the more sensitive of the pit bulls, growls at her raised voice. The dogs take yelling personally.

Yoon-hi says in a prim teacher's tone, "Oh, stop it, both of you. This is what I'm hearing. Matty's bitchy and self-obsessed. We all know that. Poor little underappreciated Tally doesn't think she's important, even though she works so very hard to let us know how much she cares about us. Not. Virginia probably didn't want to have this party but is too lame to admit it. And Katie is in her own little world, as usual. Not much of a sharer, are you, sweetie?" I flinch and think: *Not with you.*

"Tom," she adds as both Matty and Virginia sit forward in their chairs. "Good old Tom is shit-faced. How many beers have you had, buddy? Six? Eight? Maybe more?" She gestures to the empty can behind him.

He offers her a lopsided grin. "Not enough. Run out to the car and get me more, will ya, Yoonie?"

We all go silent at that. Yoon-hi drops to her seat, no doubt offended at both the nickname and the idea of Tom sending her on an errand. He lists sideways in his chair. "Wow, guys. This is so much fun. I'm the newest member of this group so tell me, shouldn't this be the part of the service where we eulogize the dearly departed? Where we say nice things about Matty's former boyfriend instead of making it about us? Why don't you start, lover boy? Tell me again how Jas and I could have been friends."

Too late, Matty seems to realize that he started this out wrong, but instead of fixing it, he makes it worse. "Huh. Well, you know, you both fell for me. Virginia, you knew Jason from before. He was sweet, right?"

Wow. How does he not get it? Virginia would never call Jason Gonzalez sweet. None of us would. And Tom isn't really asking for a eulogy. He's ticked off that we're having a service. In his position, I'd feel the same.

I rise and set my skewer and uneaten brat next to Virginia's on the stump. "I'm going to take the dogs inside. Come on, boys."

But before I get halfway to the house, Tom rocks his chair upright. "Dude. Matty. You should hear yourself. *We* both fell for *you*? You are so fucking full of yourself. Is that the best you can do? My god, you make me sick. I'm so out of here." He stumbles to his feet and weaves toward the gate.

Matty naturally goes after him. "Tom. Wait! I'm sorry. This was a bad idea. I shouldn't have asked you to do this."

"Damn straight. No, queer!" Tom howls brashly like he thinks he's made a joke. "Every one of you guys, you make me sick." He staggers, catching a toe on a rock and running straight into a wild rosebush at the fence. "Shit." He cradles a hand and kicks the bush. He flattens all the branches, then wobbles forward once again. "Go away," he screams at Matty. "I can do this by myself."

"Wait! You've had too much to drink. At least let me drive you home," Matty screams back. He makes a grab for Tom.

Tom dances clumsily away, while the rest of us stand there not knowing what to do.

"Virginia. I need help!" Matty calls.

She gives me a pleading look. "Go ahead," I tell her. "Give me a second to put the dogs up. I'll meet you in front."

I shove the dogs inside the back room and follow around the side yard to the driveway. I'm just in time to see Tom's car lurch away. My heart sinks and my lungs deflate as Matty and Virginia jump into Matty's SUV and take off after him. The sounds of their engines fade into the night.

Virginia, the only girl I've ever loved, just ditched me. Will I always come in second to her best friend?

CHAPTER TWENTY-SIX

Virginia

Tom's in the process of doing something stupid and Matty knows it, which makes him equally erratic. When we reach the stop sign at the top of the block, he barely slows the car. A vehicle coming east on Dimond slams on its brakes, narrowly avoiding us. I don't know about Tom, but we're about to have an accident.

"Pull over. Let me drive." I grab the dashboard, biting into my lower lip and tasting blood.

"There isn't time," he screams.

"Less if you kill us," I shout back. "Just do it, or I swear I'm getting out of the car right now."

Matty swerves to the curb and jumps out. "Hurry! He just went through the stoplight up ahead. Can you see him?"

Not really, but I'm not going to say it at the risk of causing more panic. I scoot across the seat, buckle up and take a deep breath to calm myself while he scrambles in on the passenger side. "Have you seen Tom drink before?" I ask. What I really want to know is if this is normal.

"Not like this. His dad has a beer refrigerator in the garage. He doesn't seem to notice if we help ourselves every now and then. Damn it, Virginia. Can you drive any slower?"

I point to a thirty-five speed limit sign. "I'm pushing fifty now." I keep my thoughts about Tom and Matty drinking Tom's father's beer to myself. Part of me almost wishes Tom would get stopped by the cops. I don't want to see him hurt, but it would serve him right to get a ticket and lose his license. How foolish can he be, taking off like that when he could barely navigate the bushes in my backyard? What if he hits someone? My father jogs these roads at night. And Matty, I'm furious with him too. He wouldn't wait for Katie to put the dogs up and join us. He just kept shouting at me to get in the car.

It's not the time to express my frustration, however because he's not in any kind of mood to hear it. We catch sight of Tom's white Ford Focus when we cross Minnesota. "I bet he's heading home." I gesture to the taillights in front of us.

Matty pounds the armrest between us with his fist. "I shouldn't have done it. I knew he was upset. I never should have suggested a memorial service for Jason."

No, he shouldn't have, but it's too late now. Tom's car careens around the corner onto New Seward on two wheels. I fill my lungs with steady breaths, praying he won't hit any red lights because I don't imagine he'll stop for them. "Call him." I gesture with an elbow to the phone in Matty's lap.

"We're almost to his house."

Tom turns left on Eagle, squealing to a halt halfway down the block at a nondescript single-story house with the porch light on. He sits for half a second in the driveway, and then stumbles out. I pull up in front beside a tree.

Matty jumps out of the car before I can shut off the engine. "Tom, honey. Please wait up." He grabs Tom's elbow. "I want to say I'm sorry."

"Ha. Sorry for what? Haven't you figured out that I don't care about you? Let go of me, you fat fucker." Tom wrestles out of his grasp.

He's hitting Matty where it really hurts: his weight. Matty's shoulders sag. He drops his hands to his sides as the front door opens and the man I saw in the polo shirt at the police station steps out. "Tom? What's going on. Are you all right?"

"I'm free, Dad. Somebody else killed Jason. The cops have got another suspect."

His father's eyebrows quirk. "I know that, son. You told us this afternoon. Remember? Are these friends of yours?" His gaze shifts from Matty to me, then back to Tom.

"We wanted to make sure Tom got home safely," I start to say, but Tom won't let me get the words out.

"That's a joke. They're not my friends at all. This here's a genuine drag queen, Pops. The other one's his hag."

Ouch. Not my favorite term. I suck in a breath. It's so dark now I can barely see Matty, but I imagine he winces. Mr. Glass does too.

"That's enough, son. You've been under an enormous amount of stress. Come inside. Let me help you."

He steps off the porch, which is enough to get Tom moving. He lumbers up the yard where his father gently takes his arm, then glances back at us. He probably wants to tell us to get the hell off his property, but he manages to lift the corners of his lips.

"I'm not sure if a thank-you is in order, but I'll go ahead just in case. I've seen you both, and I know this has been a difficult time for everyone. Take care of yourselves. We'll get through this. And now you should probably get yourselves on home as well."

"Good night." I get back into the SUV, this time on the passenger side.

Matty climbs in the driver's seat and starts the engine. "I love him," he mutters through his tears.

"Tom or Jason?"

"Both."

Ah. I've suspected as much all along. "Matty, there's nothing you can do for Jason. But Tom's been through much worse than the rest of us with the police breathing down his neck about the murder. Give him time. He'll get over this." It's the best I can offer because I'm ticked that Tom insulted us.

"What if he doesn't?"

I want to say, "Then you'll get over him." But if he'd said that to me when Katie wanted nothing to do with me last year, it would have sent me into a tailspin. "Give him time," I repeat.

He pulls away from the curb and heads back to the main road. "You just don't get it, Virginia. Everything comes easy to you."

"What? No it doesn't."

"It does. You're smart and not too hard to look at, and everybody knows that regular people don't have a problem with lesbians. But gay guys, we repulse."

I can't believe he's saying that. "That's crazy. For one thing, there's no such thing as regular people. And for another, if you think I have it easy, then you haven't been listening when I talk about how hard I work just trying to live up to Pete's reputation."

"God, I'm not talking about grades or schoolwork. Who cares about that?" He spins onto my street and comes to a stop, idling in front of my house. The fire in the backyard is still glowing, but Katie's, Tally's, and Yoon-hi's cars are gone.

"I care," I say softly.

"Well, I can guarantee nobody else does. Any anyway, you know what I mean. I'm talking about lifestyles."

I roll my eyes. "Dresses. Wigs. Makeup. All that crap?"

"No! It's not crap and you're misunderstanding me on purpose. You have Katie. I have no one. I sit with a bunch of girls at lunch."

"No one makes you do that." I take a deep breath to keep from saying something I'll regret. "Listen to me, friend. Yes, you are self-absorbed and bitchy too sometimes. But you're also talented as hell. I can't wait to see you perform again at Misconceptions. And don't forget your blog. Plenty of people seek out your opinions. But most importantly, you have friends right here who care about you. Me. Katie. Tally. And Yoon-hi. Even though you called her a liar, she still loves you."

"Not Tom," he argues, but it comes off sounding half-hearted this time.

I think I'm getting through to him. I should stop while I'm ahead, but something inside keeps me going. "I honestly don't know what Tom wants. But I gotta say you didn't do either him or Jason any favors by letting them both think they were number one in your life. By not choosing, you made them both feel insecure. Do you understand that? You practically encouraged the stupid rivalry between them. Tom truly doesn't know where he stands with you. If you love him, you should tell him, but not while he's upset. Give him a chance to calm down. Then, if you can work things out, ask him out on a real date. And stop flirting with other guys at school."

I assume he's thinking about it until he takes out his phone and turns the screen on himself.

I stare at him, incredulous. "Please tell me you're not snapping a selfie."

His lips turn downward in a pout. "I look good when my eyes get a little puffy."

I give up. Matty Brown is absolutely the most narcissistic person I've ever met. I slide out of the car and start to shut the door.

"Hey. Thanks for going with me," he adds, his voice so low I can hardly hear him. "I did hear what you said, and I can see that you make a few good points. See you tomorrow night?"

A few? "Where?"

"You know, at Amy Meeks's party."

"Surely you're not still thinking about going to that?"

"Of course, I am. We'll all go. You're my fag hag, right? You have to go." The mirth is back in his voice, the one I can't resist even when he's at his bitchiest. "Promise me, Virginia? You know how much I need you."

Something is seriously wrong with me. "Okay. Maybe," I grumble.

His laughter tinkles through the cool night air. "Say it like you mean it."

"I hate you."

"Love you, too!" He waves.

CHAPTER TWENTY-SEVEN

Katie

I'm so mad about the scene at the fire pit I can hardly see straight, but all that instantly goes out the window when I get home and find my mother sitting alone in our apartment in the dark. "He's out," she whispers.

I don't need to ask who she's talking about. Every nerve in my body sparks as I take a seat beside her on the couch. "When?"

"The day before yesterday. Sometime Wednesday morning. Denise's detective had his phone stolen on another case. He bought a new one right away and has been trying to reach her, but she didn't recognize the number so she didn't answer."

I get it. I wouldn't have either. I take Mom's unresponsive hand in mine. "Do we leave tonight?"

Her fingers come to life. "Katie, honey, I got your text. I thought you didn't want to go."

"I didn't. I don't. But I've changed my mind. I'm coming with you. Can you give me a minute to pack a bag?"

Her single working eye searches my face. "You'd really leave Virginia? You'd leave your school? Honey, you graduate in eight months."

"Doesn't matter. I belong with you." Yes, I'm angry at Virginia, but that isn't what this is about. Mom needs me, and I need her. I can't begin to express how helpless and alone I felt when she was in the hospital. I was constantly sick. Fearing she would die, I couldn't sleep. I could barely eat or study. I couldn't make new friends. Is that what loving a parent is really like? Feeling helpless that you can't do for yourself without them?

I fumble with the zipper on my jacket. "Denise said Nome has an excellent high school." Not quite true. She said there was a high school.

"Katie, no." Mom stares into my eyes, quiet for a second. "You're not going to Nome, Fairbanks, or anywhere else. You're going to stay right here. We'll all stay. You, me, Denise, and Josh. It's what Denise wants, and I do too. I won't run away from your father any longer. It's time to release myself from his power."

Hope rises up inside me. "Do you really mean it?"

"More than anything. I got that job at the flower shop today. It was my best day in a long time, and I don't want to give it up. You deserve your freedom too."

"But what if he comes for us?"

"Then we need to be ready for him. There are three of us and only one of him. I've secured a restraining order against him and Denise has alerted the neighbors. We've had new locks and chains put on the doors, and Virginia's mother has notified the police to keep an eye out for him. The super's watching out for him too. I'm not frightened, honey. How 'bout you?"

A little. But if my mom can be brave, can I expect less of myself? "Not a bit. Thanks." I put my arms around her.

"You're welcome." She holds me stiffly for a moment. "Now, hadn't you better get ready for work? You're still selling tickets at the theater, aren't you?" Her voice shifts as if concerned she's missed a crucial piece of my life while she was worried about her own.

"The theater is closed for renovations. I'll start back next month."

"Good. That's fine then. I'm glad to hear it. How about ice cream then. Or did you eat at Virginia's house?"

"Not much." Not anything.

We move into the kitchen, and I fix us each a big bowl of organic ice cream. Honestly, I'm starved, but I'm not going to spend another second thinking about Virginia, Matty, or anyone else. I'm focusing on my mom now, the one who deserves my undivided attention. The rest of them can go to hell.

"Everything okay? You're not upset about last night, are you?" Virginia asks the next morning when I appear at her garage door for the bike ride we arranged before all the crap with Jason started.

"I'm fine." I'm over it now and I'm just glad to see her. She looks great in biking shorts and a tight black top. "By the way, we're not going to Nome after all. None of us. Mom's decided we should stay."

Virginia's sober expression alters immediately into a beautiful smile. "Oh, Katie! Oh my god. That's the best news I've heard in like forever. I've changed my mind about biking. Let's stay here and canoodle. What do you say? Mom and Dad are out for the day, and Reggie's got some kind of coding competition at school. We'll have the house completely to ourselves. We can have popcorn and watch a movie. I can admire your gorgeous body—"

"Actually," I say. "I'd rather bike."

"Okay. If you're sure." She bites her lower lip.

"I am. Let's do this."

Every Saturday the two of us do something special without the group. Sometimes skiing or ice skating. Sometimes bowling in the Dimond Center if the weather's off. The plan today is to bike the Campbell Creek Trail and stop for an early lunch at Arctic Roadrunner, before making our way to the coastal trail. Our ultimate destination is Beluga Point along the Seward Highway. It's less than halfway to Girdwood. Virginia could do the whole thing and back and probably barely break a sweat, but she's more fit than I am.

It's not considered beluga viewing season, she informed me last week, yet after the full moon last night we'll likely see a bore tide, a natural phenomenon only visible in inlets. Evidently the one in the Turnagain Arm can rise ten feet. "High enough to surf?" I asked her earlier in the week when I was looking forward to it.

"Sometimes. When it's at its fullest," she replied.

It's a glorious day as we set out for the trail. Pink blossoms decorate the tops of fireweed stalks. The air is cool and crisp, not hot like it was Monday afternoon.

When we reach the restaurant, we lock up the bikes and head down an outside staircase to a creek-side picnic table. Virginia sets her backpack under an umbrella. "What would you like? I'll go in and get it."

I let her do too much for me. I need to be more independent. "I'll get it. What would you like?"

"Kodiak Islander. Small fries. Iced tea, no lemon." She gives me a funny look. "Are you sure?"

"Of course. I'm perfectly capable of ordering food myself."

"I know, but they're always busy on Saturdays. Once you order—"

"Thanks," I say. "I'll figure it out."

I go inside. The place is packed. It's past tourist season, but this is a popular spot for locals too. The fire in the double-sided fireplace is roaring. I study yellowing framed photos of famous customers on the walls while I wait my turn in line.

A moment later, a Black man with beaded dreads steps through a side door from the parking lot. My heart nearly stops. Shit. Lindley Crowe? No, thank god. This guy has a fuller face and a much more pleasant expression. He gives me a nod and steps into the line across from me.

"How's it going?" he asks, probably wondering why I'm staring.

"Great. Just great. You?"

"Great."

Where is Lindley? Has Detective Rosen caught him yet? Thankfully, Tom has stayed off social media like he promised, but if Lindley has good survival skills, he could head for the bush and avoid authorities indefinitely. Alaska is well-known for escaped criminals and military deserters. Lindley's both. I think back to trying to ask him questions when he wouldn't answer. The guy always did give off a creepy vibe.

I usually get a plain salmon or halibut burger, but at the last second I change my mind and order two Kodiak Islanders that apparently come with ham, salami, bologna, cheese and an onion ring. Like everybody else, I move aside to wait for my number to be called. How hard is that to figure out?

Virginia is crouched on the riverbank, attempting to rescue a floundered salmon fingerling when I return to the table with our food and drinks. "Darn it. It's already dead," she says with disappointment, tossing its body in the water.

"Too bad." I shrug.

She opens the sack and helps herself to a french fry. "You *are* upset about last night."

"No. I'm not."

"Really. You don't care that I just attempted a heroic fish rescue and you'd rather bike ride than canoodle?"

I know I'm supposed to laugh, but I don't feel like it. The truth is, I do care about the fish, but I wish she'd stop saying canoodle. It's Mr. A-hole Sullivan's word.

"I get it," she goes on. "Matty and me, we didn't wait for you last night. But it's not my fault. He was in a full-blown panic, thinking Tom was about to wreck his car."

I unfold the wrapper on a steaming burger and set the onion ring back inside the sack. "Matty, I understand. You didn't have to go with him."

"He needed me."

I take a bite. Delicious, although it needs more sauce.

"Katie, please. I told him he'd been unfair to Tom and Jason by letting them both think he cared about them. You've got to believe I didn't want to leave you. He screamed at me to get in the car, and I went into like, autopilot mode. I felt terrible afterward. I was furious with him and myself. I'm sorry. It never should have happened."

"Right."

Tables near us are filling up. When the wind picks up, my wrapper blows off the table. Virginia leaps up from the bench and catches it before it hits the stream. She's naturally athletic and looks good doing it, like an outfielder diving backward for a fly.

She drops the crumpled wrapper in the sack and sets her drink on top of it. "Does it make you feel any better to know that Tom called me Matty's fag hag?"

"You'd have to be straight for that to be accurate."

"I know, but still."

"A little," I admit. She smiles.

We finish lunch and climb back on our bikes. For the next half hour the muscles in my calves and thighs are golden. We pump along the flat, paved trail past streams, lakes, hikers with their dogs, and runners kicking up their heels. Virginia sees something in a pond and points to it, but between the wind and my bike helmet I can't hear her call out what it is so I just wave like I see it and keep going.

I'm exhausted by the time we cross under the highway and it isn't long before she outdistances me. I find her waiting around a curve, vertical mountain peaks on our left, the gray expanse of gently rolling water on the other side.

She blows out a breath when I pull up alongside her. "I don't know about you, but I'm wiped. Would you mind if we stopped here?" She's only saying it for my benefit. I just saw a sign for the Potter Marsh Trail so I know we're not anywhere near Beluga Point.

I get back on my bike. "I'd rather keep going, if you don't mind."

It's dumb pride that I pay for a few minutes later when we start up a steep incline. My lungs heave, and it's all I can do to keep going. I want to stop and walk my bike like the toddlers with training wheels and old people we pass are doing. I huff and puff like a pack-a-day smoker, my calves, thighs, and lungs screaming at me to stop. I'm about to give up and admit defeat when Virginia slows and gestures to a rocky outcropping shaped like a turtle in the water up ahead.

"There it is." She's barely out of breath.

"How far are we from the McHugh Creek parking lot?" I choke out between heavy gulps for air.

"Maybe three miles. That's the Kenai Peninsula over there." She takes a sip from her water bottle and points across the water to a jagged line of mountains. "It's another twenty miles or so along this same path to Girdwood."

God, she's so missing the point. The McHugh Creek Recreation Area is where we went to see the Northern Lights the night three-and-a-half years ago when my father decided we had to leave Alaska. The place has significance for me. Not, apparently, for her.

"Now you're just showing off." I uncap my bottle for a long, slow drink.

"I am not," she gripes back. Then her eyes go wide and she claps a hand over her mouth. "McHugh Creek. Oh my god, how could I have forgotten?"

"Beats me." It's the place we said goodbye to each other and cried in one another's arms for half the night. I pedal down the hill, walk my bike across the railroad tracks and drop it in the beaten, scrubby grass. I stomp over the flat part, then scrabble along the rocks, twisting my ankle a couple of times as I get close to the water. Beluga Point is peaceful but a little scary. In summer you can see fishermen wading in the water when the tide is in. It's a steep drop now, maybe twenty feet, and the inch or so of water below me has got to be frigid. The wind howls as if threatening to push me off the cliff. This is the first time I've been all the way out to the point.

I feel Virginia steal up behind me and wrap her arms around my waist. "I won't push you over the edge if you promise not to break up with me," she murmurs in my ear.

"Wow. You're so romantic." I tell myself to pull away. Instead, I lean into her sharp, thin frame. She's soft and bony at the same time, and right now I'm not sure why I love her. Only that I do.

"Do you love me?" She kisses my neck.

"No. And you don't love me either. You probably wish I was going to Nome."

"Exactly right. That way I could hop a dog sled there to prove my devotion to you."

It's so corny, we both giggle. I turn around and face her, sliding my hands around her neck to kiss her properly. "Your breath is terrible," I say, drawing back.

"Yours is worse." She pulls me close again. "I have to make myself kiss you."

"Then stop. I don't like it either."

"You stop. Promise me you'll never touch me again."

We fall away from each other, laughing so hard that she drops down hard on a large flat rock. I double over, grabbing my knees to catch my breath. Anyone who heard us would think we were crazy. We sound like eighth graders.

"I think I broke my tailbone," she complains when our chuckles fade away. She rubs her backside with a hand.

"Well, you deserve it. Don't expect me to feel sorry for you because I don't. You ran off last night with that shameless man-whore and left me alone with Tally and Yoon-hi."

"Was it awful?"

"Not at all. I love watching friends claw each other's eyes out."

"No!" Virginia starts to rise. I reach out a hand to help her to her feet. "What's wrong with us? Why are we all fighting?"

"Wish I knew. Probably Mrs. Lorner's earthquake."

"Probably. You know if she's right, the bore tide today could turn into a tsunami and sweep all the way across the railroad tracks and take out the cars on the highway. We'd better hold on to our backpacks."

We lay our jackets on the ground and sit, gazing down the inlet. Others make their way out to the rocks around us. I wish we had the place to ourselves.

Virginia takes my hand and laces our fingers together. The water below has completely disappeared now, leaving dangerous glacial silt known to suck unsuspecting people under like quicksand. We wait and wait. A couple nearby chats about where they're going for dinner. He's in favor of Simon and Seafort's. She's looking forward to trying the Cajun cuisine at the Double Musky Inn in Girdwood. They've either done their research or they've been here before.

"Are you scared?" I press my thigh against Virginia's and run my fingers up the inside of her elbow.

"Of a tsunami? Terrified. Please hold on to me." She gives me her sexy, hooded look.

Two small children balancing on rocks too close to the edge for my comfort pause a few feet in front of us. "Look, Daddy. Is that it? Is that the tidal wave?" One points at a bubbling brown wave in the distance.

"I guess so. Should be any minute now." Her father studies his phone.

When it finally arrives some fifteen minutes later, it's the kind of small flat wave you can see on any calm day at Eklutna Lake, not the Hawaiian type surfers ride in movies. I'm not sure what all the fuss is about. We stand and put on our helmets and jackets.

"Was it everything you hoped for?" Virginia asks me with a wink.

"It was perfect." I slide my hand down the back of her pants, enjoying the way her eyes go wide with delight.

"You shouldn't do that if you're not prepared for the consequences." Her voice is husky.

"Who says I'm not?" I'm already picturing a heavy make-out session on her living room couch. I'm truly not mad at her anymore, and I'm also not sorry that we came. My lungs are back to normal and my legs have that strong, tingly feeling they get after steady exercise. I'm proud I made it up the hill without stopping.

Anxiety flickers across her face. "Crap. I just remembered I told Matty we'd go to Amy's party tonight. I'll call and say we're canceling."

It makes me think for a second about Dillon Reed and his weird, vaguely threatening comments about milking snakes. But since Detective Rosen seems sure Lindley killed Jason, I have no reason to fear the freak. "Why?" I say. "I don't mind stopping by for a few minutes, if you don't."

There'll be time for canoodling later, especially if we don't stay very long. It might be nice to enjoy a real celebration with our friends now that I know for certain I'm staying in Anchorage with her.

"Are you sure?" She searches my face for signs I'm hiding something, that I'm only pretending to be fine with Matty's endless drama.

"Positive. Let's head back. Come on, I'll race you back to Potter's. Loser has to swallow a live fish."

I'm only kidding. I'd never do that. She reaches for her backpack. "You're on."

I snatch mine up faster and take off without waiting for her, scampering across the rocks back to the bikes. We've done the hard part, the steep incline. It will be downhill from here.

CHAPTER TWENTY-EIGHT

Virginia

Reggie is barely speaking to me because I still won't let him go to Amy Meeks's party. Every time we pass each other in the kitchen or on the way to the bathroom, he lets out a snort to let me know he's angry.

Please, I want to say. *Do you think I'm going to let you anywhere near a bunch of drunken high school students?* I wouldn't go myself if it weren't for Matty. The fact is, I'd rather stay here with Katie.

"I won't be late. Call me if you need anything," I say, when my ears pick up at the distinctive rattling sound of her car in the driveway.

He refuses to look up from his computer screen. "I can take care of myself."

"Fine."

"Fine."

I slam the front door shut behind me. "Do you know you have a taillight out?" I say, going around her car and climbing in.

"The building super gave me some duct tape to cover it up, but it's already peeled off. I guess I'd better get the damn thing fixed." She sighs, then adds, "Are we supposed to bring anything to this party?"

"The flyer said donations were welcome. I've got a twenty. That should cover both of us."

"And then some. Thanks."

We Google the address and discover it's in Airport Heights, an older part of town with a mix of nice and not-so-nice houses. Like Spenard and Fairview, many of the homes in older neighborhoods were built before real zoning regulations, meaning some have no insulation, others have roofs made with little more than tar paper. Amy's house is one of the better ones, a blue split-level with a gravel drive already filled with cars. More line the street. Katie squeezes Evie between two pickups in front of a boxy, log-style ranch that might have been built in gold rush days. Definitely one of the not-so-nice houses.

Music blares through Amy's open windows, and a bunch of guys play softball in the street. "Hey, Virginia. You can be on my team," a guy from my computer apps class yells, then throws the ball at me so hard I make a woofing sound when it hits me in the gut. I pick it up and throw it back with everything I've got, hoping to catch him off guard too. Sadly, it sails over his head out of reach, but that doesn't stop me from calling him a jackass. He shouts back that he loves me, which tells me he's already sloshed.

The front door stands ajar with two girls crouched cross-legged in the entrance having an intense conversation about what to wear to Homecoming. They part enough for us to step over them, and I stuff the twenty into a fishbowl full of cash while Katie grabs a couple of red Solo cups. She pours a half jigger of Vodka from a bottle into each and filling the rest with ice and Coke.

"Good?" She passes me a drink.

I smile and nod my thanks, thinking again that I'd rather be home with her and wondering how long we have to stay to be polite.

There's not a single place to sit in the living room, kitchen, hall, or even in the formal dining room where the entire table is covered with plastic cups. Kids are lined up back to the kitchen waiting to try their luck at beer pong. A guy and girl who look like freshmen disappear into a bedroom, and a girl who's standing in the hall sobs, "That's my boyfriend," then she promptly throws up all over herself.

"Let's go outside." Katie motions to a slider at the end of the hall.

"I'm right behind you." I set my drink on a bookshelf and follow her to a raised deck. A roaring bonfire fills the yard and a couple of guys shoot a basketball at a nearby tree without a hoop.

Amy breaks away from a guy in a checkered shirt and cowboy hat and comes over to hug us. "I'm so glad you guys came," she gushes.

Um, why? The breath she blows in my face is a curious blend of strawberry lip gloss and skunk weed. She stares at me with a glassy gaze.

"Matty is here somewhere. Tally and Yoon-hi are out there by the fire." She motions to the yard. "Do you know if that guy Tom is coming? The one who—" She lets her sentence go unfinished. "You don't have a drink." She peers at my empty hands. "Dillon!" she calls to the guy in the cowboy hat who's now talking to a girl with a sulky mouth. "Bring Virginia a beer."

He obliges with another Solo cup resting on the rail. Katie introduces him as Dillon Reed. "Say pretty please," he insists before handing me the cup.

"Forget it."

"Stop it, Dil. Just give her the drink." Amy slaps his shoulder playfully.

He does, then flashes his teeth at Katie. "Hey, Miss Office Aide. I was hoping you'd stop by tonight. Lil Dilly's been saying how he's been looking forward to meeting you. In fact, he was just asking about you."

Amy punches his arm a lot harder and tells him to behave himself.

Katie's face turns bright red. "Thanks for inviting us, Amy. Let's go find Tally and Yoon-hi," she says to me and heads quickly for the stairs, her boots clopping along on weathered wooden boards.

"Little Dilly?" I pull up alongside her on the patio below the deck. There are a couple of old bikes underneath it, along with a bag of soil, a trash can, and a dozen empty flowerpots.

Katie swallows half her drink in a single gulp, then pours the rest out and grabs a beer from a nearby keg. "You don't want to know."

We pass her old boyfriend, Rocky, and the hockey players, most of the football team, and a few members of the jazz band who stand around with kids from film club. Some are jumping up and down. Others rock an updated version of The Shoot, where they bend their knees and squat. Three girls fall on their asses and laugh. The music isn't quite as loud out here, but I can feel it pulsing in my chest. It makes me dizzy. The light from the moon sends an odd glow across the yard.

I take a sip from my new cup and realize I've been given Vodka instead of beer. Someone tugs my sleeve and I turn around to find Lilly Kahale, editor-in-chief of North's school newspaper, standing behind me. She's got a skinny boy with longish hair beside her.

"I'll meet you at the fire," Katie mutters, moving on without me.

Lilly watches her go, her round face expressionless. "Care to comment on the Jason Gonzalez case being solved without your help?" she asks me.

I squeeze my eyes shut, acknowledging the burn. "I thought you and I were past that, Lilly." The fact is, Lilly and I aren't friends. We never will be, but she did help out in her own small way when Katie and I figured out who killed Marisol last Christmas.

She has the grace to blush. "You're right. Ragers make me nervous."

My ears are ringing. "Me, too. Why are you here?"

"It's Mark's idea. Meet Mark." She gestures to the guy beside her. I've never seen him before, which means he's probably an underclassman.

"Hey." He nods.

"Hey yourself." Boyfriend, I'm guessing.

"So. Lindley Crowe?" Lilly presses.

How the hell does she know the name of Detective Rosen's suspect? It still hasn't been released. "You're doing a story," I say conversationally.

"Informally. I won't quote you if you'd rather be anonymous. But you gotta admit another murder in our building is news that shouldn't be ignored."

She's got a point. But even if I did know something, I wouldn't tell her. I promised Detective Rosen I'd keep my mouth shut. How did Lilly get his name, I wonder.

"There's nothing to quote. I don't know the guy." I swallow too much vodka and spit some of it back into the cup.

"Jason's killer. He worked in the cafeteria," says Mark. "We have it on good authority he was spotted in Wasilla. He's likely to be picked up later tonight."

"Good authority?"

"An anonymous source. We're not at liberty to say."

Right. "Talk later?" I'm ready to be rid of them.

They peel off, likely glad to be rid of me as well, and I see Tom coming down the stairs. Oh, yay.

Shanice is talking to Tally by the bonfire. Yoon-hi, beside them, looks put out. She folds her arms across that stupid bulky coat. Katie joins me and sets her drink aside.

"Beer?" I hold out my cup. Oops, vodka. Not beer.

"No, thanks," she says, so I set it on a table.

Somebody hands me another. What the hell? I think and drink it. I might develop a taste for it. I like the way it heats my throat.

I'm just about to ask Katie if she wants to dance when Matty shows up. He flaps his arms and elbows like a flightless bird. "God. Somebody get me a drink." None of us move, yet a Solo cup appears as if by magic in his fist. "Man," he yells, his voice sounding far away. "I feel great. Did you guys hear Rosen is closing in on the Crowe dude?" He drains the cup.

I start to ask how he heard that.

"Bullshit," Yoon-hi rudely interrupts. "Somebody made that up. Probably wanted to find out how hard it would be to start a rumor. Pretty easy, I guess, if you idiots fell for it."

My heart throbs in my ears. Did she really just say that? Now we're all idiots?

Tally gives Yoon-hi a shove that nearly knocks her off her feet. Shanice catches her arm and pushes her back upright. "What's wrong with you people? Aren't you friends?" she screams over an ear-splitting tune I don't recognize.

I glance around for another drink and spy a full one on a lawn chair. "Those days are over."

"You can say that again." Tally balls her hands into fists.

Dillon Reed sneaks up behind Katie and slides his arms around her waist. She jumps, spins around, and punches him in the chest. "Man, what the fuck!"

I'm going to hit him too, but I have to put my drink down first. When I bend over, my head spins and I nearly lose my balance.

I look up again and see a shit-eating grin spreading across his face. "Chill, Miss Office Aide. You look like you need some lovin'. Don't you want some alone time with Lil Dilly?"

"What I want," Katie growls in the back of her throat, "is for you to leave me the fuck alone."

"You heard her. Get the fuck away from her," I repeat, but the words don't come out right. It sounds more like, "Get away her fuck."

We all turn in Dillon's direction and he takes a step back, the ridiculous smile frozen on his cowboy face. "Well, damn, girl. You shouldn't have come on to me like that if ya didn't want some of this." He points to his dick.

Katie's eyeballs pop. "I didn't! You're making that up."

He's back to thinking she's making a joke. "You guys are insane. You know that, right? I'm in serious need of hooch. One of these houses…which?" He scratches his crotch and gazes at the far side of a split-rail fence where a figure smokes a cigarette on the back deck of the gold rush house. Dillon makes a running leap for the fence, clears it like a bull rider, and disappears into the dark.

"No way. Did I just see that?" Shanice stares after him.

I'm wondering the same thing, but there's no time to discuss it. Tom suddenly appears and gets up in Matty's face. He's a foot or so shorter than Matty, so technically he gets up in his neck.

"Honey," Matty starts.

Tom jabs Matty's chest with a forefinger. "Don't you honey me, you freak. I got one more thing to say to you. You. You're like an exotic pet. A peacock. The way you strut around in all that makeup and girlie clothes is disgusting. And those selfies you always take? Sad, dude. Tragic. I figured it would be funny as freak to keep you around for a bit. Like a fuck-you to my folks, but I'm so over you. All you loser freaks."

He sweeps his arm from one side to the other to make sure we know we're all included. As if there could be any doubt. "Dude. Ever wonder why y'all got your own table at lunch? 'Cause nobody else wants to sit with you. The five of you are beyond pathetic!"

He's about to walk away, but Matty seizes his elbow. I fear he's going to "honey" Tom again, but I'm wrong. "Take it back," Matty snaps.

"You think I don't mean it?" Tom lurches sideways.

Matty tightens his grip. "I know you mean it. I've tried and tried to make you happy, Tom. All you've done is bitch. Nothing makes you happy. Yeah, I made mistakes, but you're not going to call my friends pathetic. Take it back before I break your nose!"

I'm pretty sure I'm drooling, and my legs are refusing to hold me upright any longer. I make an awkward swipe at Matty's arm. Because Matty, my sweet friend, is threatening violence? This has got to be some sort of alternate universe.

Then the ground gives way beneath me.

CHAPTER TWENTY-NINE

Katie

The earth shudders. Yoon-hi grabs Virginia to keep her from tumbling into flames. Her coattail catches fire and she screams. Tally lets loose an inhuman sound and yanks Yoon-hi's coat from her shoulders. They both fall on burning embers that scatter across the lawn. The ground below me gives a series of fearsome jolts like we're all being hit by bumper cars. I lose my balance and a hairline crack opens up between my feet. Windows in the house crack. Car alarms go off. Kids scream, and the deck stairs break away from the house. They crash to the patio below, sending splintered wood flying through the air.

Everybody is yelling. Those who were dancing are thrown to the ground. They wrap the backs of their heads and necks with their hands. I'm on my knees, watching horrified as a corner of the roof of the log cabin house behind Amy's collapses in on itself.

"Katie!" Virginia wails through a haze of smoke and noise. I crawl through a tangle of legs, arms, and torsos. A chunk of brick comes soaring for my face. I squeeze my eyes shut. When

I open them, Matty is lying on the ground beside me, the brick clutched in his hand.

Just as quickly as it started, the shaking stops. Matty and I slide on our bellies, trying to reach the others. The music's gone off, but blasts from sirens and alarms and distant screaming fills the silence.

Virginia calls my name again from somewhere close.

I feel her arms go around my neck. Tally, Yoon-hi, Matty, and Shanice are suddenly with us too. We all hold one another, saying how we love each other and how glad we are that everybody is safe.

The ever-practical Yoon-hi draws back first. "Who's hurt?"

Matty clutches a bloody wrist. "Just my hand."

"You saved my life!" I kiss his shoulder, and he pats my thigh.

"Tally saved mine." Yoon-hi gazes at her friend in wonderment.

"Shanice saved both of us." Tally blinks through the lifting haze at the newest member of our group.

"Group hug. Group save." Virginia giggles through a belch. "I need a glass of water. I think I'm gonna puke." She swivels her head and vomits on the smoking remains of Yoon-hi's heavy coat. My poor sweetheart has had too much to drink. I rub her back. She shifts away and vomits again.

Matty talks about how he's never seen Virginia drunk. Yoon-hi says something about how she used to love that coat. Virginia wipes her mouth and apologizes over and over. Shanice and Tally make googly eyes at each other, and I stare up at the house, marveling that the stairs fell, yet the deck itself somehow remains standing. People all across the yard are slowly getting up. Others leave the deck to go inside and come running through a door at the bottom of the house.

"Oh, my god! My mom is going to kill me!" Amy cries. "Is everybody okay? Should we call the paramedics? What am I supposed to do?"

Remarkably, no one appears seriously injured. There's no sign of Tom, but people are starting to leave. I don't think anyone wants to be here when Amy's mother comes home, so when Tally suggests we go, we all agree and help Virginia to her feet. I sling one of her arms across my back and Shanice grabs the other. We half-carry, half-drag her through the yard toward the front of the house.

"I'm so sorry," Virginia says again, clearly mortified. "I don't drink very often, and I didn't realize I had that much."

"It's the stress," I say. "No one thinks any less of you, babe."

"I could pick up a six-pack for you on the way home," Shanice teases. Virginia makes a face at her, and Shanice double downs with, "What's your favorite? Are you a microbrewery kind of gal? Personally, I like a pale ale from Midnight Sun, but I'm guessing you're pretty hard core. Maybe a double IPA? Something stronger? Hang on." She gets out her phone as if to look it up and at last Virginia smiles.

"I probably deserve that."

"Just please don't drink around George and Abe, okay?" Shanice chuckles. "Dogs can be very susceptible to peer pressure."

"Okay. Okay. I get it." Virginia attempts a laugh, but her face is still a little green.

Tally hangs back with Matty, wrapping his wrist in a terry cloth towel that she picks up from the wreckage of the stairs.

There's one more surprise waiting for me when we get out to my car. Poor Evie is no longer parked on the street. Her front half is wedged into the bed of the pickup truck in front of her. It's crushed, the hood folded back like a flap on an envelope. At first I'm really pissed, and then the absurdity of the situation hits me. A real damn earthquake, my first! I slap my thighs and burst out laughing. Guess I won't have to get that taillight fixed after all.

CHAPTER THIRTY

Virginia

Katie says she has to get back to her apartment to check on her family, so Yoon-hi drops her off first and then drives me to my house. I ask her to wait while I do a quick walk-through to survey the damage and to make sure Reggie is okay. Luckily, he's fine. A few broken dishes and a couple of books have fallen off a shelf, but otherwise the house is okay too.

I head back outside, realizing I owe Yoon-hi more than just a thank-you and some lame apology for getting wasted at the party. We've run a successful tutoring business together for months, and we've been good friends for the last two years.

"Everything okay?" she asks.

"Fine. Um, thanks."

"You're welcome." Gingerly, she picks up her ruined coat from the back seat and drops it in the trunk.

"Before you go," I say.

"Yeah?"

"Not sure how to put this, except to confess that I'm a mess. I'm still not sure what happened to me at the party. I left one drink in the house. Then Amy's boyfriend Dillon gave me a beer, or maybe it was a vodka on the deck, and I might have helped myself to somebody else's cup at the fire. The rest is a blur. Except the earthquake part, of course. Anyway, what I'm trying to say in my weird, awkward, and still somewhat inebriated way, is thank you again for driving me home and for not giving me shit about throwing up on your coat. And well, sorry for being a jackass on the Whittier field trip too and whatever other dumb things I've done in the last few days."

Yoon-hi's quiet for a second. She shuts the trunk. "Apology accepted. Virginia, you don't remember Dillon saying he was rolling on molly?"

"What?" I blink. "I remember him hitting on Katie. That happened, right? And then, my god, he flew over a fence like a horse. Did that happen too?"

"Yeah. He said he needed more alcohol, more hooch. But there was something else. I think he spiked your drink. Maybe everybody's. People were acting nuts, like, I don't know, like everybody got wasted all at the same time. Gosh, I don't know. Maybe I'm the only one who heard it."

She shakes her head. "I'm going to have to think on that a bit. But the other stuff? The thing is, Virginia, I haven't been myself either. I don't know what got into me on the cruise. I shouldn't have called Tally an idiot."

"You said we were all idiots when we were standing around the bonfire."

Her cheeks turn pink. "I thought you said that was a blur."

"Most of it. Were you drinking?"

"Actually, I wasn't. The last few days, I find my own behavior, hmm, somewhat inexplicable." She rubs her neck.

At least I'm not the only one. "Since Jason's death?"

"Yeah. Weird, right?"

"Very. You know, you were also pretty mean to that guy Adam on the ship." I can't help myself. I want to see her squirm, if only for a second.

She sighs. "That's between him and me."

"If that's the way you want to play it."

"Oh, stop. Are we still friends?" She eyes me hopefully.

"Only if you admit it's me, not Matty, that you have a thing for."

"What are you talking about?"

"At the police station the other day you said you were crushing on me. On the ship, you claimed it was Matty."

Yoon-hi throws her hands up in the air. "I need to be more careful what I say around you. You remember everything!"

"Phonographic memory." I tap my head, sending a tiny pulse through my throat to my chest. I'm still a little dizzy.

"I think you mean photo—" She stops herself. "Cute. Can we kiss and make up now?"

"Only if you promise not to tell Katie." We give each other bear hugs and promise to talk more tomorrow.

I go inside, pop a couple of aspirin, and listen to Reggie tell me how he had to hang on to his precious computer for dear life to keep it from tumbling like a bowling ball across the floor. We exchange a hug, and then I head into my bedroom to call Katie.

"A seven-point-two earthquake, and Mrs. Lorner predicted it!" Katie answers in a rush.

"You know that's not possible." I plop down on the bed.

"Then say it was luck."

"It was luck. Earthquakes in Alaska are not uncommon. A couple of years ago we had more than fifty thousand. Shifting of tectonic plates. Ring of Fire. All that stuff." We both know all about it. We studied it last year.

She sighs. "I'm just saying it could explain a lot of things."

Like how we all turned into haters? Maybe she's right, although I have to think at least part of it was the tense situation between Tom and Jason every day at lunch.

I change topics. "Was there any damage to your apartment?"

"Not much. A couple of snaky cracks in the living room walls and another in a corner of the shower. And, as I'm sure you can imagine, Mom wasn't happy to hear what happened to my car. Denise will have to drive us to school on Monday. Hopefully, we can get a ride from Matty or Yoon-hi after that."

At least we're both okay and Katie is staying here and not going to Nome, that's what I need to remember. "Shouldn't be a problem. I'll get my car back from Pete as soon as I can. By the way, I'd like to see if we can get everybody together for breakfast tomorrow morning. You, me, Matty, Tally, Yoon-hi. Maybe Shanice."

"That's good. I like Shanice."

"I do too. She really came through tonight. I'm thinking Snow City Café. We should get there early to avoid the crowds. Or go late, same thing." The restaurant is downtown, and always busy Sunday mornings.

Katie yawns. "I vote late. Anything else?"

"God, an earthquake."

"I know. Crazy. Wonder if the animals laid down."

"Likely."

"George and Abe all right?"

"Yeah." I pat the dogs. "They miss you."

"I miss them, too."

Like always, we say, "I love you," and then yawn our good nights. I change my clothes, brush my teeth, and fluff my pillow.

I'm worn out, but sleep eludes me. Whether it's from stress, the party, or something else, I don't know. My mind swims with crazy, mixed-up thoughts of Jason, Tom, Lindley Crowe, Dillon, Shanice, and earthquakes. When I finally drift off, I fall into a troubled state, dreaming I've been poisoned.

Aftershocks rattle the windows throughout the night, but it's not until I get up the next morning that I learn the full extent of earthquake damage is still unfolding. There's a message on my phone from Mom timed just after midnight saying she and Dad are stuck between Seward and Anchorage.

The Glenn Highway is closed. A ramp connecting Minnesota Drive to nearby neighborhoods collapsed, and the National Tsunami Warning Center in Palmer issued warnings for Cook Inlet during the night.

Reggie points to the crawl across the bottom of the television screen listing all the schools that will be closed tomorrow. They include both North and Silverview, as well as all public buildings and libraries. A reporter stands with a microphone near an overpass by the airport saying there have been no fatalities reported yet, but worried family members are calling in to report loved ones missing. She gives a hotline number where you can run a hospital check to see if anyone you know has been brought in for treatment.

I call Mom and nearly stroke out when she doesn't answer right away. She calls me back a minute later to say she and Dad are both okay. They're holed up at the Kenai River Lodge and will return this afternoon, or as soon as the highway reopens.

Katie is my next call, and I can hardly keep the agitation from my voice. "Do you have the TV on? Are you seeing this?"

"Virginia!" she shouts. "The Whittier Tunnel, part of it collapsed. What if you'd been going through it today?"

For some reason, her panic calms me down. "I'm fine. Really, I am. Let's text the group and make sure everybody else is okay too."

We light up the group stream all morning. Matty's house has only minor damage, but his mom has insisted they move in with her sister in another part of town and they're on their way there now. Yoon-hi, who lives in North Aquatic Park, is okay. Her parents won't let her leave the house, and she mentions more than once how she feels like their love is suffocating her. The pipes in Tally's apartment building have burst, but the manager insists the basement flooding is minimal and safe for the time being as long as no one turns on the water. Shanice, who has been added to the stream, says she and her mom are staying at the vet's office, which has been opened as a triage center for lost and injured animals. Tom doesn't answer at all. Out of respect for Matty no one comments on it.

Breakfast at the Snow City Café is obviously out. All restaurants are closed. I hesitate, and then bring up the topic I've been dreading.

So. Last night. Anybody else feeling woozy?

No replies.

The reason I ask. I don't think I drank that much.

Still nothing. Aw, come on, guys.

Yoon-hi, help me out?

Did anyone else hear Dillon mention X? she writes.

I thought he went looking for more vodka, Matty responds.

The music was so loud, I couldn't hear anything at all, Shanice complains.

Crazy how he jumped that fence, adds Tally.

I don't get him, is Katie's contribution.

Sorry. Maybe I was wrong, Yoon-hi texts me privately.

I don't think she's wrong. But I have no idea what to do about it. If Mom were here, I'd want to get her take on it. But she and Dad have enough on their plates just trying to get home.

The news is flashing viewer-sent-in photographs of toppled trees, buckled streets, and partially collapsed buildings. TV reporters urge people to stay home as emergency personnel around the city have their hands full dealing with fires and trapped and injured people. Currently nearly a third of the population is without power. We talk about it for a bit, then gradually everybody signs off, saying they have other things to do.

Katie and I text privately for a while. Then she says she needs to make lunch, which reminds me I should too.

"Grilled cheese and tomato soup?" I ask Reggie who's barely left my side all morning.

"I'm not hungry. But sure, if you want it. Should I maybe clean up around here?"

His gaze travels around the kitchen and living room, probably seeing what I'm seeing. Dirty dishes in the sink, throw pillows scattered under the TV, George and Abe gnawing on a pair of Dad's sneakers.

Uh-oh. I run over and exchange the shoes for dog toys, setting Dad's ruined Nikes on the mantel. One of the boys must have thrown up on the hearth during the night. A yellowish substance congeals beside Mom's pinecone potpourri bowl.

I rub the back of my neck, willing the headache I've been chasing all morning to go away.

"Clean up?" Reggie's voice brings me back.

"Good idea. Mom and Dad would like that. But would you mind taking George and Abe out first?" I say, and add, "On leashes, and maybe one at a time." I'm thinking about Shanice and her mother at the vet's office. Animals panic in a storm. An earthquake would be worse.

Reggie heads for the door at the back of the house, the dogs clicking at his heels. Poor guys, they must have been scared to death when the first quake hit.

We have lunch and feed the dogs, then set to work filling the dishwasher, scrubbing dog barf off the hearth, dusting, vacuuming, and doing the sort of deep cleaning that frees my mind to wander through a maze of random thoughts. I think back to my dream of being poisoned, but I'm not sure where it came from.

Shortly after two, the doorbell rings. I hope it's Katie. I open it to find Detective Rosen on the stoop. Her back is to me as she looks out at an enormous blue spruce lying across our neighbor's driveway.

"You caught Lindley Crowe?" I can hear the excitement in my voice. It's not until that moment I realize how much Jason's killer has also been on my mind.

She turns around. "Sorry, no. Your mom called and asked me to check on you. Mind if I come in?"

I step aside and gesture to my little brother, clinging to a belt loop on my jeans. "This is Reggie. Reggie, this is Mom's friend, Detective Rosen."

Rosen brushes an ashy substance off her wrinkled shirt. "I know Reggie. How you doing, son? Your mother and I worked together before you were born. She brought you into the station her last day on the job when you were barely old enough to keep your eyes open. You've grown some since."

"Is my mom okay?" Reggie's face scrunches with worry.

"She's fine. Your folks will be home in a bit. Okay if I talk to your sister for a minute?"

He leads the dogs into his bedroom and shuts the door. I offer Rosen a cup of hot tea, which she accepts and follows me into the kitchen.

"I can't remember the last time I was here. Maybe twelve or thirteen years ago? It looks different. I recall a table over here and a yellow tile backsplash behind the stove."

I put a kettle of water on the stove to heat. "We remodeled a couple of years ago. The island's new. The backsplash is gone and the table's in the garage. Mom and I painted the kitchen cabinets ourselves."

"Nice." She slides onto a stool. "In case you're wondering, we still miss her on the force. Your mother was one hell of a detective. And now I see she's an interior decorator too. Why am I not surprised? Thanks," she says when I hand her a steaming cup.

I take a seat at the island across from her and forestall whatever else she was going to say. "Can you tell me anything about Lindley Crowe at all? I heard he was a military deserter."

"Where did you hear that?"

"From one of the cafeteria workers. Somebody else said you found him in Wasilla."

"Interesting."

"Did you?"

"Virginia, I'd love to share information with you if I could. But I'm simply not allowed. You understand that, don't you?"

"I guess." I give a disappointed shrug. "Can you at least tell me if he's been arrested?"

"He has not." She sips her tea.

I don't know what to make of that. "But he's still your only suspect because of the rat poison you found in his locker in the kitchen?"

She sets her cup on the counter. "Somebody has been telling tales out of school. Virginia, honey, I came to check up on you, that's all. If you have something you'd like to tell me, I'm all ears." She adds sugar from a bowl and stirs her tea.

Part of me wants to tell her about Dillon and the molly and the weird way he ran off before the earthquake last night, but I'm not sure it's relevant. I was wrong about Shanice and her mother being involved in Jason's death. I'm likely wrong about Dillon, too. Katie told me Dillon hated Jason, and that his father, a Pentecostal preacher, could have access to strychnine. Does that make it any more likely he poisoned Matty's ex? On the other hand, what is Lindley's motive really? That he and

Jason got into it one day over wiping down tables? None of it makes sense.

"Officers Hess and Dietrich checked the cafeteria surveillance footage from the day of Jason's death. You did too, I assume?" I already know the answer from Sullivan, but I'm hoping she might have something new to add.

"Of course. And I will say everything looked normal, if that's any help."

It's not, but I thank her anyway. How the hell then did Jason's lunch acquire rat poison? From Lindley? Really?

Detective Rosen stands and stretches. She looks tired. She's probably been up all night dealing with fallout from the earthquake and the fires mentioned on TV. From people and animals trapped in the rubble. From downed power lines and busted sewer pipes.

"I've got to get back to work now. It was good to see you, Virginia. Will you please let Katie know we're all keeping a lookout for her father should he come here?"

I need to be doing that as well. I need to focus my efforts on Katie's dad from here on out. "Yes," I say. "And thanks."

CHAPTER THIRTY-ONE

Katie

Three days after the initial earthquake, I'm calling it officially: home quarantine sucks. Yesterday Denise handed me a tube of waterproof caulk and told me to make myself useful. I think she was tired of watching me lie around on the couch all day and stare out the window.

I was glad to have something to do. I watched a YouTube video, then sealed the crack in the shower. Our super, Mr. Jacobi, said he'd tackle the ones in the living room but needed to address flooding in the apartments across the alley first. At least we're finally beginning to see recovery progress on the news. The airport and several roads have reopened. Experts, however, say the aftershocks could continue for months.

Virginia calls as I'm drying my hair Tuesday morning. "Guess what? Pete returned my car and Carl's Jr. is back in business. Do you want to go to lunch?"

"How soon can you get here?" I'm so ready to get out of this apartment, I could chew my arm off.

"Give me ten."

I wait for her in the parking lot. It's closer to forty-five minutes when she pulls up and directs Reggie to climb into the back seat. "Ready for the mission?" he asks me.

"You bet." I assume he means choosing what we're having for lunch. Anything's got to be better than the leftover beet salad in our refrigerator. Mom and Denise are vegetarians. Well, pescatarians really, since they eat fish. Mom gave me enough cash for meatless green burritos for them and chicken tenders for Josh.

I'm still deciding between the Famous Star with cheese and a chicken and waffle sandwich for myself when Virginia says casually, "How about a little field trip when we're done here?"

Reggie claps his hands together. "Any idea what kind of system they're using?"

"Hush. You'll spoil it for her." Her eyes sparkle with mischief.

"Am I going to like this?" I ask.

"I think so. Let's eat first."

We do, and then take the rest of the food back to Mom and Denise at the apartment. I understand now why Virginia was so late. Many streets are blocked with felled trees, broken chunks of concrete, and upheaved pavement. It's no wonder schools haven't yet reopened. The scent of smoke and burned rubber wafts along the streets.

"When do I get to know where we're going?" I ask once we pass the Dimond Center.

"Now. We're breaking into school."

"Because?"

"I'm still not satisfied with Lindley as the only suspect. Why would he poison Jason? Just because Jason didn't want to wipe down tables? What kind of motive is that?"

"You're thinking Dillon then?"

"Yeah. Maybe. Besides, what else do we have to do? Reggie's going to check the cafeteria's surveillance cameras. If we see Lindley hanging around the student refrigerator looking sneaky, I'll give up and wait for Detective Rosen to do her thing. If we see anyone else acting suspicious, we'll have to have a rethink."

"Anyone in a cowboy hat?"

"Or even a senior girl with long red hair."

Meaning Amy, I suppose. But I'd be surprised if Amy's involved. She isn't a doer. I don't think Dillon meant her when he said he had friends who could have poisoned Jason for him if he wanted. Virginia honks at a slow-moving car in front of us. "In any case, I'm sick of staying home."

"Me, too." Reggie bounces up and down in the back seat.

If anyone would know how to access the school's security cameras, it's Virginia's little brother. The kid can be a jerk at times, but I once saw him take apart a whole computer in under half an hour. Someday he'll figure out how to get around passcodes on phones. He's been working on an app for it.

Fifteen minutes later, we pull around the dumpsters behind the cafeteria. We get out and grab three cardboard boxes from the recycle bin.

"Here's how this is going to work," Virginia whispers like we're on some dangerous spy mission. "There was a district plumbing truck here earlier with three guys who are likely attempting to restore water to the school building. If any of them question why we're here, we'll say Mrs. Pugh asked us to pick up some of her things so she could work from home."

"And if she's here?"

"I didn't see her car when Reggie and I came by before we picked you up. But if she is, we'll say Mrs. Hicks or Mrs. Foster instead. The workmen aren't likely to ask anyway. They won't care about a couple of random students. They're only interested in repairing the earthquake damage."

"Let's go!" Reggie rubs his hands together excitedly. He must be a born burglar, a sneak, like his sister. When Virginia and I were his age we lived for this kind of adventure.

There are now two orange maintenance trucks in the circle drive. "How's it going?" Virginia asks a guy in a hard hat digging through a toolbox.

He mumbles, "Great," without looking up.

Reggie decides to try it on two men who are reinstalling the double glass doors. Clearly not all plumbers, but it probably doesn't matter. "How's it going?" Reggie aims for his sister's nonchalance.

A dark-skinned man with a gray goatee, says, "You kids shouldn't go inside. The building's closed. It isn't safe."

Reggie's eyes nearly pop right off his face.

Virginia sets her empty box on the ground. "Well, shoot. Would you mind going into the front office and clearing out Mrs. Pugh's desk drawers then? It's the first desk outside the principal's office. She said there's a plant she needs to water, and we're supposed to pick up her blue grade book. There should also be a gray folder in the bottom drawer labeled Junior Language Arts."

I'm worried they'll ask what Reggie's and my boxes are for, but the first guy glances at the second who has apparently decided to mind his own business. He's still holding up one side of the door, the cords in his neck straining. "Don't look at me," he says. "I've got work to do."

Goatee says uncertainly, "Just a plant and folder?"

"And her grade book. Oh, and she mentioned checking for her purse." Virginia points across the entry to the inside office windows. "You can see the desk right there." Damn, this girl is ballsy.

I don't bother mentioning that it isn't Mrs. Pugh's desk she's pointing at because how is he to know? He tilts his chin in thought. "All right. Go ahead. But make it quick. There aren't supposed to be any civilians in the building until we can say for sure it's safe."

"Thanks," Virginia says, which Reggie echoes.

We encounter a second obstacle when we reach the office door. Balancing her box on a hip, Virginia jiggles the handle and discovers that it's locked. She drops the box on the floor and stands back to assess it. "Huh. Well, this is a bit of an issue. I guess we'll have to go back and ask him for the master key."

Reggie gestures at fallen ceiling tiles scattered across the hall, the drinking fountain lying on its side, and lockers shaken out of their niches. "We could break the glass. Maybe no one will notice."

"They'll notice." Virginia dips her chin at the workmen.

I set my box aside and mimic her pose. "Not only that, but this glass is probably a quarter inch thick, which means we'd need a sledgehammer to break it. I think I may have another solution. Hold on a sec." I step over to the security box and punch in the code. Technically, I'm not supposed to have it, but Mrs. Foster never actually asked me not to look when she used it after our first fire drill. The same code locks and unlocks all North's doors, inside and out. I return and push the door handle. It opens right up.

"Too funny!" Virginia laughs. She grabs me around the waist and tickles me until I'm practically howling.

"Grow up." Reggie snorts. He picks up the boxes and carries them inside.

We're in full view of the men at the front door, but we continue calmly with Virginia's plan to have Reggie hack the cameras. He sits at a computer below the surveillance monitor and begins to type. "We're looking for last Monday's footage of the cafeteria, is that correct?"

Virginia leans over his shoulder as his fingers fly across the keyboard. "Any video of the student fridge that used to sit in the kitchen just past the serving lines."

"What time?"

"Maybe start with early morning? Six or seven a.m.?"

"Let's say seven. That's when the building opens." I glance back at the workmen. "Any idea how long this will take?" I don't want them getting curious and stopping by to check on us.

Reggie sits back smugly. "Already there. You do realize this isn't hacking."

"It's not?" Virginia and I both take computer apps. No surprise, code breaking wasn't listed on the syllabus. When we glance wide-eyed at each other, Reggie barks a laugh.

"Come on. You guys can't be that dense. There's no secret password. This is a simple CCTV system. Closed Camera TV? Surely you've heard of that. The cameras send a signal to this machine and the monitor above it along an NVR—a network video recorder. It's all completely digital. Most video recordings are kept for thirty days. Sometimes up to ninety. You simply look for the date, the time, and a specific camera. In this case, the one right there." He points at the monitor which is now showing the cafeteria and more specifically the big double door stainless refrigerator with Monday seven a.m. time-stamped in a corner.

"Good job, Reggie." Virginia pats him on the back.

"Honestly?" he huffs. "You could have done this by yourself. You're probably bright enough. You really don't need me."

Probably bright enough? We can't be *that* dense? What a little shit.

Virginia regards him evenly. "You're absolutely right. Go wait in the car. And you owe me twelve bucks for your lunch."

"Wait!"

"You heard me. Get out of here." She motions to the door.

"No, wait. Look, I'm sorry. I really want to help," he pleads. "Hey, if your killer didn't sprinkle poison on the dead guy's food until later in the morning you've got hours of footage to go through. Let me show you how to fast-forward this."

I hate to admit he's got a point. The display on the timestamp is now 7:02 and not a single person has gone near the refrigerator. The longer we spend in here, the more likely we'll be caught.

"What time is lunch?" he asks, probably sensing Virginia is on the fence because she doesn't respond.

"Eleven forty-five."

"Okay, then how about I fast-forward it while you watch, like a few minutes at a time."

"Not too fast," I say. "We don't want to miss anything."

I lean against Mrs. Pugh's desk to observe. It's the desk without a plant, a blue folder, a grade book, or her purse. She'd make a better principal than Mr. A-hole Sullivan. I'm delighted to look through the window and see damp, brown ceiling tiles strewn across his magazines.

"I bet I can figure it out. You probably hold this button down." Virginia reaches toward the keyboard.

"Not that one. It will erase stuff!" Reggie yelps. He glances over his shoulder in time to see her satisfied expression.

"You want to help? Then don't be such a dick," she says. "Press the button. We'll let you know if the video is going by too fast."

"Hey," I say. "Can you install cameras at my apartment building, Reggie?"

"Inside or out?"

"Either. Both. Maybe one to catch activity in the parking lot. And another in the hallway?"

"Sure. You buy them, and I'll take care of it."

"For my father, just in case he decides to visit," I tell Virginia who shifts nervously. "What?"

"Nothing. Just a dream, not important." She goes back to watching the monitor.

Reggie explains that the smaller machine at his elbow can be used to make a hard copy of the track, which doesn't seem particularly relevant. We already know the cops have seen all this.

A dizzying amount of footage flies by. It makes my eyes hurt. Reggie slows it every time anyone approaches the refrigerator. I see Tom. Matty. Lots of kids I don't know. Shanice sticks her head inside and comes out with a paper sack. Amy grabs an apple and quickly shuts the door. Miss Jamie walks by a few times and glances at it. Mrs. Lorner goes over with a bucket of cleaning supplies. She stands with the door ajar for several minutes. Lindley wipes the handle with a messy rag. He peeks inside and comes back out with a sandwich wrapped in foil. This is what the cops saw. But did he have enough time to unwrap Jason's lunch, sprinkle poison on it, and put it back? I try to recall that day. The plastic wrap hadn't looked disturbed.

"He's stealing someone's lunch!" Reggie exclaims.

We play it twice. Lindley definitely took something out, but I didn't see him put anything in it. The problem is that when the refrigerator is open you can't see inside it. The door blocks the camera, which must be high up on a wall. Virginia tells Reggie to keep going. Meanwhile, precious minutes crawl by. I keep glancing toward the hallway, expecting the two men who were working on the front doors to come in and ask us what the hell we're doing.

"Hold on. Take a look at that," Virginia yelps. "Who is that? Slow it down and play it again, Reg. Wait. Stop there."

We stare at the image of a guy with a cowboy hat pulled low over his eyes. "Is that who I think it is?"

She shakes her head. "I don't know. The hat obscures the face."

Regardless, I know we're both thinking the same thing. A guy with a cowboy hat at the refrigerator the same day Jason's little meat and cheese sandwiches were tampered with? It seems like just too much of a coincidence when ten minutes later Jason goes in and retrieves his *My Little Pony* lunchbox.

"Dillon Reed," I whisper. "Do you think he poisoned Jason Gonzalez?"

CHAPTER THIRTY-TWO

Virginia

"There's only one way to find out," I say as Katie takes a picture of the screen with her cell phone and Reggie resets the system to accept live feed again.

She puts her phone away. "I'm assuming you don't mean we should ask him. We should probably tell Detective Rosen."

I hesitate. "Definitely, but maybe not right now. She's still busy dealing with earthquake business, and we don't have proof it's Dillon since we can't see his face. I suggest we start with a friendly, or even maybe not so friendly, conversation with Amy. I've got a feeling she knows more than she lets on. If Dillon was drugging people at her party, she couldn't have been completely in the dark. After all, she agreed to let him bring the vodka."

"Yeah," says Katie, nodding. "Yeah. She wanted him to do that. Neither one of them liked Jason. And Dillon, god, he's so bizarre. The way he came up to me at her party like he actually thought I wanted anything to do with him wasn't normal. Lil Dilly, it still grosses me out."

"Little Dilly?" Reggie glances up with a smile.

"Forget it." Kate waves him down. "The other day he said he had friends at North who could get rid of Jason for him."

"Or he could come in and do it himself," I add. "Nobody checks IDs. Everybody just assumes North is safe because of the neighborhood. All Dillon would have to do is walk in like he belonged—"

"Grab a couple of empty boxes and say he was picking up stuff for a teacher?"

Not the same, but she knows what I mean. Dillon knows the school and the cafeteria. I look around to see if there's anything I can take that won't be missed and pull a bunch of discarded worksheets from the recycle bin by the copier and drop them in my box, in case one of the workers thinks to stop us and look inside. "Katie, if you're up for it, I wouldn't mind visiting Amy this afternoon. We can show her the picture on your phone and see what she has to say about it."

"I'm in," she says at once.

This is why we're a good team. We think alike and we don't let little things like fear and common sense slow us down. I shove that thought away.

"Can I come with you?" Reggie asks. "Oh, never mind. You're just going to say no. Forget I asked." At least this time he doesn't seem upset. I guess surviving an earthquake can help a person get their priorities straight. He tells Katie he can put the cameras in at her apartment as soon as she wants, and we drop him off at the house before heading back over to Airport Heights.

It's been several days since the party, yet the street is still littered with trash. Plastic cups, empty cans, and bottles. A couple of flattened rubber tubs that probably once held ice. From the front, Amy's house doesn't look that bad. There are a couple of broken windows, but the log cabin beyond it looks much worse. The roof sags at a corner and a huge tree has taken out overhead lines and most of the split-rail fence in back. Katie's car still rests in the back of a blue pickup truck. As old as it is and with as much damage as it's obviously sustained, I doubt it's worth trying to repair.

I snatch an empty vodka bottle from a bush, thinking there might be residual evidence of Ecstasy inside it, and toss it into the back seat of my car.

Katie rings the doorbell, and a few seconds later a younger girl who's a dead ringer for Amy opens the door just wide enough to peek out. Her red hair is a little shorter than Amy's, but she has the same upturned nose and smattering of freckles.

"Hi, Kathy. You may not remember us," Katie begins.

"Sure, I do." She opens the door wider and smiles around a mouthful of silver braces. "You're Katie. Katherine, like me. And you're Virginia. Mom and Amy and I helped you guys search Valley of the Moon Park for that girl you guys ended up rescuing before Christmas. I'd like to invite you inside, but I probably better not. Amy's grounded because she had a huge party the other night when Mom and I were out of town. It was the night of the earthquake. Our back steps fell off and some of the kids' parents are threatening to sue us."

"Kathy, who's that at the door?" a gravely voice speaks from another room.

"Amy's friends."

"Well, tell them to go away. I swear that girl will be lucky if I don't send her to reform school." Amy's mother comes around the door. Seeing us, she adds, "Oh, I know you! Violet and Katie."

"Virginia," Katie and I say together.

I only met Mrs. Meeks once, but I'm pretty sure she's lost weight. The red in her hair is mostly gray, and she wears an old blue housecoat over a pair of faded jeans. A half-smoked cigarette dangles from her lower lip. She grabs it to keep it from dropping on the floor.

"I'm sorry, girls. I don't mean to be rude." She motions us inside. "I thought it was that awful boyfriend of Amy's. I imagine you've heard about her party. Good lord, what a disaster. I never should have left her alone. And then with that terrible earthquake on top of everything else, we just got our electricity back this morning. Most of our neighbors, including my aunt, she lives over there, are still without." She points at the log house with the sagging roof, adding, "The power company says it may still be another day or two before they have lights."

"Sorry to hear that," Katie says politely, but Mrs. Meeks rolls over it, complaining how Amy and Dillon trashed the house and how Amy is so out of control she might just send her to live with her no-good, cheating father in New York. Either that or reform school, she repeats, and how is she ever going to pay for the damage to the house without renters insurance? At last, she asks us why we're here. Something in the midst of all this tickles my brain.

"Is this about school?" She stubs her cigarette out in an overflowing ashtray on the same console table that held a jar of cash Saturday night.

I have to think fast, so I let go of the other thought. "Mr. Spurling asked us to remind Amy about her homework. It's online. It's due next week, and he's worried she'll forget." I added the online part to explain why we're not carrying textbooks. Katie sucks in a breath as I belatedly recall World History is the only class in which Amy won't have homework because she's a teacher's aide like Katie. Hopefully, Mrs. Meeks won't think of it.

She lights another cigarette. "I can't promise she'll do it. In fact, I can practically guarantee she won't. She's upstairs in her bedroom, second door on the left."

We take that as an invitation to go up. "Were you guys at the party?" Amy's younger sister, Kathy, asks, following us halfway up the stairs.

"Sorry we missed it," Katie murmurs.

"Me, too," she whispers like she means it.

She turns back and we head down the hall to the second door on the left and knock. When no one answers a second time, Katie pushes it open, shoving aside a towel that's blocking airflow under the door. The smell of weed blows out on a thick gray cloud of smoke.

Amy bolts upright from her bed and thrusts a pocket-size bong under her pillow. "What the fuck! Oh, it's you guys. Holy shit, ever heard of knocking?" She pulls the bong back out, waves half-heartedly at the smoke, and pounds the pillow.

"Sorry." We step inside and pull the door closed behind us. "What do you want?"

"Not to intrude on your privacy," I assure her. Katie goes over to open the window, and I take a seat at a desk with a fold-down top. "We want to ask you about Dillon."

"What about him?" Amy puts her mouth inside the bong and inhales so deeply I can see her chest rise and fall. She holds her breath for a couple of seconds, then releases it. Her mom's right, she has a problem. She's just been grounded and three days later she's already high again?

I decide to start with an easy question. "Did Dillon put Ecstasy in the vodka Saturday night?"

Her eyes dart to Katie and she gives me a wily grin. "Dude gave you a hug. Figured you could use it. Did you enjoy it?"

I gaze at her, confused. Katie doesn't look at either one of us. She's too busy staring out the window. "He hit on Katie, not me."

"Good god, Virginia." Amy snorts. "How square are you? A hug. Adam. Love drug. Beans? They're all just nicknames. You never heard them? No wonder you're so uptight. It's like you've got a broomstick stuck up your ass. Dill figured people needed relaxing so they could enjoy the party. Please, at least tell me you had a good time."

A broomstick? I can feel my butt curl. "When was the last time you talked to him?"

"I have no idea. We don't keep tabs on each other. Grounded, remember?" She goes to tap her forehead and bangs her nose with the pipe. "Ouch! Why?"

"Let's move on to Jason." I signal to Katie to bring her phone over so we can show Amy the picture from the cafeteria video, but Katie doesn't seem to see me.

"Have you seen him since Saturday night?" she asks.

"I don't know. I guess not. You know, come to think of it, I haven't. He ran out of booze and disappeared right before the earthquake. Do you know my bitch mom is still going on about the party? Please. Like it's my fault there was a natural disaster? Not my fault she didn't buy renters insurance, either. That's on her. I hate this house. Who cares if we have to move again.

She wants me to go live with my dad. Like that's a threat? She doesn't like my friends, and she's always on my ass about my grades. The only class I like is Mr. Spurling's."

The one you in which you get no credit because you're a teacher's aide?

Katie turns away from the window at the same time I feel the tingle I got downstairs. "Amy, who lives over there?" she asks.

"Where?" Amy makes her way to Katie's side. I'm surprised she can stand upright.

I head for the window, too. Now I remember. Somebody was smoking on the back deck when Dillon headed for the exact same house for more liquor. It's the log cabin with the sagging roof.

Katie. Kate. Kathy. *She said she has a niece named Kate or Kathy.*

"That's my Great-aunt Yanny's house," says Amy, clearly oblivious. "Dude, someone ought to check on her. That roof is wrecked."

"Yanny what? What's her last name?" There's an urgency to Katie's voice. She leans partway out the window, then grabs my hand as if fearing Amy's going to push her out. I hold on to her, but Amy merely eyes her, puzzled.

"Lorner. You've probably seen her. She works in our school's cafeteria. Her name is Yanny Lorner."

CHAPTER THIRTY-THREE

Katie

Every now and then I'll wake up in the middle of the night with a foot cramp. I have to jump out of bed and stand flat-footed on the floor until it goes away. Occasionally, I hop up and down to release it. Denise says I probably have a calcium deficiency. Right now, my whole body feels like one gigantic cramp.

I pull away from the window. Cafeteria employees don't clean the refrigerator. Students do it. It's one more thing Jason used to complain about. But Detective Rosen wouldn't know that. None of the cops knew.

My mind goes back to the surveillance footage. Mrs. Lorner with cleaning supplies. Mrs. Lorner wearing rubber gloves. Mrs. Lorner whose husband was a biochemist. Mrs. Lorner who can't remember my name but knows the word Cholecalciferol? I'm familiar with it only because I've researched it.

"We need to go." I yank Virginia by the arm, leaving Amy sputtering something about school and homework.

"It's her," I say, when we reach the street. A noisy SUV idles across the street. I barely glance at it. "I think…oh, man, I hate to say it, but I think Mrs. Lorner killed Jason."

Virginia clutches my hand. She has no trouble keeping up with what I'm saying. "'You see a man's true colors when he's under duress. Not that children have the same sensibilities, but they learn.'"

"What?"

"That's what she said after Tom and Jason had their fight. Remember how it started with her asking him to pick up a tray of sandwich bread he'd dropped? She got called into Mrs. Foster's office with us. I thought it sounded nuts, that's why I remembered it. Katie, I think you're right. Mrs. Lorner poisoned Jason to teach him a lesson. She was insulted by the way he dissed her. He treated her as if she didn't matter."

It makes sense, yet I don't want it to be true. "Yeah. Okay. But I don't think she meant to kill him, Virginia. She said she didn't know about his heart condition." The SUV flicks its lights and the engine cuts off. It's probably another earthquake casualty.

Virginia shakes her head. "Maybe not, but I'm not sure that's important now. You do realize she may have murdered Dillon, too? The last time anybody saw Dillon was before the earthquake when he ran off toward her house for liquor. He wanted to hang on to his high, which probably means he planned to steal it from her. What's more, I bet she planted the poison in Lindley's locker, then called the police anonymously to report him. And Saturday night, Lilly Kahale's friend Mark told me Lindley had been seen in Wasilla. He said they got it from an anonymous source, but when Detective Rosen stopped by my house the next day, she didn't seem to know anything about it. I bet both calls were Yanny Lorner deflecting attention away from herself."

Yanny. I never knew Mrs. Lorner's first name, only that she was my dear sweet crazy friend. The woman who listened to every single thing I whined about. Even when I complained about Mr. Sullivan, she listened, wondering aloud if he might have poisoned Jason. Another deflection? During disasters, animals lie down so they won't fall, she'd told me. It sounded ridiculous at the time, but she was right about the earthquake.

"Dillon could still be inside her house." Virginia's voice brings me back to the present. "Or Mrs. Lorner could be hurt. Look at that roof. Amy's right that it may cave at any moment."

My eyes track where Virginia points. One corner of the house rests on the ground. Tattered curtains cover the windows. The wires lying across the yard might very well be live.

Cholecalciferol. Is the whole absentmindedness thing an act? My thoughts are all over the place.

"Katie?"

"What? Yeah. Got it. We should make sure she's okay." A small, unnerving aftershock shakes the ground. We head up a weedy walkway to a stoop and push the bell.

Mrs. Lorner opens it at once. She wears her cafeteria uniform as if she doesn't know our school is closed. "Hello. Are you selling cookies?"

What? "No. Sorry. It's me. Katie, your friend from school? And this is Virginia. You've met her."

"At school?" She coughs into her fist.

"That's right. In the cafeteria." I smell her smoky breath, just like her niece, Amy's mom.

"Oh, I do remember. Come on in, kiddo. What brings you out this way? No cookies?" She glances hopefully at our empty hands.

"Maybe next time." I wish I'd brought her cookies. The interior of the house is dim and cramped with way too much dark furniture and freaky-looking dolls on wall shelves.

"We don't mean to bother you," Virginia adds. "It's just that we saw your roof fall in the other night and wanted to make sure you're all right. Are you?"

"I think so." Mrs. Lorner flicks a light switch by the door. The room stays dark. She picks up a pack of cigarettes. The whole house reeks. But it's not just cigarette smoke. There's a worse odor that stinks like fish left too long in a cooler without ice.

"By any chance is Amy's boyfriend, Dillon, here? He came this way before the earthquake." Virginia peers at a porcelain doll with scraggly long hair and pointy white teeth.

The cigarette flames to life. "Do I know him?"

"You might," I say. "He dresses like a cowboy. We think he came to your house for vodka after he ran out."

"Hmm. Vodka. I don't think so. I don't drink. No, wait. Come to think of it, I do. My Escobar and I enjoy an after-dinner whiskey. You know, I do like cowboys. Amy's a bit of a tippler. But please don't tell her mother. I don't think she knows. Can I offer you girls a drink?"

"Um. No thanks."

Virginia squeezes my arm reassuringly, probably because she knows I'm about to lose all semblance of my sanity, then lifts her chin at a door on the other side of the room. "Could I use your restroom, Mrs. Lorner?"

"Of course, kiddo. Darn lights. You'd better let me show you. I'm afraid the ceiling fell in on the bathtub, but the toilet works."

We veer away from the kitchen where I see cans that look like vegetables or dog food, a plate of food, and a large open box of rat poison on the kitchen counter. No way in hell am I waiting here while they go off to the restroom.

The door is shut, though partially hanging off its hinges. Mrs. Lorner pushes at it gently, then kicks it open with alarming vigor. "Don't mind that one." She points at a large dark lump a few feet away.

Virginia winces at the same moment a high-pitched noise escapes my throat. Holy crap! The smell gets worse and the lump takes shape. Dreads. Cargo pants. A gray-black T-shirt stretched tight over a bloated belly. There's no doubt in my mind that we're seeing Lindley Crowe.

Mrs. Lorner stubs out her cigarette and makes a face. "Never liked that one. Wouldn't do his work. Still, he came in handy. Would you kiddos mind helping me move him out back with the other?"

"The other?" Virginia grips my hand.

"Here's the bathroom." Mrs. Lorner points. "The young man with the cowboy hat? I thought you said you knew him. Used to come around last year, but I don't recall his name. Nearly startled me out of my wits when I caught him in the kitchen. And then he had the nerve to demand one of my whisky bottles. I gave him a nice little treat instead. I don't tolerate disrespect. You know that, right? But I'm not quite sure what to do with him now."

Virginia eyes me with a look that says she's not about to step into the restroom without me, then walks in anyway. She leaves the door ajar. The toilet flushes half a second later, not enough time to do her business.

I take a deep breath, thinking that this strange woman— once my friend, I thought—will either kill us, or she won't. There are two of us. She can't force us to ingest rat poison. We'll fight her if we have to.

"Mrs. Lorner, did you hurt Lindley Crowe and Dillon Reed?" I make my tone soft in an effort to sound cordial.

"Who's that?"

I motion to the swollen corpse. "That's Lindley. I'm guessing you have Dillon in another room."

"Oh." She nods. "I think you're right. I must have. They deserved it, don't you think?"

I want to slap my face. "What about Jason, did he deserve it too?" And before she can ask me who he is, I add, "The kid at school last week, the one who dropped the sandwich buns and told you to pick them up?"

She tilts her head and pats her pockets. "Gosh, kiddo, there were several of them. But I didn't know that one had a heart condition. I only wanted to let him know he should respect his elders. That's how children learn to be polite, you know. I've said it many times. But he was gone so fast. I'm sorry." Her eyes fill up.

Several students? How did we miss that, I wonder. I think back now to vague stories of kids getting sick after lunch. Tally talked about them in the restroom when Mrs. Foster sent us in to wash our hands. And Yoon-hi mentioned them to Virginia when she saw Mrs. Foster being escorted from the building. The missed health inspection at the beginning of the year? I doubt even the most thorough of inspectors could have caught a cafeteria employee who was deliberately microdosing disrespectful kids. Mrs. Lorner is certainly crazy, but she's also careful.

Virginia steps out of the bathroom. "Would you like to turn yourself in, Mrs. Lorner?"

"Into what?" She eyes us through her smudgy, thick lens glasses.

A witch or a vampire? I fight off a hysterical laugh. This whole conversation feels like I'm stuck in the middle of a really bad movie.

"To the police. It might make you feel better," Virginia offers gently.

"Well, I don't know about that. I guess I could. They were accidents, weren't they? What do you think, kiddo? It's Katie, isn't it?" She looks at me.

At last she's gotten my name right. "I think it's a good idea," I say.

"All right, then. I'll do it. I didn't finish my dinner, but I guess that can wait. Do you think it will take very long?"

"How's this going to work? We load her in your car and drive her to the station?" I whisper to Virginia as we start back for the living room.

"I was thinking we'd step outside the house, like as far away as we can get from her stash of rat poison and call Detective Rosen." Virginia twists her head and adds, "Is someone at the door?"

All at once I hear what she hears—a hard knock followed by a crashing sound. The door falls in and the living room floods with light as an all-too-familiar silhouette fills the entrance.

CHAPTER THIRTY-FOUR

Virginia

I stare in shock at a man I'd hoped to never see again.

"Hello, Katie Kat," says Katie's father. "You've been a naughty girl, ignoring my texts and dodging my calls. By god, I've missed you. Two years, six months, and fourteen days without a word from you. The last time I saw you was in court. I protected you, you know. I refused to let my attorney question you because I didn't want you to have to talk bad about your mother. But where did it get me? It gave her way too much time to speak against me. We won't worry about that anymore. All that's going to change. Now, come give your daddy a great big hug, and then we need to get going."

Going? Going where? I don't like the sound of that. The barrel of his handgun reflects a ray of sunlight bending impossibly around him.

Katie stands frozen next to me. "What—what are you doing here?"

He frowns. "I told you, or at least I would have if you'd answered my calls. I got out almost a week ago. I came for you as soon as I could."

"Have you been following me?" She swallows noisily.

Clearly, she's afraid of him and with good reason. I step in front of her because I'm not letting him take her anywhere. He'll have to shoot me first. I recall the image I'd had the day I took the photo of the moose lying in my neighbor's front yard, the day of the blended sky. It was Katie's dad standing with a gun in a darkened doorway just like this. Just a flash across my brain, I'd thought. But now? Animals that lie down so they won't fall? An earthquake? A cold-blooded killer who can't remember people's names? If I close my eyes right now, will I wake up in my own bed? Probably not.

"I saw you in the back parking lot at Caseo's last Wednesday night. It was you, wasn't it?" I say to Katie's dad.

Katie glances at me with surprise and I realize I never told her about it because I thought my eyes had deceived me. With everything else going on, I'd stopped trusting my instincts. Big mistake. To him though, it's nothing, of course.

He shrugs. "I had to keep an eye on Katie while I put my plan in place. Sweetheart, I was watching out for you to make sure you were safe. I sat in your parking lot every day when you were at school. At night, I stayed awake outside your apartment. I was here the other night when you went to a party right over there." He waves the gun at Amy's house. "At first, I was afraid I'd lose track of you, especially at night. But then I came up with the ideal solution."

She clears her throat. "You mean because you knocked out my taillight."

"Exactly. Perfect, wasn't it? My cellmate suggested it. Most cars look alike in the dark, but it's relatively easy to follow one with a single light. I thought you might have caught on when you covered the damage with red duct tape, but it turned out all I had to do was peel the tape off. Listen, Katie Kat, we need to get going now. We've got a long way to travel and I'd like to arrive before nightfall."

"Where are you going?" Mrs. Lorner speaks up. She's wandered over to the kitchen counter. A moment ago, she'd been looking longingly at a plate of food.

He curls his upper lip. "You think I'm telling you?"

"Is it a secret? I love secrets." She pushes her glasses up her nose. "I have a couple of my own. My Escobar is a biochemist. We used to do home experiments. Measure twice. Pour once. You have to get the portions exactly right. I'm unhappy to say I've messed it up a couple of times. Escobar's gone now, one of my mistakes. The other was the poor boy at school with the heart trouble. Still, he had no need to be insolent when I simply asked him to do his job. He wasn't very nice to you young people either, was he? Him and the other one scuffled on the floor like the animals who lie down."

Katie and I catch each other's eyes. Is Mrs. Lorner engaging in another useless ramble, or does she have something more productive in mind? I know she's fond of Katie, but Katie's dad has a gun, and I don't think he'll hesitate to use it. As a group, we all seem to shift toward the kitchen. She's still standing at the counter.

She goes on for another few seconds about her ability to predict the future until Katie's dad has had enough. "My god, daughter, what is it about us that attracts the crazies? For me, it was your mother. I had no idea she was such a deviant. For you, well, I don't know. Come on now. We're done here. I'm going to have to ask you to put this on." He pulls what looks like a felt bag from a pocket in his pants. "Over your head, please. It's for your own protection. I can't let you know where we're going until I'm sure I can trust you."

Katie whimpers and Mrs. Lorner and I simultaneously shout, "Don't!"

I push Katie away from him, and Mrs. Lorner throws the box of rat poison at his face. He fires the gun into her chest and gives his head a wet dog shake. Brown flakes scatter around him like dust catching in the sunlight. "What the hell was that?" he yells.

"Rat poison, you son of a bitch. You're going to be dead in ten minutes!" Katie screams.

I try to catch Mrs. Lorner in my arms as she collapses, but she ends up falling on top of me. Mr. McRanes washes his face in the sink. "I've had enough of this. We're going. Put the damn hood on or I'll shoot your girlfriend too."

I'm helpless. In my dream, I blocked his shot. Katie sobs. I'm trapped under Mrs. Lorner's deadweight. Katie and her father walk out.

Then just as I accept that the situation is truly hopeless, the earth gives a tremendous shudder and the floor underneath me gives way.

CHAPTER THIRTY-FIVE

Katie

The terrible rumble shakes me from my stupor. It also knocks Dad off his feet. I yank off the hood, gasping for breath. Virginia barrels out of the house after Dad and me. She screams, plows headfirst into my father's back, and wrenches the gun right out of his hand. He makes a grab for her ankle. She dances away.

"Try that again and I'll shoot you. I promise."

"No, you won't."

She fires it an inch from his face. "Next one will take out your eye."

He falls back. "Let me go and I'll disappear. You'll never see me again."

"Not happening. Katie, call the police."

I've never loved her more. I wish she would take out his eye. *An eye for an eye. His for Mom's.* I'm giddy with the aftermath of fear and shock. I dial 911.

"There's a man. He shot a woman. She poisoned him. She poisoned the guy lying in her hall. Others, too. Come at once."

"What is the nature of your emergency—never mind. Tell me where you are?" The operator starts over.

"Airport Heights. It's Mrs. Lorner." I have to put my head between my legs before I faint. Virginia guides me to the stoop and takes the phone. "Is she dead?" I ask her.

"Not sure," she says and gives the operator our address. "Hurry, please. Yes, I'm all right. Virginia Eaton. Katie McRanes. Yanny Lorner, and Paul McRanes." She hangs up.

"You saved me." I wrap my arms around her neck.

"You saved me last time in the shed." She means last Christmas. "Katie, god. The floor collapsed. I was trapped. But then I pulled my feet free from the crawl space. Are you hurt? Did he touch you? I could still shoot him. Nobody but us will know. Just say the word."

I hiccup through my tears. "I'd like that very much, but no." She kisses my face and neck. Dad starts to move, and she gets up and presses the gun firmly to his temple.

"Do it. Get up. Try to leave. Please. I dare you."

He stops and puts his hands behind his head. "Do you want to hear my side?"

"No."

We wait. Virginia holds me tightly, telling me a story about a dream she had of a cat and a moose and a man who dared to point a gun at me. I cock my head, staring at my car resting in the back of someone's truck. The SUV I heard when we came out of Amy's house is now parked in front of Mrs. Lorner's cabin with the passenger door open. I scoot so close to Virginia that I'm half sitting in her lap.

"I think I know where he was going to take me. Remember that bison hunt I told you about? How he marched Mom and me through snow and ice for days?"

"You stayed in a hunting cabin. Afterward, your mom gave up meat." Virginia kisses my neck.

"Yes, there. It's remote. I might have never gotten away. You saved me."

"I love you."

"I love you even more."

The police come. Then Mom and Denise. I don't remember calling them.

Detective Rosen hauls Dad to his feet and cuffs his hands behind his back. The ER people bring Mrs. Lorner out on a gurney. They follow with Lindley, and then Dillon.

It's crazy that Dillon's still alive.

Dad tells Rosen that Mrs. Lorner snatched his gun away and shot herself. He tried to stop her. Lies, all lies. Mom steps up and slaps his face.

Mr. and Mrs. Eaton arrive next. Rosen takes a statement from me and then Virginia. Amy and her mom and sister come out of their house. Rosen signals two uniformed cops to take Dad away.

I break down again. "She, Mrs. Lorner, will she live?" I cling now to Denise. Virginia saved me, but Mrs. Lorner tried to also, the batty lady who listened to all my problems.

Rosen gently pats my shoulder. "Go home and get some rest, hon. We'll talk more tomorrow."

EPILOGUE

Virginia

Mrs. Lorner died Thursday at the hospital. For a while, the doctors thought she'd make it. At one point, she opened her eyes and spoke in detail about fatally dosing Jason and her dear late husband, Escobar, the scientist. Both accidents that she deeply regretted, Escobar's a bit more than Jason's, I imagine. She didn't seem to feel nearly as bad about Lindley and admitted that she'd lured him to her house by threatening to notify the military police that he was a deserter, then poisoning him and framing him for Jason's death. She also confessed to planting the rat bait in his locker and telling Lilly and Mark that he'd been spotted in Wasilla.

"Delays help, don't you think?" She patted her sheets absently, no doubt searching for a cigarette.

She talked with Katie several times, sometimes calling her Kathy or Kate, but usually just kiddo. We knew who she meant because she mentioned Katie's thumbnail diet and her horrible father who needed to go to prison for a long, long time. Around midnight, she closed her eyes a final time and drifted off. One of the nurses told us it wasn't unusual for a patient with a serious chest wound to suddenly pass away.

On Friday, Mrs. Foster came back to school. Katie was immediately reinstated as an office aide and Sullivan was sent packing. I pity whatever school has to take him next.

We assumed the Homecoming game and dance would be canceled, but Mrs. Foster said it would be good for everyone's morale to carry on as usual, as much as such a thing is possible. We had another major aftershock this morning.

Katie and I skipped the football game but we're here at the dance with our friends tonight. The gym has taken a beating, but decorations hide most of the damage. When the music starts, a loud thudding beat, I grab Katie's hand, thinking it's another aftershock.

"You're fine," she says. "We're both fine."

"I guess Dillon will be too. He got out of the hospital this morning," I tell her. "Oh, and Mom told me Detective Rosen identified the cowboy hat from the surveillance video at the refrigerator as belonging to someone else."

"I'm surprised Rosen shared that. She's so closed-mouth."

"I have my ways." I offer a wink.

We wait for a minute until a slow song comes on, and then we wrap our arms around each other to dance. The gym is pretty crowded. If I squint I can just make out Tally in the top section of the bleachers with Shanice. Good for them, I think. Yoon-hi sits alone, and Tom is nowhere in sight. I wish Yoon-hi's parents would lighten up, but I'm not going to pretend I'm sorry about Tom's absence. Matty deserves better. He's over at the side, talking with a trans girl named Emory. He sees us and waves.

A few seconds later, I spot Mrs. Donovan chatting up one of the cheerleaders. She's here as a chaperone, I guess. I'm just glad Tally's over her.

I wonder, did the last couple of weeks really happen the way I remember them? Tom and Jason's fight. Jason's seizure. The wild wind and hot weather. The crazy blue-gray sky. The cat and moose communing in my neighbor's yard. We spent two weird evenings gathered around outdoor fires, friends who stopped being friends for a while. It almost feels as if it never happened, until I recall Katie's father standing in Mrs. Lorner's doorway with a handgun. What would I have done if he'd shot Katie or taken her away from me? Could I have gone on without her? Could I go to college and live my dreams without the girl I love? I don't want to think about that. I pull her close and whisper to her that I love her.

The song ends and Mrs. Foster steps up to the microphone. She waits for the gym to get quiet.

"I want to thank everyone for your wonderfully supportive emails and phone calls," she begins. "I'm glad to be back at North, although I will say Mr. Sullivan did an admirable job in my absence."

"Boo!" we all yell.

She waits patiently for everyone to settle down again. "I'm also happy to announce that my dear friend Mrs. Pugh has accepted a permanent post as North's assistant principal. I'm sure you'll welcome her as I have. And now, I'd be grateful if you'll bow your heads for a moment of silence in memory of a student we recently lost. I'm not sure how many of you knew Jason Gonzalez. As a freshman and sophomore he attended North, then left us for a year to work alongside his father in his dream job, he called it. For those of you who did have the pleasure of his acquaintance, I imagine you were familiar with his sharp tongue and cutting wit. He also had a self-deprecating sense about him that many may never have known.

"Jason suffered through several heart surgeries as an infant and later, debilitating illnesses in his childhood that he was loath to share with others. He was often in a fair amount of pain, yet he told me once he never wanted to be a burden. I believe he used humor as a way of dealing with the hardships life dealt him."

Unbidden tears drip down my cheeks. "I don't think I ever really knew him."

Katie blows a breath out through her cheeks. "Me, either."

We allow the minute to pass in full, then Yoon-hi, Shanice, Tally, Matty, and Emory all join us on the dance floor. It's a fast song now and we joyfully throw our hands high in the air in celebration of our friendship.

Author Notes

On March 27th, 1964, the second largest earthquake in recorded history struck Alaska's Prince William Sound. Today, nearly sixty years later, you can still see evidence of the tsunamis that followed outside of Girdwood (and other places) where the land dropped an estimated five to ten feet and ocean saltwater swept over trees, soaking their limbs and roots and thereby creating the "Girdwood Ghost Forest."

I first came up with the idea of a natural disaster having strange and unforeseen effects on friendships in 2018 when I was teaching and a magnitude 7.1 earthquake hit just north of Anchorage, AK, tearing roads apart and shaking buildings to their core. Schools were closed for a week and there was quite a bit of damage, but fortunately no fatalities. The fact is, tens of thousands of earthquakes are reported every year in Alaska, and yet even with modern technology, there is still no way to predict them. Take that, Mrs. Lorner!

One other quick note. When I wrote the first draft for this I, like everyone else, had no idea what havoc COVID-19 would inflict on the world. Yoon-hi casually mentions it in chapter three, and after some debate, I decided to leave it the way it was.

This is my second novel with characters Virginia and Katie, and their friends, Matty, Tally, and Yoon-hi (pronounced Yoon-hee). My appreciation goes out to my dear friend Kimberly Smith for hosting a debut party for my first book, *Can I Trust Her?*, and as always to my beautiful wife, Cheryl, who is my sounding board and the first to read my stories in their rawest form.

I also owe a huge debt of gratitude to the wonderful women at Bella Books for publishing both novels, and to my incredible editor, Ann Roberts, who is kind, sharp, and all around amazing. Ann's keen insights made this a better book. You can find her stories at Bella Books as well. I recommend them.

Last, but in no way least, my thanks to you for reading *Is She Lying?* If you have enjoyed the writing, I would greatly appreciate a review on Amazon. They really do help other people discover new books. And I love hearing from you. Feel free to get in touch! You can contact me through my website www.franceslucas.com and say hello to me on Facebook and Instagram at franceslucas.author and find me on TikTok: @ flucas72.

Best wishes and happy reading to you all.

More Titles from Bella Books

Mabel and Everything After – Hannah Safren
978-1-64247-390-2 | 274 pgs | paperback: $17.95 | eBook: $9.99
A law student and a wannabe brewery owner find that the path to a fairy tale happily-ever-after is often the long and scenic route.

To Be With You – TJ O'Shea
978-1-64247-419-0 | 348 pgs | paperback: $19.95 | eBook: $9.99
Sometimes the choice is between loving safely or loving bravely.

I Dare You to Love Me – Lori G. Matthews
978-1-64247-389-6 | 292 pgs | paperback: $18.95 | eBook: $9.99
An enemy-to-lovers romance about daring to follow your heart, even when it's the hardest thing to do.

The Lady Adventurers Club - Karen Frost
978-1-64247-414-5 | 300 pgs | paperback: $18.95 | eBook: $9.99
Four women. One undiscovered Egyptian tomb. One (maybe) angry Egyptian goddess. What could possibly go wrong?

Golden Hour - Kat Jackson
978-1-64247-397-1 | 250 pgs | paperback: $17.95 | eBook: $9.99
Life would be so much easier if Lina were afraid of something basic—like spiders—instead of something significant. Something like real, true, healthy love.

Schuss – E. J. Noyes
978-1-64247-430-5 | 276 pgs | paperback: $17.95 | eBook: $9.99
They're best friends who both want something more, but what if admitting it ruins the best friendship either of them have had?

9 781642 474770